SHINJUKU SHARK

VERTICAL.

SHINJUKU SHARK

ARIMASA OSAWA

Translated by Andrew Clare

VERTICAL.

Published by Vertical, Inc., New York.

Originally published in Japanese as *Shinjukuzame* in 1990 by Kobunsha, Tokyo.

ISBN 978-1-932234-37-4

Manufactured in the United States of America

First Edition

Vertical, Inc.
1185 Avenue of the Americas 32nd Floor
New York, NY 10036
www.vertical-inc.com

EDITOR'S NOTE

What is Japan's most popular crime novel series?

If you were to put the question to a man on the street in Tokyo—or to a woman, for that matter, since the protagonist of the book you hold has an enviable following among ladies—the answer is likely to be *Shinjuku Shark*. The nineties, when the series made its debut, was *Shinjuku Shark*'s decade, not only for the police procedural genre or the wider crime novel category but also for Japanese *mystery*.

It sold; not only did it sell, wildly, but the franchise was adapted to the screen (both the big and the small) and even to *manga* comics form. It racked up the best prizes, too. The first installment, published in 1990, won two, the Eiji Yoshikawa New Writer Award and the coveted Japan Mystery Writers Association Award. Only three years later, the fourth installment garnered Mr. Osawa the Naoki Prize—nominally granted to the best genre novel of the preceding half-year, but in truth the semi-official recognition of sustained excellence in popular fiction.

Shinjuku Shark is one of those rare series about which fans state with genuine conviction and pride: "It gets better with each volume." Far from losing steam, it has continued, with force, well into our new century—the latest and ninth installment, published in 2006, won the Japan Adventure Fiction Association Award. The same year also saw Mr. Osawa assume chairmanship of the prestigious Japan Mystery Writers Association that so presciently smiled upon the inaugural volume of his epochal blockbuster.

It is something of a scandal that the work has not been translated sooner.

Some of the details of this first installment may seem a little dated. The Berlin Wall has fallen but not yet the Soviet Union, causing the Japanese police to be rather more concerned about leftist extremism than they would be today. Answering machines do not register the hour of incoming messages, and cell phones have yet to supplant car phones and bulky mobile phones. The influx of sex workers from the rest of Asia into seedy Kabukicho is here a "new" development. But this first installment, from nearly two decades ago, is the one that launched the hit franchise—and for good reason. It is still the best place to start if you're looking for a heck of a ride.

For reasons that will become clear to those who turn the page and treat themselves to the story that unfolds, this note shall not be signed "Ed."

SHINJUKU SHARK

1

Samejima heard the scream as he was folding up the jeans and polo shirt he had taken off.

He hesitated for a moment, then locked the door of his locker. The key was attached to a wristband by a piece of velcro tape.

As he came out of the locker room, with a bath towel wrapped around his waist, he heard the scream a second time. There was a sauna room at the end of the corridor leading away from the locker room. Just before the sauna was a lounge and a nap room.

The scream had come from the nap room. It was large—about twenty *tatami* mats in area, but only one light bulb was switched on and it was extremely gloomy.

The sauna was on the top floor of a building near Shin-Okubo station, which housed a number of different business concerns. It was the fifth time in two weeks that Samejima had set foot in the establishment.

This particular sauna was well known to those with a predilection for such places. Its patrons bathed and then sized one another up in the lounge before settling themselves down together under blankets in the nap room. One always heard the sound of frantic, heavy breathing and the regular creak of beds.

Samejima stopped in front of the nap room. Suddenly a young man came bolting out of the darkness. His cheeks were red and blood trickled through his fingers as he pinched his nose.

"Help me," he said, crawling for cover behind Samejima. He looked like he was about to burst into tears.

Samejima transferred his gaze back to the doorway of the nap room. A well-built man, who looked as though he was chasing the younger man, appeared in front of him. Both the older man and the young man were stark naked.

The older man was in his early forties and had close-cropped hair. He looked as though he would have been muscular when young, but his body had since run to middle-aged fat—evidence of too much eating and drinking. His chest and stomach were pale, but his arms and the nape of his neck were suntanned.

The man noticed Samejima and stopped in his tracks.

"What do you want?" he said, in a low voice. He seemed annoyed that his pleasant little game had been interrupted.

Samejima remained silent. The man glared at him and said, "You got a problem or something?"

He seemed to have decided that Samejima was some kind of upstart; Samejima, who was thirty-six, looked a good ten years younger than he actually was. He wore his hair long at the back, just past the nape of his neck. He carried very little excess fat and was slightly built. He kept in shape by jogging, but he was certainly no weakling.

He glanced down at the young man, who was clinging to his feet trembling.

The older man growled, "Who the fuck are you? You wanna say something?"

"This is the kind of guy you are, is it?" Samejima said calmly, staring at the man.

"What?"

"You like beating up on people?"

"So what?"

The man took a step forward, but Samejima stood his ground. He knew the man was flustered.

Samejima looked down again and asked the young man, "Do you like it—being beaten up?"

"No I don't. I hate it. It hurts." The young man shook his head vigorously from side to side. Specks of blood sprayed from his nose onto Samejima's feet.

"He says he hates it," said Samejima, looking up again at the older man.

"You motherfucker…" the man cursed, then switched to a matter-of-fact tone. "You've got a big mouth. This's got nothing to do with you." He cocked his head to one side and looked Samejima up and down. Samejima felt the man's eyes were drawn in particular toward his left hand and his cheeks.

Samejima speculated as to his occupation. He wasn't a *yakuza* gangster—that much was certain. Had he been a *yakuza,* he would have shown his hand before the conversation had gotten this far.

"You've got your reasons for coming here, right? You've no business asking me what I'm doing."

Samejima didn't say anything.

"I came here for a good time. You getting in my way like this reminds me of my job. I've seen your face somewhere before."

"Is that right?"

"Wait here. And don't go running off."

He seemed to think nothing of the young man now and kicked him like a dog before walking off toward the locker room. He barged his way past an office worker who was getting changed and turned around chuckling to himself.

The man watched Samejima to make sure he stayed put and smiled contentedly. He took the locker key from his wrist and opened the door.

"Go on, get out of here," Samejima said to the young man.

"What?"

"Go into the lounge or somewhere."

"But…"

"Go rinse your face with cold water," said Samejima, watching the older man thrust one hand into his open locker.

11

"Thank you."

The young man slipped away, anxiety and fear on his blood-speckled but chiseled face.

The older man returned, clutching a black leather-bound police notebook in his hand.

"Ah." He stopped, noticing that his prey had gotten away. He didn't follow him; instead, he thrust the notebook in Samejima's face.

"So what?" said Samejima.

"Don't get cute with me, kid!" the man exploded with rage. He seemed to have assumed, wrongly, that Samejima would back down when he saw the police ID.

He tried to strike Samejima across the cheek with the notebook, but Samejima caught hold of his wrist.

"Oh that's just great, it really is. How do you fancy a trip to the police station, you son of a bitch? I'll beat the crap out of you." The man shook himself free of Samejima's grip and grabbed him around the neck, pulling his face in close to his own.

"Cut it out. You're not the only one with one of those," said Samejima, still in the grip of the older man.

"What?" The man looked Samejima in the eye. It was only then that he seemed to sense something more in this long-haired man than the twentysomething youngster he'd taken him for. "Who the fuck are you?" The man drew in a breath. "You're not...?"

"You don't trample over someone else's territory and flash your ID."

Samejima slowly removed the man's hands from around his neck and gripped the wrists tightly. The man had a look that said "Oh, heavens."

Samejima held his gaze; the other looked down at the floor, and his bottom lip was trembling. "That little punk, I thought he was up to something—theft, something... I was just about to check him out."

"You mean picking pockets, stark naked in a sauna bath?"

The man kept his mouth shut. Then he blinked and quickly said, "Which station? Shinjuku?"

"If I tell you then you'll have to tell me. I don't think that's a good idea, do you?"

"No, you're right. Wouldn't do."

Samejima let go of the man's hands. "If you want to do shit like this, you should stick to your own neighborhood."

The man was lost for words.

"I'll be seeing you."

The man's mouth gaped open.

"I'll be seeing you," Samejima repeated.

The other closed his mouth. A shadow of frustration flitted across his face, but he remained silent and stepped back a few paces, then made for the locker room.

Opening his locker, he looked back at Samejima several times as he put on his underwear. Samejima watched the man put his tie around the collar of his white shirt, and then walked off. He peeped into the sauna room and the hot and cold baths. He didn't see the face of the man he was looking for, so he returned to the door of the nap room.

He'd done it dozens of times before, but looking around inside was as awkward as ever. Coming into the room full of entwined men often resulted in shouts of anger—he was mistaken for a peeping tom. The one he was searching for wasn't in the nap room either.

Sofas were laid out in the lounge, and the TV was left permanently on. A waiter, barefoot and wearing a uniform with a bow tie, was leaning against the counter where drinks and light snacks were served, gazing at the TV.

To one side was a sign: *Customer services not included in waiter's duties.*

Samejima cast a cursory glance at the faces on the sofas and went on into a room at the back that contained a number of dressing tables. The room was rank with the smell of cheap cosmetics. There was a row of mirrors and washbasins along the wall; above the taps were shelves with sundry cosmetics.

The young man was sitting in front of the dressing table farthest away.

It looked as though his nosebleed had stopped. He was gazing miserably at his swollen face in the mirror.

Samejima stood behind him, and he turned around with a start.

"He's gone now."

"That's a relief," muttered the young man, holding his face with both hands.

"Do you come here often?"

"No, not really," said the young man, shaking his head. "Once or twice a month. Why?" His voice was fawning, self-indulgent.

"Was that your first time with that guy?"

"Yeah. But I've seen him before. He likes skinny types. I wouldn't have guessed so looking at him."

Samejima looked around. No one else was in the dressing room.

"Do you know a man called Kizu? He's thin, well tanned, has a tattoo on his left shoulder."

"What kind of tattoo?"

"A scorpion."

The young man opened his eyes wide and stared at Samejima in the mirror. "Is he your lover?"

"My lover's friend." Samejima averted his eyes.

"Really?"

Samejima felt the inside of his knee being caressed. He looked down. The young man was scraping the inside of his knee with the nail of his right thumb.

"I know him. And something else. I like you."

Samejima scratched his chin. "Listen. I'm sorry but I don't have time. Let's get together next time. Where did you meet Kizu?"

"When can I see you?"

"How about next week?"

"When next week?"

"Friday, same as today."

The young man nodded. "Around the same hour. I'll be waiting for you."

"So, where did you meet Kizu?"

"At a bar in west Shinjuku called Agamemnon. He showed me his tattoo."

"Made out with him?"

The young man shook his head. "His lover was there."

"Isn't that you?"

"No. Someone else."

"Ah."

Samejima nodded and placed his hand on the thin shoulder of the young man, who in turn placed the palm of his own hand on Samejima's and said with a smile, "See you next time."

"Yeah, next time."

Samejima noticed the young man was becoming aroused and averted his eyes again. It was almost twice the size of the older man's and seemed incongruous against the small frame.

He returned to the locker room; the older man was nowhere to be seen. Samejima opened his locker and put on his bleached jeans and white polo shirt. His watch showed 9:10 p.m. He recalled he had a date.

A live concert by the band Who's Honey was on until 9:00 p.m. He had promised to go and meet Sho afterwards. There'd probably be three encores, lasting about fifteen minutes; then she'd return to her dressing room and spend another ten minutes putting away her gear. If he didn't arrive at the live house by 9:30, Sho would be in a bad mood. He'd promised three weeks ago to meet her this evening.

"Don't make promises you can't keep," Sho always said.

If they went to the trouble of arranging a date and he broke it off at the last minute, she gave him hell. And the date this evening was the rare one that Samejima himself had suggested.

He pulled his shoes on and took the elevator. He'd completely forgotten about the date until that morning. Of course, he wouldn't admit that to Sho; her hot temper was renowned within her band. Once, during a concert at the live house, she became so incensed by a young punk who'd interrupted the prelude to her song that she smashed a *saké* bottle over his head.

Samejima left the building and hesitated, wondering how best to get there. The TEC Hall, where Sho's live concert was being held, was in Kabukicho, Ni-Chome, midway between Shin-Okubo station and Shinjuku station, slightly closer to Shinjuku.

He wouldn't make it in time if he took a cab. He'd be better off walking or riding the Yamanote line one stop to Shinjuku. The sidewalk that cut through to Kabukicho from the eastern exit would no doubt be congested.

Samejima caught sight of a green car on the inner track of the Yamanote line pulling into the station from the direction of Takada-no-baba. He sprinted as it was coming in alongside the platform. He didn't have time to buy a ticket; pulling his police ID out from the hip pocket of his jeans, he showed it to the station employee at the gate and bolted down the stairs.

The train had stopped and opened its doors. They closed just as Samejima dove into the carriage.

Sweat coursed down his back. He may as well not have bothered going to the sauna. But he'd gotten the information he was after. He leaned against the doors and gazed down on the streets as the train approached Shinjuku.

Kabukicho was, as ever, a seething mass of people.

The crowds weren't too bad around Shinjuku Street, but they became worse from the junction with San-Chome by McDonald's. People waiting for the traffic light spilled off the sidewalk at the Yasukuni Street crossing in the direction of Kabukicho.

It was normal for a weekend except for the number of uniformed police officers standing in the vicinity of each intersection. The increased police presence was on account of a garden party for a state guest to be held the following day in the Shinjuku Gyoen Imperial Gardens.

Samejima wondered how many police officers were deployed around the main trunk roads, Shinjuku, Yasukuni and Meiji. There had to be at least a thousand in Shinjuku Ward alone.

The deployment of uniformed officers wasn't limited to the area around the Imperial Gardens but extended to more or less all the wards of the Tokyo metropolis. Police checks were particularly thorough in Shinjuku Ward, and Minato Ward, where a number of foreign embassies were concentrated.

The scale of the operation equalled that normally reserved for a state funeral, and the number of officers from the Metropolitan Police Force being insufficient, it looked as though they'd requested the assistance of the neighboring prefectural police forces of Chiba, Saitama and Kanagawa.

"Police everywhere tonight," said one of the pedestrians waiting for the light to turn green.

"Fine by me. We can drink safely tonight—won't be bothered by *yakuza*."

"Well yes, but…"

Samejima didn't catch the rest of the conversation. The lights changed, and the tide of people, as if pushed from behind by a great force, surged across Yasukuni Street.

Samejiima looked at his watch: 9:27 p.m. Sho would soon start to look for him.

He ran along, weaving in and out of the rows of cars that were momentarily stopped on the crossing, like gaps in a broken comb.

Yasukuni Street was backed up with cars as well as with throngs of people.

The main cause of the problem was illegal parking. It was made worse by the riot police buses that were being used for spot checks. They were blocking the lanes of traffic in front of the intersections.

The road opposite the Koma Theater was the busiest pedestrian street in Shinjuku at night. The whole area was crowded with pachinko parlors, arcades, bars, coffee shops, noodle stands, peep shows, restaurants, massage parlors, opticians, Chinese restaurants, cabarets, mahjong parlors, night clubs, loan shark and gangster offices. All of these establishments were housed in multi-purpose buildings. On the top floor of a quiet bar was a massage parlor, in the basement of the opticians was a dance club, and the mahjong parlor in the basement of the coffee shop was a front for the local gangster office.

The street was teeming with people coming to and fro; it wasn't possible to walk any quicker than the crowd's snailing pace. If you fell out of line, you just ran headlong into a cabaret loudspeaker blaring out the evening's entertainment or the revolving signs of an arcade.

The flow headed for Kabukicho slowed down as soon as it had crossed Yasukuni Street. It seemed almost as if walking itself had been the purpose of coming to Kabukicho.

Despite the crowds, Samejima hurried on, slipping past couples, evading the unyielding shoulders of drunken office workers, dodging the flowing hair of young women.

The intermingled smells of alcohol and food and dust from the air conditioners seemed to absorb the scent of perfume and body odor, and the further into Kabukicho the crowds went, the stronger and more pronounced the smell of Shinjuku became.

Samejima stopped as the TEC Hall came into view, opposite the Kabukicho Plaza. A small group of people had gathered in front of the arcade. The onlookers came and went quickly. It was a fight. Samejima knew intuitively that *yakuza* were involved; a brawl between ordinary people would have attracted a much larger crowd. In Shinjuku, a fight involving the *yakuza* never invited many onlookers. Afraid of being drawn into the fray, passersby lingered only for a moment.

A couple, out for a stroll, moved away from the crowd, and Samejima was able to see what was going on.

He tutted to himself. It was hardly what you'd call a fight; it was more like a lynching. Three men had formed a circle and were kicking a man who was crouched on the ground. One of the assailants held their victim in place by his collar. The man on the ground was slumped face down. He was hardly putting up any resistance.

Samejima remembered seeing one of the assailants before—one of the punks loyal to the Hanaigumi *yakuza* clan. The other two looked as if they were similarly connected.

Samejima quickly scanned the neighborhood. There was no sign of a uniformed police officer. It was clear that the man on the ground had lost the will to fight. It didn't look as though his attackers were intent on killing him.

"You stupid…" was the thought that first occurred to Samejima.

The Shinjuku police were already stretched to the limit due to their garden party duties.

The Police Organised Crime Department, *Marubo*, was fairly strong and had put pressure on the various *yakuza* clans. Accordingly, gang members, particularly in a bunch, didn't go out of their way to pick fights with ordinary members of the public. The man who was being beaten up didn't appear to have any friends of his own. Maybe they'd run off or gone to call the police.

If he was alone, he must have done something in his drunken stupor— impersonated the gangsters perhaps—to provoke such an attack.

The *yakuza* wouldn't have gone so far if they'd simply caught the man's gaze in passing.

Samejima detested the *yakuza*. Strangely enough, many officers preferred the *yakuza* to ordinary law-abiding citizens.

There were those who hated the *yakuza*, like Samejima, and others who were on quite familiar terms with them. It was the *yakuza*'s values that Samejima despised most of all.

But there were officers who fraternized with the *yakuza*, claiming they understood the *yakuza* more than they did ordinary people.

Samejima sighed and took a step toward the gangsters. *Yakuza* gangsters, unlike the *bosozoku* bike gangs, knew how to inflict pain without killing. Even if Samejima left their victim alone now, two weeks suffering from bruises and a nosebleed would be all.

Having stumbled across the scene, Samejima was unable to pretend he hadn't seen it. The irony suddenly struck him that if he stopped to save this man from taking a beating, he'd surely take one from Sho.

But he couldn't think of that at the moment. He took another step forward. Two new faces joined the onlookers.

The punishment being meted out by the gangsters had almost come to an end.

It happened as Samejima came closer to the fight. The Hanaigumi gangster swung back his right leg and prepared to deliver a final kick. Samejima casually swept the gangster's other leg from under him. The gangster, who hadn't been paying attention to his rear, found himself with no supporting leg and fell squarely on his back.

"Hey, you fucking…"

"What the hell, you asshole."

The other two gangsters, faces red with anger, turned and faced Samejima.

"Stop it," said the gangster on the ground to his two accomplices, having looked up and recognised Samejima.

"Who the fuck do you think you are?"

Samejima twisted the wrist of the gangster who had grabbed hold of his collar.

"Please, let us go. These guys don't know who you are."

Samejima ignored the gangsters and looked down at their victim.

"What do you mean, boss? This son of a bitch kicked you down."

"Just shut up, you prick. Let's get out of here."

Their victim didn't appear to have suffered any serious injuries. His lip was split, and blood was running from his nose, but otherwise he didn't seem too badly shaken up.

Of more concern was the state of shock he'd be in at having been treated so roughly in a public place. It wasn't at all uncommon. The psychological damage from a beating by gangsters in an amusement quarter like this one always stayed with the victim. Even after the physical wounds had healed, the victim avoided such places and developed an almost pathological fear of gangs and violence.

Samejima squatted down in front of the man.

"Are you okay?"

The man was still young, in his mid-twenties.

Blood and saliva were stuck to his upper lip and under his chin. He screwed his eyes tight shut and moaned slightly. He smelled faintly of alcohol. He didn't appear to have consumed a large quantity of *saké*, but he was definitely drunk. He wore jeans and a T-shirt and a short coat made of a thin black material. A black earphone cord attached to a portable stereo protruded from his coat pocket.

"Hey," Samejima shook the man's shoulder again.

The man muttered something indistinct. It sounded to Samejima like "fuck you."

"Can you stand up?"

"Shut up!" The man brushed Samejima's arm away. He spat on the ground. "Fuck off and leave me alone!" His eyes opened wide and he stared at Samejima. His bloodshot eyes were filled with tears. Dark bruising was starting to appear on his left cheek.

Just as Samejima thought he ought to take him to a police box, the man got shakily to his feet. He placed his right hand on his side where he had been kicked and doubled over. When he stood straight up again, he was taller than Samejima had imagined. He was fair-complexioned, but not frail.

"Wait a moment," said Samejima, placing his hand on the man's shoulder. But the man gripped his hand violently and shoved him away. The pain from where the man's nails had dug in knifed through Samejima's hand. The man stared at Samejima through eyes partly hidden by a long fringe. They were dark eyes.

"Dammit," the young man spat.

The other pocket of his coat bulged with rolled-up paper. It looked like a movie pamphlet or something similar.

The man headed toward the station, tottering. It was hard to say whether this was because he'd been beaten up or because he was just plain drunk.

Samejima had a lasting impression of those dark eyes.

As the man's back was swallowed up in the Kabukicho crowds, Samejima inspected the back of his hand. The man's nails had left two deep welts in his hand.

The Hanaigumi gangsters had disappeared without a trace.

Samejima felt strangely annoyed. It wasn't that he was expecting any words of thanks. He'd discarded such indulgent expectations long ago. Shinjuku was, after all, different.

Police officers who worked the streets were considered fully fledged after they had three to four years of experience behind them. With officers assigned to the Shinjuku force, it was one year. This fact alone was indicative of the volume of accidents and crimes occurring there.

Samejima had been a street cop some eleven years ago, only for six months. In that short time he'd come to appreciate just how tough the Shinjuku police officers were.

In this town there were two laws: crime law and the law of the jungle. The local residents were, generally speaking, well versed in both of them. Without exception, people who lived in Shinjuku earned their living there as well. So long as they lived in Shinjuku, they learned all about those two laws.

Samejima caressed the wound on the back of his hand and began walking. The gallery had by now dispersed and only a handful of onlookers remained, gazing curiously at Samejima.

The TEC Hall was diagonally opposite the Kabukicho Police Box. The concert hall was located in the second-level basement. Samejima went on past the Shinjuku Koma Theater and Toho Assembly Hall and turned the corner at the police box.

On duty until 10:00 a.m. the next day, the police officer stood in front of the police box. He noticed Samejima and saluted. He was still young, maybe twenty-five. Senior officers were not assigned to the Kabukicho Police Box. The oldest officers there were thirty-five.

Samejima stopped. He couldn't decide whether to report the incident. All he needed to say was that there'd been some trouble. But neither the attackers nor the victim would be found at the scene of the incident. Added to which, the uniformed police officers were tired, having been on special alert for days now. There seemed little point in having them rush to the scene of a crime when nobody was there.

Samejima casually returned the salute and tripped down the steps of the TEC Hall. He pushed on the concert hall door and was greeted by the sight of empty seats. The only light came from the wide stage. The band's gear had all but been stowed away.

Sho was sitting on the edge of the stage, dangling long, bare legs over the side. She was wearing a rather racy leather mini-skirt over black tights. She pushed back her fringe with its purple-colored streaks and lifted a glass to her mouth.

She noticed Samejima and lowered the glass.

"You're late, you jerk."

She pursed her lips, but she didn't appear to be all that angry. The concert couldn't have gone too badly.

"My fault, I'm sorry."

Samejima stopped several paces in front of the stage and looked up at Sho.

She was twenty-two. Who's Honey was her second band. In her previous band she'd doubled as both the bass and vocals; in Who's Honey she only did vocals.

Her volatile temper was written all over her handsome, well-defined features.

Her dress sense wasn't gaudy. Her everyday appearance conveyed ample natural sex appeal.

Occasionally Samejima jokingly called her "Rocket Tits," referring to her 88cm bust and barely 60cm waist. To make matters worse, Sho usually went on stage braless. Her excuse seemed to be that she couldn't shout properly while wearing a constricting device. They had become acquainted a year ago.

"Your meeting's finished?" inquired Samejima.

Sho nodded and gulped down her drink. She emptied the remaining ice into her mouth and set the glass down. Then, swinging her legs and using the momentum, she jumped down from the edge of the stage. She seemed confident that Samejima would catch her. Indeed, Samejima had already taken two steps forward, and caught her in his outstretched arms. Her soft body, giving off a slight fragrance of cologne mingled with perspiration, fell into Samejima's chest.

"Hey, that was a pretty crazy thing to—"

Sho smothered the rest of his words with her lips. Prizing his teeth apart with her tongue, she forced her ice cube into his mouth. She pulled away and looked into Samejima's eyes and let out a deep throaty laugh.

"You joker," said Samejima at last, having crushed the ice and swallowed it.

"But it tasted good, didn't it?"

Some of the live house staff were still on stage, but Sho didn't seem to give a damn what they thought.

She slipped out of Samejima's arms. "Where shall we go?"

"Are you hungry?"

"Yeah, I'm starving."

"How about we eat some *yakiniku*?"

"Sounds good to me."

"What about the other guys?"

"You want to treat us all?"

Samejima shrugged his shoulders.

"Did the concert go well?"

"I'd give us 80 out of 100."

"That's pretty good, isn't it? Worth celebrating."

Samejima stood on tiptoe so he could see the back of the stage. There were four members of Who's Honey besides Sho. It was a simple rock band with just drums, guitar, bass and keyboard.

"They're not here anymore."

"What's up? Are they all ashamed of Her Ladyship's behavior?"

Sho grinned. "They said they didn't want to eat with a cop."

"Assholes."

Samejiima grabbed hold of Sho's collar.

"Hey, that hurts! Violent cop! Someone call the police!"

"If you make any trouble, I'll cuff you and take you down the cells."

"You mean, take me to the room at the back and do dirty stuff to me?"

"You bet. You've absolutely no idea how enormous a police officer is. A pro-wrestler would be put to shame."

"Oh! Oh!" moaned Sho, lowering and twisting her body and gyrating her hips. She looked up at Samejima and said, "Such a big—talker!"

Samejima forced a smile and shook his head. "Whenever I bump into the officers from juvenile crime I'm afraid they're going to start talking about you."

"No way. I'm an uptown girl from Yamanote."

"Come on, let's go," said Samejima, executing a mock karate chop with his hand.

It was a little after 11:00 p.m. when they left the *yakiniku* restaurant on Kuyakusho Street. Between them they had gone through four servings of beef flank, two portions of salted tongue, and four bottles of beer.

Sho always had a healthy appetite after a stage performance—probably because she put everything into her singing.

While they were eating, she talked about the performance. There'd been about fifty people standing in the TEC Hall, which had a seating capacity of a hundred and fifty.

Sho's band performed live five times a month mainly in and around Tokyo.

A month ago they'd decided to sign up with an agent. They planned to release their debut album in the next six months. Sho had written the lyrics of nearly all thirty of the Who's Honey original songs. Samejima had helped out with a few of them.

They walked along Kuyakusho Street in the direction of Yasukuni Street.

A year ago, when he first met Sho, Samejima had been on the trail of a group who were selling the chemical cleaning agent toluol. Although the group was described as such, it was just a bunch of young guys in their late teens and early twenties. The members were all former classmates from junior high who, not belonging to any *yakuza* clans, made some small-time money for themselves by stealing quantities of toluol from a paint shop and selling it to guys they knew.

One of the teenagers, a seventeen-year-old former *bosozoku* bike gang member, was stabbed by one of the local *yakuza* thugs. The teenager, stabbed in the thigh, died of shock from loss of blood. Soon afterwards, his attacker surrendered himself to the Shinjuku Police Station. The wholesale group disbanded a short while later because of the incident.

The self-styled leader of the group was the boyfriend of one of Sho's friends. He hadn't inhaled the toluol himself; instead he spent pretty much all the money he'd managed to save on buying apparatus for his band and on studio rental costs. Sho's friend had volunteered to manage the band and worked part-time as a bar hostess, pouring all her salary into the band.

The leader had disappeared, and in order to track him down, Samejima had gone to meet the girl at Sho's apartment, where she'd been staying.

At the time, Sho had been living in a one-room apartment near Yoyogi station.

Samejima knew he'd never forget the first time he saw Sho's face, when he called at her apartment and she opened the door for him. She had great black bruises around her eyes, and her lips were swollen to twice their normal size. Samejima later discovered that she'd been beaten up by *yakuza* gangsters who were looking for the toluol group leader.

"Show me your ID."

Those were the first words Sho spoke when he told her he was a police officer. Samejima opened the ID page of his police notebook and showed it to her through the gap in her chain-locked door.

"Are you alone?"

"I'm alone."

"I thought detectives always went around in twos."

Sho contorted her swollen lips. It took Samejima a while to realize she was smiling.

"I always work alone. Who did this to you?"

"*Yakuza*," Sho answered frankly.

"Where were they from?"

"I've no idea. What is it you want?"

"I'm looking for a friend of yours—Mika Akizuki."

Sho shrugged her shoulders. "Wait a minute."

The door closed. When it opened again, Mika Akizuki was standing in the doorway where Sho had been. Sho was in the back of the room; she wore a set of headphones and was staring at a music sheet. She was dressed in jeans and a tanktop, while Mika Akizuki had on a one-piece mini-skirt.

"Can I come in?" asked Samejima.

Mika turned to look at Sho; unconcerned, she earnestly scribbled annotations on her music sheets.

"What's she doing?"

"Coming up with lyrics. She's got to put a song together by tomorrow," answered Mika, her expression serious.

Samejima and Mika faced each other in the apartment's narrow kitchen.

"Are you looking for him? Kakkun?" Mika said first.

The group leader's name was Katsuji.

"Yes, I am."

"Are you going to arrest him?"

Samejima nodded.

Mika let her long hair fall forwards over her downcast face. She covered her face and hair with both hands and kept very still.

Samejima waited.

After the pause, Mika's voice came disconnectedly through the gaps in her fingers. "I…tried my best…to help Kakkun. I loved his music… He was so easygoing, so gentle and kind to me… He had a lot of fans, but he said I was the best… Even that horrible business… I'm sure Kakkun did it for the band…"

"Does he know they're after him?"

Mika nodded.

"I was almost caught yesterday, but Sho saved me. So they beat her up instead."

Samejima looked again at Sho. She had a troubled look on her face as she erased something she'd written down.

"Does she know all about it?"

"She doesn't know anything. But she still helped me out without asking any questions, saying we're buddies." Mika sighed and sniffed, "But it's no good anymore. I can't go on covering up for Kakkun. Because of me and him, Sho was beaten up like that."

"She didn't ask why? She just protected you and took a beating from the *yakuza* for her trouble?"

Mika nodded, her face still buried in her hands.

"Did she file an injured person's report?"

"No. I told her to. But Sho said if she made a complaint, it would cause trouble for me and the others."

Samejima knew Mika was appealing for help. At first, she didn't want Katsuji to be caught, but now that the *yakuza* were after him she was concerned for his safety. She obviously thought it would be better for him if he were arrested.

"Where is he?"

"Will you help him? Kakkun?"

"I'll see what I can do. If you prefer, I won't say I heard his whereabouts from you."

"Really?"

Samejima nodded. "That's a promise." And he meant it.

Mika told him where Katsuji was hiding out. It was a live house in Kichijoji.

"I know the place. I'll go there right now." Samejima stood up.

"Wait, I'll go too." Mika sprung to her feet.

Samejima looked at her face and shook his head from side to side. "You'd better not. If he sees you with me he might jump to the wrong conclusion."

"I don't care. Take me with you."

It was just as Samejima was trying to reason with her that Sho spoke up. "I'll go with you two."

Samejima looked at her and said, "The people who did that to you might be watching the place."

Sho stood there, expressionless. "They've no reason to kill me. And if you're there I'll be fine."

"They never forget a face, those guys."

"I've nothing to do with them. I'm not even selling paint thinners."

It was better than going there alone with Mika.

"Okay, let's go," said Samejima.

Samejima and Sho went into a small gay bar on Kuyakusho Street called Mama Force. It was run by a "Mama" who used to be a coal miner.

It was early and the bar was almost empty. A man sat at the counter, which was designed to accommodate eight people, reading a book, with a whiskey and water set down in front of him. The Mama, who was dressed in woman's clothes, sat with her legs crossed behind the counter, looking down at a paperback.

"Well what a surprise, I haven't seen you in a long while."

The Mama put her book to one side and stood up. The man at the counter also knew Samejima.

"It's been a long time, Tobita-san," said Samejima, sitting down and leaving a space between himself and the man.

"He's such a bad customer! Sitting in the bar and spreading out his legal precedent books," barked the Mama.

Samejima smiled.

Tobita was a court-appointed lawyer. He had a law office together with a fellow attorney over in west Shinjuku, where he specialized in criminal work.

Tobita smirked. He was of average height and wore glasses, and his hair was neatly parted at the side. He was well known for never wearing his lawyer's badge after hours.

"I heard that before long the real-estate loan sharks will be looking at this place too. You could use me as a kind of bodyguard."

"It's no laughing matter," retorted the Mama. "I'll be delighted if they show up here. I'd sell up if the price is right. Having a lawyer loitering around here all the time is more trouble."

Sho bowed toward Tobita. "It's been a long time."

"Ah, you look well, dear."

It was Tobita who had defended Katsuji.

"Thank you for your assistance back then."

Sho had addressed the lawyer in a courteous manner. Samejima stared at her. "So you can speak politely to people, as long as they're not police," he said.

"Shut up!" came her reply.

The Mama burst out laughing and lined up on the counter a bottle of Jameson's whiskey and an icebox, then took out some glasses. For hors d'oeuvres, there was shellfish boiled in soy sauce.

"Mama, do you know the bar Agamemnon?" asked Samejima, picking up his whiskey and water.

"I know it." The Mama, who was about to pick up her paperback once again, looked at Samejima.

"What kind of a joint is it?"

"It's a private club. Non-regulars hardly ever get in. And if you're straight they'd sense it right away."

Samejima let out a sigh. "Do you know any of the bar staff?"

"I know a young guy who works behind the counter there, from when we used to be over in Ni-Chome. Why do you ask?"

"I wonder if I can get him to help me out a little."

"Hmmm, I wonder. It all depends."

"I want him to let me know if a certain customer shows up."

"That could be difficult."

"It would be better than me going there and asking all sorts of questions, wouldn't it?"

"Yeah, I have to say they wouldn't be too happy if you turned up there. Those clubs hate the *yakuza,* but they hate the cops too."

"I don't want to cause any problems for the bar. I plan on making the arrest only once the customer has left the premises."

"What did he do, this guy?"

"Illegal manufacture of firearms."

Tobita, who had been feigning indifference, suddenly looked up.

Taking no heed of him, Samejima continued. "One person has died and another been seriously injured thanks to a gun he supplied. Three weeks ago."

"Hey, wait a minute," said Tobita.

Samejima lifted his glass and drank some whiskey and water.

"Is that the guy I think it is?"

Samejima deposited his gaze to the back of the bar.

"The guy with a tattoo on his left shoulder?"

At length, Samejima turned to face Tobita. "Yeah, it's him. Thanks to your plea bargaining he came out of prison the end of last year. He got himself a new place to live and now he's back working hard as ever at his old trade."

Plea bargaining was the tactic used to extract a confession in return for a reduced sentence. Tobita turned pale.

Samejima continued to talk: "But it's not your doing really. By nature he's the sort who likes making guns. Even in prison, if he could lay his hands on the tools, he'd probably make them out of metal bars and a toothbrush. All he does is make the things, he doesn't care about what happens after that. Whether a person dies, or ends up spending the rest of his life in a wheelchair, is of no concern to him."

"Perhaps, rather than sending him to prison, it'd be better to crush all his fingers," said Tobita conversationally.

Taken aback, Samejima looked at Tobita. Tobita's expression was dead serious.

"I may be a lawyer, but it doesn't mean I believe all my clients are innocent. There are some that I'd give a harsher sentence than the public prosecutor asks for."

"Is that true in this case?"

"On a strict interpretation of the law, the requested four-year sentence was too severe. The problem is that the case was judged only on the basis of the charges brought by the public prosecutor. The problem, as far as the law was concerned, wasn't that he manufactured firearms with the result that those firearms were used to kill people. That's just the way the law is, and we all have to work within the boundaries of the law."

"There are some people I'd like to sentence to death even though they haven't killed anyone," said the Mama.

Tobita nodded in agreement. "I agree with you entirely. Taking another's life is the most serious of crimes as far as the law is concerned. But people commit much more inhuman acts under so-called lesser crimes. If you compare the case of a parent who kills an ill child out of despair for its future, and the case of a crook who cheats an old person out of his entire fortune, the law will treat the killing of the child as the more serious crime."

"I think you'd make a better prosecutor than a lawyer," said Samejima.

Tobita smiled. "I couldn't have become a public prosecutor. I only just scraped through my bar exam."

Samejima nodded, and looked at the Mama. "Can you arrange for me to have a conversation with the guy at Agamemnon?"

The live house at Kichijoji had already been staked out by the *yakuza*. While walking from the station with Mika and Sho, Samejima noticed a Mercedes parked close by that he had seen before.

"Wait here."

He left them behind and walked up to the Mercedes and rapped on the driver's side window. The junior boss, who was commanding the *yakuza* on watch, peeped his face out.

"I'm with the Shinjuku Police," said Samejima, without giving the man a chance to say anything. "Move your car from here and go back to your office."

The *yakuza* knew Samejima's face but didn't know of his reputation for how he dealt with gangsters.

"Who are you to order me around? What are you, a traffic cop? If you're with the Shinjuku Station, you don't have the jurisdiction."

There was another young gangster in the passenger seat, and the *yakuza* was clearly trying to demonstrate he was in control of the situation by his bullish behavior.

"Get out of the car," Samejima said curtly.

The *yakuza* ignored him and tried to wind up the open window. In the same instant, Samejima whipped out his special police baton and shattered the side window.

The special police baton was a weapon that many plainclothes officers routinely carried around with them. It was made of metal and was approximately an inch in diameter and a half-foot in length. With a flick of the wrist it could be extended to a foot and a half.

Having witnessed the window of his cherished car being smashed, the *yakuza* flew out of the car, his face contorted with anger.

"You bastard!"

Samejima grabbed hold of the man's cheeks and pounded his face against the broken window. With his face pressed against the broken shards of glass, the *yakuza* let out a moan.

"There, how'd you like that? It's called '*ban kake*'. You got any complaints?"

Ban kake was a method of questioning a criminal suspect. Knowing that if he resisted, he would be arrested for interfering with a government official in the exercise of his duties, the *yakuza* quietened down.

"You get out too."

Samejima ordered the lackey in the passenger seat to come out. Then he had them place their hands on the roof of the Mercedes while he searched them.

A mountaineers' knife was inserted in the lackey's jacket.

"And what do we have here?"

"I've no idea."

"That's just great."

Samejima splayed his legs and kicked him in the groin from behind.

"What the hell are you doing? You're taking things too far!" shrieked the junior boss, looking over at the gangster squatting down on the ground. "You don't do this kind of shit in the middle of a busy street. Even *Marubo* wouldn't behave like this."

"Well, I'm not like *Marubo*. I don't give a shit about you losing face."

A sharp intake of breath. Then: "What the fuck. Where the hell are you from then?"

"I'm Samejima, from Crime Prevention. You'll do well to remember my face."

The instant he heard Samejima's name, the *yakuza* had a look of regret on his face.

The similarity of the values shared by the police and the *yakuza* manifested itself in the completely vertical structure of their respective organisations. An order from above was absolute, and transgression was not permitted. As a result, those further down the chain of command developed a like-minded predisposition.

It was all bound up with the concept of honor among men and the resultant chivalrous notion of returning favors, of honest giving and taking.

The relationship between the police and the *yakuza* was one of give and take, of granting the other face-saving concessions.

In the case of a conflict between gangs, the purpose of many criminals handing themselves in to the police wasn't solely to achieve a reduced sentence. The practice was also instrumental in allowing the *Marubo* a means of saving face—it helped maintain a mutually satisfactory co-existence.

While those in high official circles within the police force expressed their intention to annihilate violent groups, those police officers operating on the ground knew that the gangs would not be broken up so easily. The prevailing attitude on the ground seemed to be that gang members would be easier to deal with if the police could identify the various organisations, rather than let them dissolve and have matters take their own course. *Marubo* didn't do things the way Samejima did them. Another cop would have put it differently: "This is a matter of face, please leave for now." And a detective from a department other than *Marubo* would only act after consulting with *Marubo*. The *yakuza* would then receive prior warning of any intended action.

The only detective in the Shinjuku force who singularly failed to operate on this basis was Samejima. His methods caused waves within the police force but were even more disliked by the *yakuza*.

Samejima was a detective who didn't grant any concessions. If no prior warning was given, there was unrest in the *yakuza* camp; they had to be afraid of being hauled off to prison for committing even minor crimes. One reason for the existence of a relationship of concessions and prior communication was the desire on the part of the police officers to avoid the mountain of paperwork associated with making an arrest. It would begin with an application for an arrest warrant; then there would be a demand for support, the arrest itself, the investigation, and the preparation of the deposition. Even if matters progressed that far, the case often came to an end because it couldn't be referred to the Public Prosecutor's Office on the grounds of inadequate evidence. If that happened, all the work would have been for nothing, and on occasion the case and the police would be censured by the prosecutor. As a result, and leaving aside confessions, which were easily obtained from those criminals turning themselves in to the police, there developed a relationship whereby it was difficult to make an arrest even where the person was a known gang member.

"Shit!" the *yakuza* continued to rail.

Without saying a word, Samejima snapped a set of handcuffs onto his right wrist. He fastened the other end to the door handle of the Mercedes.

The other stared in disbelief at the unfolding events.

"Come on, give me a break will you?"

The *yakuza,* still fastened securely to the car door, had begun to notice the scrutiny he was getting from passersby.

"You're not going to leave me here like this, are you?"

Samejima levelled a cool stare at the *yakuza.* "What's there to complain about? Your buddy's in violation of the Firearms and Edged Weapons Law, and you're guilty of interfering with a government official in the exercise of his duty."

"Okay, okay. I'll get out of here."

"It's a little too late for that," said Samejima, turning around and walking away.

The *yakuza*'s scream sounded loud behind, but Samejima didn't look back.

"Let's go," said Samejima, returning to where Mika and Sho were standing waiting.

"Were they staking out the joint?"

"Yeah."

"I wonder if Kakkun is okay," said Mika, looking like she might start to cry again.

"He'll be okay, for the moment. The *yakuza* must have assumed someone will call the cops if they go into the live house after him, so instead they'll be biding their time waiting to ambush him when he comes out. They may have brought some subordinates—they're likely to be surrounding the live house."

"Are you going to bring him out alone?" asked Sho.

"I'm going to try."

"You're pretty weird."

"You think so?"

Samejima stood at the entrance to the live house. The place was in the basement of a long, narrow multi-purpose building, and the walls of the stairwell leading down to it were covered in graffiti.

Samejima lit a cigarette and scanned the area around him. He took in a likely looking Toyota Crown and a Nissan Cima parked nearby. There was also a group of gangsters with a mobile phone in the coffee shop across the road, looking their way through the window.

Samejima remembered seeing a car phone in the Mercedes. It seemed the junior boss didn't intend to make an appearance in person; instead he meant to issue his commands from a distance. It looked as though the total number of gangsters keeping watch was no more than eight or nine.

The door to the live house was closed with a sign on it that read: *Under preparation. Opening soon.*

The *yakuza* clearly intended to rush Katsuji all at once when he came out and carry him away to some unknown destination.

Samejima stamped out his cigarette, and said to Sho, "You know Katsuji, don't you?"

"Of course," answered Sho, holding Samejima's gaze.

"What's he like?"

"He's got a great voice. He can make people weep with his Blues. Especially women. A bastard, but his songs are the best."

Samejima looked away. A *yakuza,* with a mobile phone receiver glued to his ear, was staring down from the second-floor window.

"All right. You go down and bring Katsuji up. I'll wait here. If he comes up the stairs himself he'll be giving himself in. If I have to go down and get him it'll be an arrest. Tell him that."

Sho took a deep breath. "What about Mika?"

"She'll be here with me. If he says anything, tries to make a problem, tell him that we've come here to protect him from the *yakuza*. If that's not true, then there's no way Mika would have told us where he was hiding out."

"I understand. But what about the lookouts?"

"You can tell him about them. If we leave, then they'll raid the place and tear him apart."

There was a brush of air, and Samejima looked around. Sho was already halfway down the stairs leading to the basement.

"I haven't, have I?" said Sho, bathed in red and green light from the stained glass lampshade.

"What?"

"I've never been to your apartment."

"No you haven't, come to think of it."

Samejima knocked cigarette ash into an ashtray, which was balanced on his bare chest.

After leaving Mama Force, they'd gone to Sho's apartment in Shimokitazawa. Sho lived in a one-bedroom apartment in a multi-story apartment block that also housed a video rental shop and an ice cream store. She'd moved out of her apartment in Yoyogi nearly six months ago.

"Can't I go sometime?"

"It's not like you to say that. Do you think I've got a wife there or what?"

"Don't be stupid."

Sho turned over to face Samejima on her semi-double bed, and her full breasts pressed up against his left shoulder.

"Are there things about you that you still haven't told me?"

"Of course there are. If I tried to tell you everything I've done in my life it would take me thirty-six years."

"Quit fooling around! I think the reason you keep me away from your apartment is there's someone you don't want to know about me. I don't mean a woman, but some guys who don't like you."

"If I was that bothered about it then we wouldn't be able to walk around together in Kabukicho."

"Well, in that case, why is it?"

Samejima didn't answer. As he drew on his cigarette, the nail marks on the back of his hand stood out in relief in the glowing light of the cigarette tip.

"What have you done to yourself?" said Sho, noticing the welts on his hand.

"I saw a fight. I tried to break it up and got this."

"That's not like you. You messed up."

"Probably. I'm full of scars where I've messed up."

"On your neck too?"

Samejima laughed.

When they first slept together, Sho had asked Samejima why he wore his hair long. Without saying anything, he had scooped up the long hair from the back of his neck and shown her. Just above the nape of the neck was a six-inch scar running diagonally across the hairline. Sho didn't ask any more questions about it at the time.

"How did you get that scar on your neck?" said Sho, staring into Samejima's eyes.

Samejima gazed at his own reflection in her big black pupils. The scent of soap. Sho's eyes were serious.

"It was a Japanese sword."

"A real one?"

"No. It was a replica without an edge. Had it been the real thing it wouldn't have left a thick scar like this. Either that, or it would have taken my head off altogether."

"Did the guy realize it was a replica when he attacked you?"

"I wonder. I don't think he remembered—he was all wound up. If he'd wanted to kill me he should have stabbed me with it."

"You were lucky it didn't break your neck."

"First it hit my shoulder, and then it skidded onto my neck. It would have been dicey if it had struck my neck directly."

"So he was trying to kill you."

Samejima stubbed his cigarette out in the ashtray without replying. He could feel the warmth of the flame on his chest as it passed through the porcelain base of the saucer.

"Was he a *yakuza*?"

"No."

"So, an ordinary decent guy took out a *katana* and tried to kill you?" Samejima removed the ashtray and propped himself up.

"He was police."

Samejima remained where he was. Sho knocked on the door and had one of the live house staff let her in. It was close to ten minutes before she came out again.

"Kakkun," said Mika.

Samejima turned around and looked down the stairwell. A tall man with short hair was coming up the stairs behind Sho. He had sunken cheeks and big eyes, the perpetual sulky face of a malcontent child. There was a certain look about his eyes that seemed peculiar to him, a mixture of dissolution and arrogance.

Katsuji looked up at Samejima blankly. He looked tired of being on the run.

After looking sympathetically at Katsuji's face for an instant, Samejima looked back again at the surrounding area. The *yakuza* had disappeared from the window, and the car doors of the Cima and Crown were open. A group of *yakuza* appeared from the entrance to the building with the coffee shop. *Yakuza* also climbed out of the cars and stood to the side of the vehicles staring in Samejima's direction.

The *yakuza* who had come out of the coffee shop surrounded Samejima and Katsuji, Sho and Mika. There were five of them.

The gangster with a mobile phone took a step forward. He was still young. Twenty-five, six. He had a fair complexion and was heavy set, with a watchful look about him. He wore a double-breasted pinstriped suit without a necktie.

"The key." The young gangster spoke with a hoarse voice. It was a severe voice that didn't go with his age. "The junior boss told me to get the key to the handcuffs."

The words were polite, but his manner of speaking was brusque. He held out his left hand.

"Is that all you want?" asked Samejima, looking the gangster straight in the eye.

"That's all," said the young man without blinking. "The junior boss is embarrassed, being cuffed to the car like that."

Without averting his gaze, Samejima fished the key to the handcuffs out from his trouser pocket. He decided that when the time came, he would truss this young man up and make sure he was the very first of this bunch to go to prison.

"What's your name?" asked Samejima, still holding the key in his hand.

"Makabe," replied the young man. He kept his eyes trained on Samejima.

"Is it your turn to go down next?"

Without saying anything, Makabe bowed his head slightly.

"I'm Samejima, of the Shinjuku force."

"I know. 'The Shark.'" Makabe raised his head and looked Samejima squarely in the eyes.

"How do you know my name?"

"I keep my eyes and ears open in the territory. It's a *yakuza*'s job to know these things."

"Your boss didn't recognize me."

"I must apologize," said Makabe, in a subdued voice. His eyes remained focused on Samejima.

Samejima dropped the key into Makabe's hand. "You can return the handcuffs to *Marubo* when he makes his rounds."

"No. I will return them to you," said Makabe.

"Why?"

"To conceal the shame."

"You think your boss has suffered shame?"

"How else would you describe being trounced by just one man in the middle of the street?"

Samejima drew in a long, slow breath. He could feel the pit of his stomach slowly start to knot. Makabe was not a typical *yakuza*. Usually, where his adversary was a police officer, a *yakuza* gave up and accepted the situation.

Samejima nodded. "Is that right?"

Makabe nodded back. He didn't do this deliberately to intimidate. But, in terms of sheer presence, he by far exceeded his superior.

"I'll be seeing you." Makabe executed a bow, with a menacing glint in his eye. Slowly he changed direction and walked away. He hadn't paid Katsuji any notice.

Samejima watched as Makabe climbed into the rear passenger seat of the Cima. It was clearly an older man that opened the car door for Makabe. Samejima knew deep down that he would have a run-in with this Makabe in the near future. And he knew it would not be resolved easily.

Makabe's face was imprinted in the back of his mind.

He stopped a passing cab and bundled Katsuji into the back. As Mika was climbing in, Sho said, "I'll go home from here."

"Get in. Some of those punks might still be loitering about."

"They've no issue with me," remarked Sho, as she began to walk away.

The door closed and the taxi set off.

For a while nobody said anything. Katsuji had his eyes closed, with his head resting against the seat. Mika on the other hand had her eyes wide open and was staring at the seat in front.

Katsuji spoke, still with his eyes closed. "I guess they'll kill me in prison."

Mika glanced from Katsuji to Samejima.

"Don't you think?" added Katsuji, searching for a response from Samejima.

"What makes you think so?"

"That bunch. They won't forget about me. They'll get me for sure."

Samejima laughed.

Offended, Katsuji lifted his head from the back of the seat. "What's so funny?"

"They don't have that kind of time on their hands. Besides…"

"Besides? What?"

"You're not really that much of a big shot."

Katsuji glared at Samejima in silence. But after a while, he exhaled loudly. It was a sign of pure relief.

"Kakkun…"

Katsuji didn't reply.

"Kakkun." Her voice dissolved into tears.

Katsuji stared vacantly out the window.

"Are you angry at me, Kakkun?"

Samejima slowly looked at Katsuji's profile. An uncertain smile had settled on his face—not quite abandonment and not quite self-contempt.

"When I've done my time, I'll carry on with the band again. Come and watch me, won't you?"

Mika started to cry. Samejima transferred his gaze back to the windscreen.

The following day Samejima paid another visit to Sho's apartment.

It was just after 9:00 a.m. Just as he was coming up to the apartment, Sho came down the stairs, dressed in jeans and trainers.

She noticed Samejima and stopped halfway down the stairs. She had a paper bag and a portable stereo in her hands.

"Are you going out?"

"I thought I'd go out and get some breakfast." She looked over the road toward a family restaurant.

"Do you mind if I join you?"

"Is there something you want?"

Without answering the question, Samejima said, "Did you finish the song lyrics?"

"Not yet. I sat up all night doing it, but it's not right," said Sho, as she came down the remaining flight of steps.

They walked straight over toward the family restaurant. It was deserted. Samejima sat down opposite Sho, in a booth in a corner at the back of the room.

Sho ordered, and then put on her earphones and took out her music sheet from the paper bag.

"It's okay. I can hear you talk," she said, and switched on the stereo.

Samejima sat in silence, sipping weak coffee and staring at Sho.

Sho used the fingertips of her left hand to beat time while she scribbled notes on a sheet of notepaper. She inscribed a number of verses.

She wrote "the worst," and then scratched it out in favor of "the pits." Then she gazed at "tears of steel" and "hollow concrete laughter," and circled "tears of steel." She paused, and wrote, "we need to be happy," and stared at it with a frown.

It seemed she was having trouble getting the phrase right and nothing else was coming to mind.

Samejima could hear the keyboard melody as it resonated from Sho's earphones. Sho was also humming the tune down her nose.

Samejima read what she had written down so far.

Get away, everybody says get away right now, this town is the pits, Shinjuku, nothing but crying voices every night, every night,

Get away, everybody says get away right now, this town is the pits, Shinjuku, nothing but grief, today, and tomorrow too,

But stay here, we'll drink up a hundred gallons of tears, don't tell us we need to be happy,

A joy you don't know, is here after midnight,

Get away, everybody says get the hell out now, this town is the pits of darkness, nothing but crying voices every night, every night,

Get away, everybody says get the hell out now, this town is the pits of darkness, nothing but grief, today, and tomorrow too,

But stay here, we'll drink up those tears of steel, don't tell us—

Sho appeared to be struggling to come up with something satisfactory for the second phrase beginning with "But."

Samejima watched Sho as she stared earnestly at the lyrics with her lips pursed.

They had been sitting at the table for almost ten minutes, and Sho continued to look at her music. It seemed she had decided to concentrate on composing her lyrics until Samejima said something.

"Will you make a record out of it?" said Samejima, breaking the silence.

Sho raised her eyes, and shook her head without saying anything. When Samejima said nothing further, she looked down at her work.

"In the second verse, rather than 'the pits of darkness,' how about 'a core of darkness'?" Samejima suggested.

For a while Sho didn't say anything. But then she picked up her pen and changed "the pits" to "a core."

"You won't get anything for that, you know."

"I know."

Sho lifted her face and glared at Samejima. She looked angry.

"If you don't like it then do it how you want. I shouldn't have said anything. Sorry," said Samejima.

Sho's mouth relaxed with a puff of her cheeks. "It's rock. We're not talking traditional Japanese *enka* here."

"You don't look the type to be performing in a long-sleeved kimono."

Sho looked up at the ceiling and exhaled, "Okay, what do you want?"

"Did something happen, yesterday?"

"Yesterday? You mean on the way home? No, nothing really." Sho shook her head. "Is that it?"

"Don't you want to file an injured person's report, about the bruises on your face?"

"No, I don't."

"Afraid they'll get back at you if you do?"

Sho looked at Samejima in amazement. "You really hate the *yakuza* don't you."

"What makes you think so?"

"What makes me think so? I get the feeling you never pass up an opportunity to get at them, that's what. You'd have them arrested for spitting in the street if you could."

Samejima looked out the window in silence.

"I don't feel like filing a report. It's not that I'm afraid, it's just a hassle having to do it, that's all."

"Really?" said Samejima, reaching out for the bill.

"So, why is it?"

"Why is what?"

"Why is it that you hate the *yakuza* so much?"

Samejima looked at Sho. "It's not just the *yakuza* I hate. I'm not too fond of people who break the law but who think they're decent citizens so long as nobody finds out what they've done."

"If you put it like that, Japan is full of people you hate."

"That's right. But this country's too soft on the *yakuza*. Officially, we're seen to take a tough line with them, but in reality, there are thousands of *yakuza* out there involved in murder who're free to carry on business as usual."

Sho listened quietly.

"The tool of their trade is fear. The *yakuza* are frightening, and they like to make people think they are, in order to bleed them dry. An ordinary person knows that he'll have a tough time if he's caught up in *yakuza* business, so he gives in to their demands. If he goes against them and is attacked and injured, the gangster goes to prison but the damage's already been done."

"But that's taken for granted, isn't it?"

"I don't like things that are taken for granted. As soon as something's taken for granted, you'll have some people manipulating the situation to their advantage. People who, in spite of being self-respecting businessmen, use the *yakuza* to collect their debts and demand the transfer of real estate. I get more annoyed with those guys than I do with the *yakuza.*"

"But, the powers that be don't think that way?"

"That's true."

"The police only seem to arrest people who commit minor offenses. They turn a blind eye to the really bad things being done by the likes of politicians and big business. Right? Everyone thinks so. But you can't say that, or they accuse you of being naïve. That's the way the world is, they say. So, you just have to be smart and live as easy a life as you can."

"It's not about being smart. People who think that way get what's coming to them in the end."

"And what if they don't?" said Sho, with a challenging glint in her eye.

"Then I'll make sure they do."

"What, because you're a cop? Because you carry a badge and pack heat?"

"No, that's not why."

"Then why? You could be hurt, killed, even. Aren't you afraid?"

"I'm afraid."

"Yesterday, you smashed up a *yakuza* car. You pushed that self-important junior boss around. If you weren't a cop they'd have killed you for sure."

"You may be right."

"So why then do you talk so big? Do you think that cops are better than everyone else or something?"

"That's not what I think. But I don't like the idea that I do it just because it's my job."

"You're a show off, aren't you? When it comes down to it."

Samejima smirked. "I may be that, as long as I'm not arrogant with it."

Sho looked at Samejima in astonishment.

"Ordinary people hate the police if they pick up a speeding ticket. But they like the police if they save them from a quarrel with a drunk. Don't they?"

"You aren't arrogant?"

"The only bunch who think I'm arrogant are the ones who are *truly* arrogant. They can't tolerate anyone else throwing their weight around."

Sho looked hard at Samejima's face and said, "Why do they call you 'The Shark'?"

"It's my name. It's taken from Samejima. *Same* as in shark."

"Is that it?"

"That's it."

"Isn't it because, to those guys, you're like a shark? The way you close in on your prey all of a sudden and devour them?"

Samejima didn't respond.

Sho caught the waitress's attention and had her take the plates away. She lit a cigarette and looked straight at Samejima.

"My hope is that one day people who call me that will disappear from Shinjuku."

"You mean, criminals?"

"Yeah."

Sho blew out smoke, and caught Samejima's eye. "But if that happened, Shinjuku would turn into a pretty dull town. Nobody would go there for a good time."

"Maybe. But at least it won't be like in your song."

Sho nodded in agreement. And then she beamed radiantly. When she smiled, her forbidding expression changed completely; her face took on a bright, childlike innocence.

"Do you like rock?"

"Yeah, I do."

"As in, 'Only Jimi Hendrix is real rock'?"

"Up to Deep Purple. Just kidding."

"Why don't you come along to my next concert?"

"Yeah, I'll do that," Samejima said.

And that was just what Samejima did. Two weeks later, at a live house, Samejima discovered that the lyrics to the song "Stay Here" included "a core of darkness."

The live concert came to an end and, just as the audience began to leave, Sho looked out from her dressing room with a towel around her neck and called Samejima over.

"What did you think?" Sho was soaked with sweat. "It wasn't too bad, I'd say."

"Now who's arrogant?"

Sho glared at Samejima. The lyrics to "Stay Here" hadn't changed all that much from when Samejima first saw them, and the part after "we need to be happy" was just the same as the first verse.

Samejima took out a sheet of folded paper from his jacket pocket. "This might help."

"What is it?" Sho took the sheet of paper and opened it. She read over it once and opened her eyes wide in astonishment.

"It's a nice song. But it ends weak," he said.

"Did you write it?"

"Yeah. If you don't like singing someone else's words, you can throw it away."

Sho folded the paper in two and secreted it in the neckline of her costume. The complete new lyrics for the second verse of "Stay Here" were written on the piece of paper.

"Let's go for a drink. But if you start behaving like a cop I'll ask you to leave. I'd like to show this to the band leader."

"I'll wait downstairs," answered Samejima.

Samejima waited until Sho fell asleep and then slipped out of bed. He dressed in the clothes he had dropped on the floor and went quietly to the entrance to the apartment.

Sho woke up as he unfastened the chain and turned the doorknob.

"You going home?"

"Yeah."

"We're doing another concert the beginning of next month. We're going to announce our professional debut. Come along and watch," said

Sho sleepily. "Only this time, be there from the beginning."

"Yeah," Samejima said again.

There was a thud as Sho's head hit the pillow.

"You liar!"

"Good night."

Samejima opened the door.

"If you don't show up I'll call the police," murmured Sho, as if talking in her sleep.

2

Out of a total of 600 regulars assigned to the Shinjuku Police Station, there were 285 uniformed officers.

From among this number, seventy-two officers were assigned to the three Shinjuku police boxes located at Kabukicho, the east exit and the west exit. Each police box had twenty-four officers divided into four squads of six men, and each squad rotated through daytime duties, first watch, second watch and off duty.

There were seven sections at the Shinjuku Station. Each was under the command of an inspector, who acted as section chief and in turn was responsible to the station chief, a senior superintendent, and his deputy, a superintendent. The sections were: General Affairs, Accounts, Guard, Crime Prevention, Crime (Investigation), Traffic, and Patrol.

Samejima was assigned to Crime Prevention, a section primarily tasked with juvenile protection and public morals-related issues, but also the illicit sale of narcotics, stimulants, thinners and toluol.

He lived in a one-bedroom apartment at Nogata in Nakano Ward. He had lived there since his assignment three years ago to Shinjuku Station. Before that, he had lived in a Metropolitan Police dormitory.

This was the second time Samejima had served with the Shinjuku force, although the circumstances this time were quite different.

His first assignment had been at the age of twenty-four when he had suddenly been ordered to report for practical training as an assistant police inspector. This was straight after he had graduated university and passed his civil service exams.

General candidates who had graduated from either high school or college became eligible to sit the police sergeant exams after serving as an ordinary officer for four years, in the case of a high school graduate, or one year, in the case of a university graduate. In order to be able to take the exams for assistant inspector, a candidate who had already made sergeant was required to serve a further three years, for high school graduates, and a further year, for university graduates. After that, both categories of candidate would have to serve an additional four years in order to become a full inspector.

Samejima's practical training with the Shinjuku police force took place during a nine-month period while he was studying at the Police Academy. At the age of twenty-five, Samejima graduated from the academy and became a police inspector.

He had achieved full inspector status in a little under eighteen months since obtaining his bachelor's degree, while the earliest a candidate could ordinarily achieve this would be thirty for a high school graduate and twenty-eight for a university graduate.

This illustrated well the marked difference in treatment within the police organization between "career" officers and "non-career" officers.

When Samejima had first been assigned to the Shinjuku Station, he had been seen as very much someone who was on loan. He was an important article not to be soiled, and the police officers with whom he had been placed treated him with kid gloves.

That was to be expected. A "career" police officer like Samejima, having been promoted to inspector with two years on probation on the Metropolitan Police, could, at the earliest, advance to the rank of superintendent before the age of thirty during the course of postings at both the local and central levels.

Even in a station as large as Shinjuku, the rank of superintendent was equal to deputy station chief. Such a position would carry with it great responsibility, including taking care of the needs of the fraught veteran section chiefs and their daily concerns. It would be rather like a subsidiary company's site manager suddenly being promoted and welcomed as an employee by the parent organisation.

In the following eight years, Samejima came to appreciate some of the serious problems inherent in the type of career system adopted by the Japanese police organization.

Samejima's rank was that of inspector. By rights, he ought to have been at a level equivalent to section chief in Crime Prevention. However, Samejima was merely another investigator within that section. Added to which, there wasn't a single detective who was willing to be his partner.

The reason for this was not only that Samejima had failed to conform to the requirements of the career system, but also his colleagues' perception that he was a loose cannon: an officer who refused to tow the official line within the rigid police organization.

At the age of twenty-seven, Samejima had been assigned to a certain prefectural police headquarters. As a natural stage in his career path, he joined Section Three of the Public Security Department. The majority of career officers rose through the ranks having served in one public security post after another for various provincial police forces. The Third Section of Public Security was tasked principally with the surveillance of anarchist groups and, in particular, those organizations with left-wing connections.

There was also a Public Security Investigation Agency, which had broadly the same characteristics as the Public Security Department. While the agency investigators did not have tools akin to the powers of arrest and search enjoyed by police officers, curiously they too carried out the surveillance of left-wing activists. One method frequently employed was that of cultivating an inside informer—the putting in place of a spy.

There were various ways of infiltrating an organisation with a spy. One method was to bribe a would-be informer. Another involved an investigator making an approach to an activist and, under the pretence of sharing a common interest, becoming friendly with the activist. At this point, the investigator would disclose his true identity and force the activist to cooperate by making veiled threats to let the other activists know about their friendship. Once such cooperation had been secured, the activist would typically be remunerated. Information would be obtained through this classic "carrot-and-stick" method.

However, the existence of two government offices with more or less the same purpose—the same could also be said of ordinary police and narcotics law enforcement—failed to promote a sense of cooperation, resulting rather in intense rivalry.

Both the police and the investigators were vehemently anti-communist. As a result, left-wing activists were routinely persecuted without the slightest sense of guilt on the part of law enforcement.

The Public Security Third Sectio to which Samejima was assigned, as chief inspector, wished to infiltrate the extremist faction of a left-wing organization. The location was a provincial city, but it was also the seat of the local prefectural government. While the population was small, it had at one time been made up of mine workers, providing a rich breeding ground for left-wing activism.

At the time, there had been an assistant inspector called Kamegai serving under Samejima's command. Although a high school graduate, by his mid-thirties he had progressed through the ranks to assistant inspector through hard work and a record number of arrests. However, as was frequently the case, he was right-wing and had an abnormally strong sense of his perceived power as a police officer. A fervent anti-communist, he had also shown signs of sympathizing with right-wing activists. While the senior officers in the prefectural police force were cautious, they had seconded Kamegai to the Public Security section in charge of countering left-wing activity.

Even Samejima, who had just arrived in his new post and had yet to appreciate the nature of the locality or the character of the men under his command, gradually began to sense the danger signs from Kamegai.

Strictly speaking, it was rare for a career police officer to actually lead an investigation. An assignment to prefectural police headquarters was treated more as a fact-finding secondment necessary in the advancement to superintendent.

Generally speaking, even when a subordinate committed a real blunder while under a career officer's command, the organization would sympathize—provided there were no serious consequences—and the matter did not unduly impact the career officer's promotion prospects.

Kamegai was respectful in his own way toward Samejima. However, it was quite clear that as a local police officer, he wasn't of a mind to obtain permission for all his investigative activities from a newly arrived career inspector.

Kamegai's first words to Samejima after his arrival were: "This place has great food and *saké*, sir. You should take a break from all those tough exams you have to sit."

Career officers assigned to the provinces were, to a greater or lesser extent, welcomed in much the same way. As far as the local non-career officers were concerned, contact with the newly arrived career officers was nothing more than a brief interlude and had no real bearing on their future.

Broadly speaking, the career officers were divided into two types. The first were those who, conscious that they were outsiders, took care to make sure they were not a burden to the local officers. The other consisted of those who considered the brevity of their assignment to be irrelevant and had a strong sense of responsibility, and who tried hard to understand the men under their command.

Samejima was of the latter type.

"Thank you," he had replied, "but nobody has ordered me to take it easy. I intend to devote myself to my duties immediately. I dare say there will be things I can learn from you, too, and I hope I can count on your cooperation."

It was clear that Samejima's attitude had incurred the ill will of Kamegai.

Samejima straightaway requested a member of the section staff, who had some time to spare, to submit to him the documentation, together with supplementary explanation, relating to all ongoing investigations.

Samejima wasn't surprised to learn that afterwards Kamegai had called him an "impudent greenhorn grind."

Kamegai had been desperately trying to install a spy in the extremist faction of a certain left-wing organization. "I'm gonna smash those guys one of these days," he was in the habit of saying.

To be sure, the Prefectural Police Public Security Department was paying close attention to this organization, particularly as there had been casualties, including fatalities, from an internal struggle several years earlier.

Then, Kamegai found out that an investigator from the local Public Security Investigation Agency was trying to make contact with a member of the organization.

The member's name was Fuchii. He was a twenty-three-year-old cram school teacher. As yet, his experience as an activist was slight, and he had participated in one of the organization's gatherings simply because one of his colleagues was also a member. Fuchii had been targeted by a veteran investigator called Kanekura. Kanekura discovered that Fuchii belonged to a beach fishing club and approached him by becoming a member himself. Kamegai found out about Kanekura's scheme from an acquaintance of his in the Maritime Self-Defense Force who had seen Kanekura and Fuchii on one of the fishing trips they frequently went on together.

Fuchii had yet to gain the trust of the other members and wasn't privy to details of the organization's planned activities. As a result, Kanekura's approach was relatively easily.

The important cells in the organization would not easily have allowed contact with someone they didn't know. They certainly wouldn't have revealed their addresses and real names to anyone other than a fellow activist.

It appeared that Kanekura had taken time to develop his relationship with Fuchii; he had also waited until Fuchii had become a more trusted member of the organization. Of course, during this time, Kanekura kept his true identity a closely guarded secret.

Unfortunately, Kamegai disliked Kanekura.

"That guy Kanekura's like a fucking leech. Always doing things underhand…"

Several weeks after discovering Kanekura's plan, Kamegai and one of his detective friends arrested Fuchii on suspicion of committing a road traffic violation. The interrogation took place not at the prefectural police headquarters, however, but at a drive-by restaurant managed by one of Kamegai's relatives. Once they had gone through into one of the restaurant's private rooms at the back of the building, Kamegai announced that he was a police officer with Public Security. He proceeded to inform Fuchii that Kanekura was an investigator and stared fixedly at Fuchii as he turned pale with shock.

Kamegai showed Fuchii two sets of photographs. One set was taken with a telescopic lense and showed Fuchii enjoying himself fishing with Kanekura. The second set were of dead bodies from the internal violence several years earlier.

Fuchii began to tremble while he was looking at them.

"If you so much as mention what I've told you about Kanekura to your friends then you'll end up like this too," said Kamegai.

Fuchii fell silent, his whole body quivering. Kamegai grabbed hold of his shoulder and pulled him in close.

"I have a job to do. But I don't like playing games like Kanekura. When your people meet, I want you to send me information. Whatever happens, we'll look after you, that's a promise. How about it?"

"I—I need to think it over."

"That's fine. Think about it as long as you like. We won't arrest you. Even if you escape to another town we won't come after you. But your friends are different. It doesn't matter where you hide, they'll come after you. And when they find you, they'll beat your brains out. Do you know how they do it? There will be several of them, and first they'll break your legs. Then, when you can't move, they'll take it in turns to beat your head in with a steel pipe—you know, like splitting a melon with a stick. And they'll beat you as if their lives depended on it, because if they don't, they'll be suspected of being an informer. I hear the inexperienced guys have trouble doing it because they're puking up all over the place. They always let those guys go first, so you don't get to die quickly. You'll die slowly, your head split open, writhing around in agony, covered in blood..."

Fuchii was "converted." He agreed to become Kamegai's spy.

Samejima was told this by one of Kamegai's colleagues who had been there at the time. He found out about Kamegai's intimidation following an informal complaint to the Third Section by the local head of the Public Security Investigation Agency who had received a report from Kanekura to the effect that his infiltration scheme had been obstructed.

Upon learning how Kamegai had handled the situation, Samejima was seized by rage. The methods were unlawful and dangerous in the extreme. If his threats became known to the left-wing organization, Fuchii's life would be in danger.

Samejima severely reprimanded Kamegai. In addition, he forbade any contact with Fuchii.

Kamegai took it personally. This young superior had taken away from him the one chance he had of finally crushing the extremist faction. With his face a livid color he said, "An inspector who will be leaving this town in a year has no right to meddle in our affairs."

Samejima answered calmly, "If I find out you've approached Fuchii after today, even a phone call, I'll request the department head to have you removed from Section Three. Do you understand?"

Kamegai's face turned pale and expressionless. A look of hate, like hellfire itself, came into his eyes. He turned quickly around. As he left the room he muttered under his breath, "Asshole, are you so afraid of losing your job?"

Kamegai had failed to grasp that Samejima was genuinely concerned for Fuchii's life.

A few days later, Fuchii was attacked in his house by an armed gang. He survived but, as a result of the injuries sustained to his brain, was left in a permanent vegetative state. Moreover, his younger brother, a university student, had been there at the time and suffered injuries to his spinal column so severe that he would have to spend the rest of his life in a wheelchair.

Photographs showing Fuchii meeting with Kanekura were scattered around the scene of the crime.

The Prefectural Police's First Section and Public Security, Third Section established a joint investigation headquarters, following which they arrested half the armed gang members—four men out of eight. The cram school teacher colleague who had enticed Fuchii to join the organization in the first place was amongst their number. The remaining four members had been called in to help from other prefectures and were professional hit men.

Although there was a search for named suspects, two members failed to be apprehended.

On the day the investigation headquarters was disbanded, Samejima was in the basement car park of the Prefectural Police Headquarters.

It was a little after 8 p.m. when Kamegai came down to the car park. He appeared to have drunk a fair quantity of celebratory *saké* at the headquarters and walked unsteadily.

Eventually he managed to insert the key in the door of his car and climbed inside. Just as he eased forward, Samejima stood in front of his car.

Seeing the silhouette in the beam of light, Kamegai stamped on the break pedal and brought the car to an abrupt halt.

"What the hell're you trying to do?" screamed Kamegai from his window.

Samejima looked at him and said, "I'm arresting you for driving under the influence of liquor."

"What the fuck."

At length Kamegai realized it was Samejima and took in a sharp breath.

"Get out of your car."

The two hadn't so much as spoken to one another outside of the job since Fuchii had been attacked, and all the while the joint investigation headquarters had been operating.

"What kind of stunt is this?" said Kamegai in a thick voice, looking down at the object Samejima had in his hand. It was a pair of handcuffs.

"As I said, I'm arresting you."

Kamegai climbed out of the car.

"Very funny, Inspector."

"It was you who sent the photographs, wasn't it?"

Kamegai remained silent. A faint smile appeared on his lips.

"You tipped them off and Fuchii was beaten up."

Kamegai turned away. "I dunno what you're talking about."

His neck, flushed from drinking, glistened with sweat. It was just before the end of the rainy season, and the air in the underground car park was stale and heavy with humidity.

"You must be feeling pretty pleased with yourself, annihilating that gang just as you'd planned."

"Yeah, that's about right," said Kamegai, fixing Samejima with his gaze. There was a glint in his eye. "I don't give a damn what happens to those Commie bastards. Having those pieces of shit kill each other like that was a great success for the Third Section. Has the Chief Inspector got anything to complain about?"

"Thanks to you, the whole of Section Three is smeared in shit as well. What you did was worse than those pieces of shit."

Kamegai's mouth slackened for a brief moment. In the next instant his left fist shot out and struck Samejima in the pit of the stomach. Samejima groaned and bent over, and Kamegai grabbed and twisted his hair. "You think you're smart as hell don't you, kid? How'd you like to be buried alive? Oh yeah, I know a local contractor, a right-winger. He'd love to do it, you asshole."

Kamegai pounded Samejima's forehead against the bonnet of his car. Samejima started to black out and fell flat on his back in the car park. Kamegai kicked him in the chest.

"This is a pretty rough neighborhood. Nobody would bat an eyelid if a new officer lost his way and ended up down some old mine shaft."

Kamegai spat on Samejima's face as the latter looked up. "Sounds like you're pretty friendly with these 'wingers," said Samejima, breathing heavily. Blood streamed into his eyes from the gash on his forehead.

"It's better than siding with those Commie pieces of shit like you do," said Kamegai, looking quickly around the car park. He looked as though he really wanted to finish it there and then.

Samejima's right hand moved. He lashed the handcuffs he had been holding against Kamegai's shin.

Kamegai cursed and leapt out of the way.

Samejima placed one hand on the car and levered himself upright.

"I've done quite a bit of research since I arrived here. Four years ago, the labor union representative of a mining corporation was killed in a hit-and-run incident. He was hit by a contractor's truck being driven by a nineteen-year-old apprentice, who later turned himself in to the police. But the scene of the incident was next to a disused mine which had nothing to do with the contractor and was nowhere near the apprentice's apartment. The victim's family said that he'd been called out by phone in the middle of the night. Just before the incident, a detective by the name of Kamegai had been seen in his patrol car in the same neighborhood. Of course, that was hushed up, and nobody knew who had called the victim out. It was treated merely as an accident."

Kamegai was staring at Samejima, his face devoid of emotion. Then suddenly he started to climb into his car.

Samejima grabbed hold of his shoulder. Kamegai shrugged him off but Samejima recoiled and struck him in the side of his head with his elbow. Propelled by the impact, the opposite side of Kamegai's head hit the roof of the car and he slumped to the floor.

Samejima gripped Kamegai's collar and hauled him to his feet.

"How do you like that? Trash like you shouldn't work as a police officer."

Kamegai let out a roar and shoved Samejima away. He leapt on Samejima, who'd fallen backwards against another car, and squeezed his neck with both forearms.

Samejima brought his knee up into Kamegai's groin. At last, after the third kick, Kamegai released his grip and fell backwards. Samejima threw a straight right at Kamegai's grimacing face. The impact of the blow on Kamegai's crunching nasal bone reverberated down his fist. Kamegai collapsed onto his own car.

Kamegai showed no sign of getting up after that. Samejima, his breathing ragged, turned his back to retrieve his handcuffs from the floor.

"Die!"

The roar of anger sounded behind him. He didn't have a chance to turn around. He felt a jolting impact from the top of the shoulder through to the nape of his neck and fell forwards.

Looking up with his hands on the floor he saw Kamegai wielding a Japanese sword above his head. He had apparently taken it out from where he kept it in his car. He gripped the scabbard tightly in his left hand. With his crushed nose, and covered in blood, Kamegai's face was barely recognizable.

Samejima twisted his body away just in time. The tip of the sword hit the floor and sent sparks flying. His neck was on fire and he watched as blood dripped to the floor.

Kamegai seemed to remember suddenly that the sword was a reproduction without an edge. He gripped the handle with both hands and held the sword at waist height.

"I'll run you through."

He thrust the tip of the weapon towards Samejima. Samejima dropped to the ground and swept his attacker's leg. The pain was terrible and he felt unable to stand up again and fight. Kamegai lost his footing and faltered. But the force of his thrust continued and the tip of the sword passed through the side window of the patrol car. The noise of the glass shattering echoed around the car park.

Kamegai's arms had gone through the window up to his elbows. By wriggling around, trying to free his arms, he managed to cut them on the broken glass. He was covered in blood.

Samejima crawled to where he had dropped his handcuffs. Facing down, blood oozed down his neck and dripped from the point of his chin onto the floor.

His vision was impaired and his body felt abnormally heavy. Even so, he managed to pick up the handcuffs and, before Kamegai could extract himself from the window, fastened Kamegai's ankle to the bumper of the car.

Then he leaned against the door of the patrol car and fell unconscious while waiting for help to arrive.

Seven months later Samejima was ordered to transfer to the Guard Section of the Metropolitan Police's Defense Department. This was the section in charge of guarding the Imperial family.

Kamegai had received a disciplinary discharge, but there had been no criminal indictment.

The top-ranking officials within the Metropolitan Police organization at first appeared to consider transferring Samejima to an internal administrative department like personnel or health and welfare after his stint with the Guard Section. However, perhaps because it was decided that he would be unsuited to that sort of position given his temparment, Samejima's next transfer was to Public Security, External Affairs Section Two.

He had not advanced beyond the rank of inspector.

Three years later, at the age of thirty-three, another incident occurred. Externally, the incident was treated as the suicide of a superintendent assigned to the Metropolitan Police's Public Security Department, Public Security, Second Section.

The reason for the suicide was given as a nervous breakdown brought on by overwork. The superintendent concerned had been a classmate of Samejima and had climbed the ranks in the police force with relentless speed.

Several days before his death he left a letter with Samejima. The reason for this was clear. He knew that Samejima could no longer achieve the same level of advancement in his career.

Samejima knew the truth behind the suicide. The senior officers within the Public Security Department also knew that Samejima knew. It reached the point where Samejima's life was at risk if he were to continue his career as a police officer. Samejima had unwittingly become enveloped in a secret feud within the Public Security Department's administration.

The feud was as yet unresolved, and both sides were desperate to learn what the final words of the superintendent had been. The factions tried various means of extracting the contents of the letter from Samejima, including applying direct pressure, bribery and intimidation. For both sides, the existence of the letter was potentially explosive.

Samejima ignored their entreaties. He had no allies among the senior officers of the Metropolitan Police.

Only one person remained neutral in all of this: the Chief of External Affairs Second Section, who was approaching retirement. When he discovered that Samejima had no intention of resigning as a police officer, he recommended that he be transferred to the jurisdiction of the Shinjuku Police Station.

"Even if you resign, your safety can't be guaranteed. If anything you might be in a more dangerous position. In which case, this transfer would be better for you than staying here."

Needless to say, this was an unprecedented personnel move. Samejima was effectively being demoted.

For both sides in the feud this proved an expedient way of ridding themselves of a nuisance. The arrangements were made with exceptional speed and the letter of appointment for the transfer to Shinjuku Police Station was delivered to Samejima.

The reason why the Shinjuku Police Station was chosen was plain enough. Including within its jurisdiction Japan's largest amusement district, the police officers assigned there were kept busy twenty-four hours a day.

The brass were afraid of sending Samejima away to somewhere beyond their reach. They watched for any sign of him plotting to expose the truth behind the feud while he worked in his unimportant job.

Samejima became the responsibility of the station chief and was assigned to the Crime Prevention Section. To the section members he was a fallen idol. Moreover, he was an idol who possessed a bomb that might one day shake the police organization to its very foundations. Samejima had no intention of dealing with the situation by defusing that bomb. He didn't say as much, but he let it be known to all about him that Samejima was far from finished as a detective.

"That guy's dangerous to be with…"

"He'll get wasted one of these days…"

Whispers in the locker room had the effect of increasingly isolating Samejima. He was forced to become the only lone criminal investigator in the Shinjuku police force. On the face of it, he had colleagues and a desk in the detectives' office, but in reality Samejima was alone.

He carried out most of the dangerous investigations and arrests solo. Samejima's activities were a mystery to his fellow police officers. It wasn't that he concealed what he was doing. If he were asked, he'd talk about most of it. It was simply that nobody asked him.

After three years of going it alone, Samejima claimed the record within the Shinjuku police force for the rate of major arrests made, with the result that he'd come to be known as the "Shinjuku Shark." It was a nickname born of the fear felt toward the lone wolf detective who approached his prey silently and attacked without warning.

3

He had been to Shinjuku three times already this week. Since the beginning of the month he had been fired from two part-time jobs.

At his second job he had been given a real hard time by one of the senior employees before being canned.

I really hate people like you taking things easy all the time, pleasing yourself in life and shirking at your job. I can't tell if you're alive or dead half the time. Boy, do I detest people like you. Take a look at yourself in the mirror. You've no direction in life. I don't want idle good-for-nothings like you around here.

He secretly called the senior employee "Mad Dog."

Mad Dog liked to give the impression he was giving his all to the job. But in fact he was the kind of asshole who'd jump to attention and shout, "Yes sir, I'll get it done right away" as soon as the company president said anything to him.

His colleagues privately referred to the senior employee as an arse licker. But in truth Mad Dog wasn't even as smart as that.

He realized this when one time after work Mad Dog took them to a bar and, drunk on draft beer and *chuhai*, began to lecture them:

You see, what you have to understand is that it's a tough world out there. If you don't try your hardest you'll have your feet swept out from under you. If you slack on the job, you can bet someone will be watching you. To cut a long story short, even today, with that purchase slip...

His colleagues pretended to be impressed and listened attentively. But really they hoped Mad Dog would pick up half the bill. Mad Dog couldn't be expected to pay for everything. Though he was a full-time employee with the stingy company, everyone knew that Mad Dog wasn't paid such a big salary. They only listened out of pity for him. Of course, Mad Dog wasn't aware of this. He was a simple-minded braggart. And because he was a braggart, the drunker he became, the more he talked and the more his tone became that of a well-respected company president. Moreover, after he had finished boasting, he underwent a sudden change, his tone becoming conciliatory, as if he were having a heart-to-heart talk with colleagues:

But you're all good people. You work as hard as you can, I know…

It was laughable, and saying such things made him appear all the more idiotic.

Hey, what's the matter? You're hardly drinking. Don't tell me you can't hold your liquor. The more you drink, the more you'll be able to drink.

He tried to explain that he had a weak constitution when it came to alcohol.

What're you muttering about? I can't hear you if you don't speak up. Weak constitution? That's just an excuse, an excuse I tell you. You're always full of excuses.

Mad Dog had shaken his head from side to side with a pitiful smile on his face:

I don't understand what this fellow's thinking, I really don't.

No, that's not right. He works hard. It's just that, well, he's a bit gloomy, that's all, one of his colleagues came to his rescue.

At first he had thought that only this colleague was his friend. That perhaps they shared interests in similar things.

However, that wasn't the case. Once, the colleague came to his apartment. Although he had looked at his model guns and handcuffs, and the posters on his wall, he didn't show any interest. Neither was his colleague interested when he talked about movies and videos.

The colleague was fairly considerate, with a pleasant enough face, but he felt there was something missing. He went to stay at his apartment once and understood the reason.

Sitting right in the middle of his colleague's six-mat room was a Buddhist altar, about as big as a Western-style wardrobe.

How much was it?

One point two million yen.

He said nothing, just stared at his colleague.

I paid for it with a loan. It's pretty tough making the payments. But, I've changed since I got it. I can concentrate on what people are saying now, and I don't get into fights anymore. It's like I've found the real me.

He wanted to ask how and where his colleague had come to buy the altar. But in the end he didn't bother. He knew that if he asked, his colleague would get serious and begin counseling him about something. Those types liked to recruit more followers to their organization. There was something slightly creepy about them, like their purpose in life was to increase the numbers of their group and go together to study sessions, exchange meetings and similar gatherings.

So he felt like saying, "You of all people have no reason to call me gloomy," but he didn't.

When it came down to it, they were all a bunch of jerks. How could he explain himself to idiots like them if they couldn't even see how idiotic they were?

You're a nerd, are you?

He was momentarily startled when Mad Dog said this to him. He knew better than anyone that he wasn't a nerd. Yet, from the outside, maybe he did look like one. He studied his colleague earnestly, wondering what he would say to Mad Dog. His colleague didn't say anything. He just sat there with a slightly sad expression. If his colleague had said anything like, "Yes, he is a nerd," he'd have gone ahead and blabbed about the Buddhist altar.

It seemed his colleague knew that, too. Seeing him from his apartment to the railway station, the colleague had said: *If they find out about my Buddhist altar, I'll probably lose my job. So please keep it to yourself.*

Don't worry, it's nothing to do with me, he had replied, before taking the train.

He hadn't gone directly home that day. Instead, he'd gone to a "police shop" in Shinjuku called Marksman. The store manager, Igawa, understood him better than anyone. Igawa called him "Ed." Ed was the name of a detective who appeared in the *Ironside* TV series that made up a large part of his video collection. In the original series, besides Ironside and Ed, there was a woman detective called Eve. Eve Whitfield.

Ironside was a detective with the San Francisco Police Department who went around in a wheelchair. Ed was his sidekick, the archetypal detective—he liked this character best. He also had other series in his video collection: *The Mod Squad*, *Hawaii Five-0*, *The F.B.I.*, *The Felony Squad*, *The Search*, *Starsky and Hutch*.

He had also collected certain domestically produced series like the "Macaroni" and "Blue Jeans" segments of *Howl at the Sun*, part of *The Special Mobile Investigation Unit*, *Lonely Cop*, and the early seasons of *License: No Mercy*. He had tried to get hold of *Lone Wolf*, also starring Shigeru Amachi, but couldn't find it.

"Marksman" was a police fashion and model gun store. It dealt mainly in uniformed police equipment—most customers having a mania for dressing up in uniforms—and catered for their fickle tastes in types of police baton and holsters. But Igawa appreciated his tastes and whenever he came across something of interest from the world of the plainclothes detective, he would let him know straight away.

Amongst the best items in his collection obtained so far from Marksman were a plainclothes detective's holster with a cover, and a police ID pocket book. On the cover of the pocket book were the words "Fukushima Prefectural Police."

He had actually wanted something embossed with the Metropolitan Police logo but this proved too hard to come by. He even had an L.A.P.D. badge.

The holster was flat and triangular in shape, too narrow to house a New Nambu revolver. According to Igawa, it might have been from the 1940s when, unlike today, the type of sidearm used by police officers wasn't standardized. It may have belonged to a detective who carried an automatic.

The type of automatics most prevalent at the time were the Colt M1911 from America and the pre-war 1910 Model Browning of which there was a large stockpile in Japan. Judging from the size of the holster, it was almost certain to have been a Browning.

He had been in second grade at junior high school when he started to become fascinated by the world of the detective. He spent all his time watching detective dramas on television.

He loved the moment when the detective flashed his police ID. He always thought it would be boring to be a uniformed officer. If you wore a uniform, everyone knew right away you were a police officer. It was a wonderful feeling to see the villain's face when the plainclothes guy took out his ID and badge and revealed he was a cop.

And of course, they had guns. They would pull open their jackets and whip out their pistols from the waist or a shoulder holster. How many times had he practised that in front of a mirror?

His speciality was to feint suddenly with his left hand while quickly pulling out a gun from behind his back with his right hand—the "FBI quick draw." With this sort of draw, it was better using a 2.5-inch Magnum revolver rather than a large automatic.

"Police!" he would shout, flashing his ID.

The villain would panic and draw his gun. In the next instant he would pull out his own gun from under his jacket and blow the bad guy away. Then he would turn to his buddy, and say: "Call an ambulance."

And, of course, the bullet he fired would have penetrated the chest. The bad guy would always die before he arrived at a hospital.

It wasn't fashionable to wear handcuffs suspended from a belt in a leather case the way the Japanese police did. It was much better to have the cuffs showing: hanging out from the trouser waistband. The combination of gun and handcuffs peeping out casually from under the jacket was the mark of the plainclothes detective.

What if, by chance, the people walking indifferently by him in the crowded streets of Shinjuku realized all of a sudden he was a plainclothes detective? His heart started to beat with excitement at such thoughts.

Girls, attractive girls noticing his revolver, would draw back, eyes wide with fear.

It's okay, I'm a police officer, he would say with a smile.

He remembered laughing at a similar scene on a plane in the movie *Die Hard*. Everyone thought the same way.

Today, once again, he had gone into Shinjuku to visit Marksman.

He had phoned Igawa to ask: "Have you anything of interest at the moment?"

"Yeah, I think I might have something of interest, Ed. I've a set of PC internal photos and a tape recording of a wireless conversation."

"A tape?"

"A conversation between PC and PS on the police wireless network. A customer of mine listens in to things like that—he brought it in. He comes by quite often with things."

Anybody knew that you could intercept local emergency wireless traffic from the police and fire services using a modified pocket-size radio receiver of the sort that could be picked up on the market.

"What kind of conversation is it?"

"Traffic accident, and, someone had their purse snatched, I think. Then there's something about inspectors' movements and warnings. There's some pretty amusing stuff on there too."

"Can I listen to it?"

"Yeah, no problem. Why don't you come over?"

From his apartment to Shinjuku he could travel direct on the Seibu Shinjuku line. He could get there in half an hour without changing trains.

It was a little after 2 p.m. when he came out of the east exit of Shinjuku station. He had gotten out of bed close to midday and called Marksman from a neighborhood restaurant. To get to Marksman, he needed to walk from the Seibu Shinjuku station alongside Shokuan Street in the direction of Kiou Shrine. Marksman was on the second floor of a mixed-occupancy building near the shrine. On the first floor there was a CD and record store dealing in Indies music, and in the basement was a comic store. Kabukicho's hotel district was close by, too, and the area immediately surrounding the building looked a little out of place with so many young people there.

He had only ever been into Shinjuku to visit Marksman or to go to the movies, or perhaps a bookstore or some such place. He wasn't interested in arcades, much less bars and dance clubs. Except that, if he were a detective, he wouldn't mind chasing a criminal through a dance club. He could play out a violent gun battle with the criminal in the middle of the floor as dozens of screaming girls tried to run away. He would take a bullet in his left arm as he shielded a girl from the criminal's line of fire. Needless to say, the criminal would be gunned down in the end.

The girl he'd saved would fling herself into the arms of the selfless detective. *It's okay. It's only a scratch*, he would say, with a self-effacing smile.

Afterwards, he wouldn't give the girl so much as a second thought. After all, he had saved her in the line of duty.

Even were he to fall in love, his next dangerous assignment would be waiting for him. He just didn't have the time for relationships.

His imagination played out various scenarios as he wound his way to Marksman. It was far more enjoyable imagining these things while walking the streets, than when in his apartment. There were even some guys who routinely visited Marksman while carrying a model gun and wearing a SWAT uniform under their suit. But they never looked right in a suit and they were too puny for a SWAT uniform; it just made them look pitiful.

It was laughable to see those guys with a Smith&Wesson M59 slung under a dark blue suit, wearing white socks and black leather shoes. If he were to become a detective, he was sure he would never wear white socks with a suit. Besides which, a dark suit was more appropriate for an FBI agent. If anything, a police detective looked the part if he were more sloppily dressed, in jeans or cotton trousers and a jacket.

American detectives always packed a gun, so a jacket was essential. Japanese detectives only carried guns in TV dramas; everyone knew they didn't really. In fact, gunfights between detectives and criminals seldom occurred in Japan. If they did occur frequently, then no doubt Japanese detectives also would start carrying guns.

Just before he got to Kiou Shrine he noticed a red flashing light. There wasn't just one but a number of lights. Moreover, there weren't just the usual black and white police cars there but also gray and black unmarked patrol cars and even a mobile unit from the Criminal Identification Section.

His heart suddenly started to beat faster.

It was the hotel area in Ni-Chome, the second district of Kabukicho. Some incident had occurred; and, judging from the number of police cars parked in the vicinity, a person might have been killed.

Whenever there was a shooting incident involving the police, he would be sure to collect the newspaper articles and put them in his scrapbook. The majority of incidents ended with warning shots being fired, and most of those again involved uniformed officers. Generally, plainclothes detectives would use guns to break through a barricade in order to rescue a hostage. That sort of serious incident happened only once a year, if at all. The first cases that came to mind were those where a body was discovered in a love hotel. It was quite common to hear about a woman being murdered in a Kabukicho love hotel.

A hotel employee, thinking it suspicious that the guest hadn't made any attempt to leave and go home, would take a peep into the guest's room. That was when they discovered the body.

As if attracted by some unseen force, he drew nearer the flashing lights and the crowd that had gathered to watch. An inspection of the scene of the crime was underway.

A rope had been stretched across the area, and there was a chalk outline of a person on the road surface. Dark blood stains covered the area.

The incident had taken place on a narrow road between two love hotels. There were two human outlines. Triangular plastic boards bearing letters, "A" "B" "C" and on, had been placed here and there on the road. A criminal identification officer wearing an armband was taking photographs from various angles.

He thought maybe it was a traffic-related accident.

Then he noticed two bicycles over on their sides next to the chalk outlines. They were painted white, and he knew at a glance that they belonged to the police.

Two men appeared from a love hotel adjacent to the scene of the crime. They flanked a woman of about sixty.

It soon became evident that the men were detectives. One of them had his pocket book open, and they both wore wireless receivers in their ears.

They were gathering information. What on earth had happened?

Camera lights flashed and a detective moved around, his nose close to the road surface, as if sniffing out clues.

He found himself standing in the front row of onlookers.

"Move back. Please move back."

A uniformed police officer, standing at the edge of the rope and wearing a "Crime Prevention" armband, waved his arms in the air. He wore white gloves on both hands.

"Excuse me, what happened?" he summoned the courage and asked.

The police officer didn't answer and stared expressionless at the sign outside the love hotel.

"A police officer's been murdered," said a man standing directly behind, who looked at first sight like a *yakuza* gangster with close-cropped hair. He looked scary, but his voice wasn't at all.

"A police officer?" he repeated, looking at the man.

"It seems they were gunned down. Both of them."

He looked back again at the bicycles lying in the road. So, the bicycles belonged to the police officers that had been murdered.

In the cordoned-off area, besides the uniformed police officers, there was a man wearing dark blue overalls. A wireless dangled from his left hand and crackled with noise. After a burst of static, the wireless began to jabber in a mechanical tone. It wasn't clear enough to catch properly, but it was evident from the man's following actions that he had been summoned somewhere.

"Yes, this is Hamura. I'm at the scene of the crime."

"Metropolitan Police, Public Security Section Three and Mobile Investigation heading to the scene."

"Understood, checking out," the man replied into the wireless and lowered his arm. He shifted his gaze from the mid-distance to the crime scene.

Breathing hard at the thought of two police officers being gunned down, he was feeling choked.

Was it a gang? No, more like the work of an extremist group.

He could almost feel the tension in the air around the crime scene. This wasn't just any murder. Colleagues had been killed.

If this were in a movie or on TV, this was the point where the heroic detective, having hurried to the scene of the crime, muttered: "Dammit."

Then he really heard someone clicking his tongue. It was the man wearing the dark blue overalls, the detective called Hamura. He had clicked his tongue in irritation while staring at the crime scene. He was annoyed—probably thinking he would arrest the culprit someday for sure...

A shiver of excitement and tension ran through him, fixing him to the spot. Then, his head felt strangely hot and his mind began to whirl at high speed.

He wanted to cross the rope. He wanted to become a detective—a member of the investigation team—and chase down the killer.

The murderer had killed the police officers with a gun. From the next day on, all detectives would undoubtedly be armed. They would hold an investigative meeting and collate their information. He wanted to be there. He wanted to become a part of the team.

This wasn't a world of his making; it was the scene of a real-life murder. All that separated those on the inside from those on the outside was one length of rope.

If he could just get inside by showing the uniformed officer nearest the rope his police ID...

The officer was sure to salute and lift the rope for him. He heard a siren.

It wasn't the repetitive staccato type, but a long drawn-out wailing siren. He turned around and realized the number of onlookers had nearly doubled.

"Get out of the way!"

Without warning, a uniformed officer extended his gloved hand. The crowd suddenly divided in two as if a passageway through a theater audience had been prepared.

Six men passed through. All of them wore dark blue or gray suits and looked a little like well-built businessmen.

Hamura approached the lead man and saluted.

"Thank you for coming so quickly."

"Who's in charge here?" asked the man wearing glasses, who was in his mid-forties.

"Criminal Investigation Sub-Section Chief Sotoyama. He's over there."

"Thanks," said the man, striding over the rope.

Tension once again filled the air with the arrival of this team of six men.

Who were they? They were certainly very senior; they had to be detectives with sufficient experience to lead the investigation of an incident as serious as this.

The plainclothes detectives looked as though they were moving about purposefully. Since the arrival of that man they were working all the more enthusiastically.

If he were in that man's position…

But wait—that role would surely be tedious. There was no way that man would run down the criminal, gun at the ready.

As he had always known to be the case, he'd prefer to be the sort of investigator who hunted for clues at the scene of the crime and pursued the murderer.

Toward the rear of the roped-off area, by the chalk outlines, stood the man with the glasses listening to an explanation from a detective of about fifty who had been there from the outset.

He wanted to be there. He wanted to stand behind the rope and discuss the crime with the other detectives and assist them in forming an impression of the faceless murderer.

In that instant it struck home again that this wasn't a product of his imagination but the real scene of a criminal investigation. That single length of rope signified clearly to him that he was an outsider.

Those who were able to go beyond the rope were the privileged few. He wasn't a police officer. Nor was he his much-admired detective.

Even if he couldn't carry a gun, and even if he had to dress like a businessman, he still wanted to be a detective, if that would allow him to cross the rope.

And if that were not possible, he would content himself with being a cameraman or a newspaper reporter. An eyewitness, even, would be better than nothing.

He felt bitter that he was unable to offer even the smallest scrap of information to the investigators.

If only he had seen or heard something—or apprehended the murderer himself...—he would probably be standing on the other side of the rope now.

This was the first time in his life he had been at the scene of a crime, and a murder at that.

The fact saddened him. He was an outsider, and he couldn't bear the thought that he was nothing other than a mere onlooker.

Before long, several TV broadcast vans appeared. The crime scene became a hive of activity for a different purpose. Newsmen and women carrying television cameras and microphones formed a line by the rope.

The male announcer wearing a neat suit and lively female reporters turned to face the cameras and began to speak. Most of the onlookers turned in their direction.

In particular, the crowd gazed curiously at the female reporters who had taken great care of their makeup and hair.

And then he understood.

They weren't *in*. They may have been reporting how terrible it was that these police officers had been gunned down in broad daylight, but they made no attempt to go beyond the rope, indeed they were not able to do so.

The only people beyond the rope were the police officers and the victims, and, of course, the murderer.

He remained in the same spot for what seemed like an eternity.

Night came, and still the rope was not untied.

He would stay there, until the rope was untied.

Until the rope is untied…

He said this over and over to himself, like an incantation.

He was hungry, and he needed the toilet. But, unsure whether he would ever see the scene of a criminal investigation again, he wished to burn the image into his memory.

4

It was the Mama from Mama Force who decided on the first floor café terrace of the building in Aoyama. It was three days after Samejima had paid a visit to Mama Force with Sho. Samejima had taken a call from the Mama at his home at seven that morning.

"You're pretty early, aren't you?" he said when he realized who it was.

"I'm not early. I've just got back home," said the Mama.

"You worked right through the night?"

"My night is about to start. Anyway, I'm calling about the guy who works at Agamemnon."

"Does it look like you can put me in touch with him?"

"He can meet you today. Your day, that is. My night."

"What time?"

Samejima had just returned from jogging. His T-shirt and sweat pants were wet with perspiration; he felt as though he might catch a cold. Running an hour every morning was Samejima's daily routine.

"He said around 4 p.m. is good for him. He can meet you in Shinjuku, before he goes to the bar."

"Shinjuku's no good. If we bump into anyone who knows my face it would mean trouble for him."

"Okay. How about Aoyama? Close to my place."

"That's a pretty nice neighborhood to live in."

"It's one of those out of the way sort of places you can live in without being bothered by anyone."

"It's probably okay. Whereabouts?"

"There's a café terrace on the first floor of the Aoyama Twin Towers. There are two cafés and it's the one facing the quadrangle. They serve a nice cup of tea."

"Okay. 4 p.m., right?"

"3 p.m., if we're meeting there."

Samejima dropped by the police station a little before 2 p.m. and heard the report.

At around 1305 hours an emergency call was received reporting the sound of gunfire in front of the Hotel Montana in Kabukicho Ni-Chome, X, X Block. The caller, an employee of the Hotel Montana, discovered on the road fronting the hotel the bodies of two police officers who had been on patrol, and called an ambulance. The two officers, both assigned to the Kabukicho Police Box, were named as Fusao Onoue and Toshimichi Saka. Officer Onoue died at the scene of the crime and Officer Saka died before reaching hospital. The station's Criminal Investigation Section and the Metropolitan Police Criminal Investigation First Section are currently looking into the matter. All station personnel are to remain on high alert and watch out for any suspicious persons in this district.

Onoue and Saka had both been in their twenties and worked out of the Kabukicho Police Box.

Samejima, preparing to leave, stood up from his chair. His desk was separate from those of the other section members and was positioned next to the desk of the section chief.

"Samejima," Section Chief Momoi called him over.

The detectives' room of the Crime Prevention Section was deserted. Most of them were out having a late lunch or on investigations.

Samejima stared at Momoi without saying anything.

Momoi was a somber-faced man of fifty-two with grizzled, un-oiled hair. He was an inspector, the same rank as Samejima. He had eighteen years of service with the Shinjuku Station.

Although a non-career officer, at one time there had been great hopes for Momoi's advancement through the ranks. But it was said that his future and his hopes had been taken away from him by a traffic accident that happened fourteen years ago. Stopped momentarily at a tollgate on the expressway, Momoi's family car had been hit by a truck whose driver had fallen asleep at the wheel.

The truck driver died, as did Momoi's son who was about to turn six. His wife sustained serious injuries and they divorced later.

It was said that ever since that day, Momoi had become a "cadaver" himself.

Momoi never smiled. His expression remained set, and he hardly ever attended meetings. An ordinary Section Chief of Crime Prevention would take the lead in guiding and educating juvenile delinquents by going out in the street and actively engaging in crime prevention. Not Momoi.

Day in, day out, he sat in his section chief chair casting his eyes over paperwork with his old man's glasses.

There was a rumor that Samejima's assignment to Crime Prevention had been forced on Momoi. But the reality was that Momoi had been the only chief who hadn't declined to take Samejima on the grounds of disruption to teamwork.

The man who effectively carried out Momoi's role in his place was an assistant inspector called Shinjo, who had continued to ignore Samejima since the latter's assignment. He appeared to be working on collecting points in Crime Prevention in the hope of gaining a promotion and transferring to Public Security.

"It's a problem for our section too. The section chief's like a cadaver. We can do without someone else who's going to pull us down." Shinjo said this deliberately within Samejima's earshot. Momoi was also there at the time, but his expression remained the same.

"Did you know Officer Saka?" Momoi said in a quiet voice.

"I knew him," Samejima nodded.

Saka wasn't a career officer, but he'd become a police officer after graduating from college. His father was a member of the Shinjuku Ward Assembly and was in the running for being the next ward chief.

"You're after Kizu?" asked Momoi.

"Yes."

"Are you close to running him in?"

"Kizu's just come out of jail, but he makes it no secret that he's resuming his old trade. Whether he's overconfident, I don't know, but he's made a pile of money. He'd probably sell his country if he'd make money out of it."

Momoi said nothing.

"If I can figure out where he's hiding out, let me nab him."

"Do as you please."

Samejima nodded and left the Crime Prevention Section room.

Tension filled the air at the Shinjuku station. Preparations were underway to put in place police cordons and to set up a special criminal investigation headquarters.

At the moment there were no criminal investigation headquarters at the station, which was very unusual for Shinjuku police. The number of serious crimes occurring within its jurisdiction was marked.

With the state guest garden party having only just finished without incident, Samejima thought, the case must be a real headache for the station chief.

The murder of police officers would likely be seen as being related, and the Metropolitan Police's Public Security Department would certainly become involved. If Public Security's elite, with their overbearing style, joined the investigation, there was bound to be friction. It was often said that Public Security was a "vacuum cleaner." They'd absorb all information without divulging any of their own.

If this vacuum cleaner were to partake in the investigation, it would make things very difficult indeed. The legwork in obtaining information would be done by the army of people at the crime scene, while the job of piecing it all together and making sense of it would be left to Public Security.

It might have been the same Metropolitan Police organization, but there was little or no cooperation between the Criminal Investigation First Section, which handled murders, and the Public Security Department.

There was even some doubt as to whether Public Security would respond to a request for materials from Section One.

Samejima left his office and headed in the direction of the railway station.

The Shinjuku Police Station was located in west Shinjuku. Perhaps it might have been better placed in east Shinjuku, where Kabukicho was. But the traffic there was always congested; police wouldn't be able to use patrol cars as freely.

The traffic tailbacks on Shinjuku and Yasukuni Streets had become chronic. A patrol car responding to an emergency call could end up stuck in the garage because of the gridlocked traffic. Instead, there was a large police box situated at Kabukicho. During the late-night hours, when incidents occurred with greater frequency, it was far quicker to dispatch police officers by bicycle.

Samejima got off the subway at Aoyama and went into the designated café terrace. Cakes were on display in glass cases, and the deep sofas opposite lines of tables spoke volumes about the nature of the locality. The customers at the tables were a mixture, not just businessmen discussing their businesses, but also housewives on their way back from shopping trips. These housewives, however, were quite well-dressed and didn't look as though they'd ever worn a kitchen apron. The topic of their conversation was likely to be about their country retreat, golf membership, and such.

The Mama was sitting alone on a seat toward the back of the café terrace. As she had hinted on the phone, there was a pot of tea on a reserved table. She had on large-framed sunglasses and wore a hat pulled down low at the front. She wore a loose blouse together with wide pantaloons.

Her face was devoid of cosmetics.

She looked up from her paperback as Samejima sat down opposite. "Have the tea. With plenty of sugar and milk." A waiter in a tuxedo appeared next to them, but Samejima nodded and he walked away wordlessly.

"Thanks for taking the trouble."

"Don't mention it. Town's upside down, isn't it." The Mama closed her book.

"All kinds of guys," answered Samejima.

The Mama nodded in agreement, and gazed at his clothes.

He was wearing a light green suit and a hemp shirt with no tie.

"The color suits you. Your girlfriend's choice?"

"I chose it."

"Why Samejima-san, I'm surprised. You really look quite smart. I like smart-looking guys."

"Now you're scaring me."

The Mama grinned. "Don't worry. I'm too fond of that girlfriend of yours." Then she raised her left hand slightly.

Samejima turned around to see a short-haired, thin young man coming in through the café terrace entrance.

"There's Fuyuki. Don't you go scaring him now."

The youth was wearing a white shirt and tight-fitting jeans. He was the type of young guy you saw anywhere but for his large eyes, like a frightened bird's, and red lips.

"Hello," he said, to neither of them in particular, as he stood at the side of the table. He had a quiet voice.

"Have a seat. It's okay. This is an old friend of mine, he won't give you a hard time."

Samejima nodded. "A long time ago Mama-san dumped me. I've not been able to hold my head up since."

A smile appeared on Fuyuki's face. "She's had a lot of police officers, isn't that right?"

"Idiot. He's just joking," said the Mama.

"But it's true that you've had a lot of cops," Samejima added.

Fuyuki looked from Samejima to the Mama, and Samejima took out his business card. It contained only his home phone number and the Crime Prevention Section number. There was no reference to the police or any other title.

Fuyuki took the card and bowed. "I'm Fuyuki, from Agamemnon."

"I heard about you from Mama. Let me get straight to the point: you know a man called Kizu? He has a tattoo of a scorpion on his left shoulder."

"I know him. He's a fairly regular customer," Fuyuki replied quietly.

"When did he last show up?"

"Yesterday. Around 11 p.m."

"You mean on a Sunday?"

"We're open on Sundays, too."

"Was he alone?"

"He was yesterday, yes."

"Does he stay long?"

"It varies. Sometimes he stays about an hour then goes home. Other times until closing time."

"Until closing time?"

"Supposed to be about 3 a.m."

"Same as my place," said the Mama.

"It's supposed to be 3 a.m., but if the customers are people we like, the place stays open right through the night."

"How many times a week does he stop by?"

"Once or twice. But before the last time he hadn't been in for about ten days."

"I heard he has a lover."

Fuyuki nodded.

"What's his lover like?"

"He used to work in the bar—a guy called Kazuo. He was in a *bosozoku* bike gang. Pretty mean-looking sort."

"How old would he be?"

"Kazuo? Twenty, twenty-one."

"Has Kizu only recently started seeing him?"

"It seems. I get the feeling Kazuo really looks up to him."

"Looks up to Kizu?"

"That's right."

"And Kazuo brought Kizu to your bar?"

"That's how it looks."

Fuyuki had the habit of using words like "looks" and "seems."

"Are they serious about each other?"

Fuyuki nodded. "The other day Kazuo was sucking him off on the sofa."

"Does that kind of thing happen a lot?"

"Hardly ever. The mama doesn't like that kind of stuff. Having said that, she used to be afraid when Kazuo was together with Kizu. He'd be somehow stronger and our mama couldn't say anything."

"Why did Kazuo quit working there?"

"There was a complaint from one of the customers."

"A complaint?"

Fuyuki looked at the Mama's face.

"It's okay, you can say what you like."

"Once, Kazuo went back with a customer. It seemed they'd gone to a hotel together. In the morning, when the customer got up, Kazuo was gone and so was the money in his wallet."

"Did he report it to the police?"

Fuyuki shook his head. "The customer was an ordinary salaryman. He had a wife and children and couldn't bring himself to file a report."

"Are they living together now? Kizu and him?"

"I don't know. Maybe."

If they were, then Kazuo would know about Kizu's trade—possibly even helped with it.

"Where did they become acquainted?"

"I heard it was at a snack bar. After he left our place he used to help out there."

"Where was it?"

"I don't know the name. I think he said it was over towards Monnaka."

"Monnaka?"

"Monzen Nakacho. Near Kiba."

"Has he quit that job now?"

"Yes."

"Where does he live?"

"I don't know. I asked him once but he didn't tell me."

"Are you working today?"

Fuyuki nodded.

"If Kizu shows up again, will you let me know? Or Kazuo—even if he's alone. Call my number on the card, make it sound like you're talking to a friend."

"How?" Fuyuki sounded anxious.

"Is the bar a small place?"

"Yes. You get about twenty people in there and it's full. So I can't get into any weird conversations."

"You could just say, 'Can you return the video I lent you?'"

"Return the video?"

"That's right. If Kizu is nearby, it'd be better not to use my name."

"Does he know you?"

"He does."

Samejima chose not to mention the fact that he'd been responsible for sending him to prison once in the past.

Fuyuki stared silently at Samejima. At last, he said, "Will you give me something in return?"

"What do you want?"

"Money."

The Mama looked at Samejima.

"How much?"

Fuyuki spread out his fingers.

"Fifty thousand yen?"

"Five hundred thousand."

Samejima let out a sigh. "I can't afford that much. You've got to understand, Kizu is a bad guy. He makes his living illegally manufacturing guns. People are shot and killed with the guns he sells. More could die. I want to stop him."

"And what happens if he finds out I'm helping you?"

"Don't worry. I'm not going to arrest him at your bar. I'll get him once he's come away from there. There's no way I'm gonna tell him I found out his whereabouts from you. And if I catch him this time, he'll go down for five years."

"If he did find out from someone, he'd try to get his own back. Kizu's *yakuza* isn't he?"

"Kizu isn't a *yakuza*. He doesn't belong to any organization. He has business dealings with the *yakuza*, but he doesn't pledge allegiance to any one clan. So nobody is going to retaliate on his behalf."

Fuyuki thought about it, then said, "So what's the payment?"

"I'll give you fifty thousand."

He thought for a while. Then: "Can you pay now?"

"I can give you half now. You'll get the balance once he's arrested."

If Samejima were with Public Security, a cooperation fee could probably be paid straightaway. But with Crime Prevention, he wasn't even sure they'd pay half. Pushing money around without need of a receipt was Public Security's speciality.

"Okay, let me have it."

Samejima took out his wallet. He was left with only a few thousand-yen notes.

"If that's all." Fuyuki took the money and stood up.

Samejima noticed then that Fuyuki hadn't ordered anything.

"Wait a minute. Will you give me your real name and address?"

Fuyuki gave him the info from where he stood. Samejima decided from what he'd been told that it was the truth. He lived at Koenji.

"Can I have your telephone number as well?"

The number began with the district code for Suginami Ward and seemed credible enough.

"Okay. Thank you. I won't say anything about this to anyone. I'll wait to hear from you."

Once Fuyuki had left the café terrace, Samejima quickly took out his pocket book and made a note.

"He's pretty hard-headed, don't you think?" said the Mama in disgust. "Five hundred thousand? He's an outrageous little brat. I wouldn't be surprised if he doesn't bother going to the bar today."

"That's a possibility," said Samejima, putting his pocket book away. He intended to call Agamemnon and check to see if Fuyuki had turned up for work. If he hadn't, then he'd watch the vicinity of the bar and wait for Kizu.

The worse case scenario was Fuyuki tipping off Kizu. If Kizu knew he was being followed, he might just go to ground, in which case it'd be difficult to trace him for a while. It was to sniff out Kizu that Samejima had visited the sauna in Shin-Okubo.

"I wonder why he hangs around Shinjuku. If it's young boys he's after, he might as well be going to Roppongi or Akasaka," said the Mama.

"The world's a small place for the bad guys. Just like ordinary people, they have favorite places they like to hang out. They dislike places they're not familiar with—even more so than ordinary folk. In the end they always go back to Shinjuku."

"You mean go back and get arrested? What idiots."

"Only an idiot would do something bad enough in the first place to get himself arrested," Samejima said.

5

By the time Samejima returned to the station, a police cordon had already been put in place.

Checkpoints had been established on the principal highways throughout Shinjuku and the tailbacks were worse than they'd been the week before. The object of these checks wasn't just the vans and trucks of extremist groups that they were looking out for, but also private vehicles.

Not even the officers involved believed these checkpoints would result in the arrest of the killer. But if this was the first in a planned serial killing of police officers, then it could prove effective in preventing further incidents.

Of course, it wouldn't have the desired effect if the murderer stayed put in Shinjuku. If that were the case, they'd probably get the information they needed through their inquiries. The detectives in Criminal Investigation were concentrating all their efforts on extracting information from their usual network of sources.

A Special Investigation Headquarters had been established at the station. In preparation for the press conferences, the number of liaison officers at the station saw a surge.

The first press conference started at six in the afternoon. There were a large number of officers present in the conference room, largely due to the paucity of information so far obtained in relation to the crime.

Samejima had just finished his paperwork and was getting ready to leave for home. With the press conference underway, there was nobody else left in the section.

"It's been a long time."

Samejima looked up from his desk.

A man wearing a dark blue three-piece suit was standing in the doorway to the Crime Prevention Section. He was tall and powerfully built; his hair was neatly parted at the side, and sharp almond-shaped eyes sat in a light-skinned face.

Samejima nodded.

The man's name was Koda. He had joined the force the same year as Samejima.

"How about we grab some food from the section canteen?"

"What do you want?"

"Now hold on a minute, that's no way to address a superintendent," Koda laughed. He was shrewd and possessed the requisite innate disposition of a police bureaucrat: duly sycophantic with those in charge and firm with his subordinates.

"I'm just about to leave for home."

"Two of your comrades have been murdered. Don't you feel like putting in a little overtime? For fellow troopers."

When Samejima's former colleague from Public Security Section Two committed suicide, Koda was already a young leader of one of the factions. He'd pressed Samejima on several occasions to hand over the letter.

Samejima stared quietly back at Koda. "I'm sure they'd be bursting with respect for you if they heard what you just said. 'That's just like that great superintendent of ours'…"

"Lay off, will you? I came here to talk about arresting your colleagues' killer," said Koda, moving closer. "You know we're holding a press conference. How about you going along and sitting in?"

"The conference is Criminal Investigation Section One's responsibility. Our job is to work discreetly in the background." Samejima took out a cigarette.

"I'm working over here for a while and just thought I'd show my face and say hello."

"So am I supposed to salute you every time we bump into each other in the corridor?"

"There's nothing wrong with observing regulations. If you like, I could get you into Special Investigation Headquarters. If it went well, maybe you could return to the First Section."

Samejima pretended to think about it and lit his cigarette. He blew smoke slowly at Koda.

Koda drew back a step. "Still smoking?"

"Get out."

"What did you say?" Koda sounded pissed.

"I've got more than enough to keep me busy right now. Get out."

Koda's eyes suddenly grew cold. Showing his anger was a part of his playact.

"It usually takes twenty years to reach superintendent. If you're not careful, you'll be an inspector for the rest of your career."

"It's none of your goddamned business."

Koda moved his face in close. "It's not *your goddamned* anything. It's 'superintendent' to you. Show some respect for your senior officers. You want to know something? I've disliked you right from the beginning. If you talk to me like that I'll see to it that you spend the rest of your career in this detectives' room. You can enjoy hanging around with your drug-pusher friends."

He turned his back before Samejima had a chance to say anything. As he was about to go out through the door he spat, "A fool who doesn't realize he's a fool is an even bigger fool."

Samejima remained silent and stared at the doorway Koda had just gone through. His face had been emotionless all the time Koda had been in the room.

He breathed out heavily and stubbed his cigarette out in an ashtray.

Samejima looked up suddenly as the door to the section opened again.

In the doorway stood a large-faced bald man wearing threadbare trousers, a tie with a ridiculously small knot and an over-sized jacket. Both his hands were thrust casually into his jacket pockets. The pattern of his jacket and the color of his trousers hardly matched.

The man moved unsteadily into the room and without saying anything picked up the pack of cigarettes from Samejima's desk. He took one out and lit it.

"The superintendent wanted to know where Crime Prevention was, so I told him. Did he give you any trouble?"

"Not really."

"How's it going with Kizu?"

"I found a bar I think I can use."

"Really?" said the man, his cigarette still in his mouth, as he moved over toward the grilled windows.

"How's it going down there?" asked Samejima.

"I've never seen such a commotion."

"Looks like a gun was used."

"Yeah, that's right."

The man looked down at the entrance to the Shinjuku Police Station, unconcerned about the lengthening column of ash falling from the tip of his cigarette.

His name was Yabu and he was from Criminal Identification.

He had an established reputation for his skill in ballistics testing and had been invited on a number of occasions to work for the Metropolitan Police, but each time he'd turned them down.

He often said he'd wanted to be a doctor but gave up on the idea because his name, "Yabu," meant "quack" in Japanese.

It was Yabu who had deduced that a gun made by Kizu was responsible for a murder four weeks earlier.

Yabu looked at Samejima in a vague sort of manner. "The proprietress of the Hotel Montana said she only heard one shot. It seems to have made a terrific noise. Our inquiries in the neighborhood also confirmed one shot."

Samejima silently returned Yabu's glance.

"Officer Saka, or should I say assistant inspector—he got a posthumous double promotion—and Onoue were on patrol cycling diagonally two abreast. Saka was in front and Onoue was slightly to his left at the rear. We only found one bullet, in Saka's body."

"One bullet?"

"One bullet. It had been fired diagonally from the left rear of Onoue. It entered from below the left shoulder blade and more or less passed through the chest cavity. Then it hit Saka squarely in the back, ruptured his right lung and lodged itself in his ribs. Onoue died instantly, and Saka died approximately ten minutes later from loss of blood."

"What kind of gun was it?"

"We took the bullet out of Saka's chest. It was crushed flat, but it certainly wasn't from a handgun."

"What about a hunting gun?"

Yabu nodded. "It could have been a rifle. We're verifying the caliber right now."

"It had to be a rifle."

"Compared with a handgun, the bullet from a rifle contains far more gunpowder. So naturally it also has a much higher degree of penetration. That's because it travels faster. It also depends on the caliber. Take a handgun. With a Magnum .44 revolver, the bullet travels at an initial velocity of 360 meters per second; with a 9mm automatic Luger it's 340 meters per second, and a New Nambu Special, like the one you guys use, is only 278 meters per second. If you convert that to kilometers per hour, we're talking a thousand kilometers per hour. Now, a rifle, like a 30-30, the type commonly used in Japan for hunting deer and wild boar, has an initial velocity of 728 meters per second. And if we go a little bigger, the 30-06 for example, we get to 890 meters per second, which is 3,200 kilometers per hour. The bullet from a handgun travels initially a little slower than the speed of sound. But a bullet from a rifle is two or maybe three times faster. Maybe Onoue didn't even hear the gunshot."

Yabu said all of this without a pause.

"From how far away was the shot fired?"

"That's the problem. It's extremely difficult to work this one out. If we had an eyewitness it would be easy, but we don't. In that neighborhood there are likely to be fewer people passing by during the daytime than at night. The only thing is, a bullet, you see, has an interesting characteristic. It's greatest point of penetration isn't necessarily the point at which it leaves the muzzle of the gun. The bullet from a rifle in particular oscillates as it leaves the barrel."

Yabu removed the shortened cigarette butt from his mouth and started to elaborate.

"As you know, in order to allow the bullet to run true to its target, the barrel of the gun is rifled. A bullet, a bit like a bolt turning in a nut, is rotated as it leaps from the gun barrel. A round from a rifle, of the type I'm talking about, has a long, narrow head compared with a round from a handgun. Both the cartridge and the bullet itself are long and narrow. As a consequence, the bullet always rotates with the base oscillating slightly. But this oscillating movement corrects itself at a certain distance in flight—generally between 100 and 150 meters. After that it continues rotating and flies straight. Eventually, if it doesn't hit anything, it begins to lose its forward momentum because of gravity and air resistance and, like a spinning top just before it falls over, starts to oscillate again and finally drops to the ground."

"So, basically, what you're saying is that a rifle would have more destructive power if fired from a slight distance?"

"Destructive power is different from penetration. Think about which would have the greatest effect: being stuck by a needle or being beaten with a hammer. Destructive power and speed don't always go hand in hand. A slow moving bullet will become lodged in the body. A bullet that passes through its victim doesn't necessarily cause much damage. In the present case, the bullet that passed through Onoue stopped in Saka's body. It appears to have had a relatively high degree of penetration, and it wouldn't be all that surprising if it were a rifle bullet fired from a fairly large caliber weapon."

"You mean the rifle was fired at point blank range?"

"That's the greatest likelihood. Even if you don't apply this logic, considering how narrow that alleyway is, unless the shot came from high up somewhere it's hard to see how it could have been fired from a distance."

This ballistics expert never touched alcohol. Nor did he take much exercise. He perspired too much for that. But as an investigator he was absolutely first-rate. Simply being good at making inquiries and pursuing and arresting criminals wasn't the mark of a top-notch investigator. Yabu always gave full rein to his imagination. The detectives at the scene of the crime didn't have the time or inclination to do so. Yabu's imagination was far removed from mere flights of fancy and was always based on the circumstances and the evidence.

Samejima listened to his thoughts. The other detectives at the station only wanted results; they weren't interested in how Yabu arrived at his conclusions. Samejima listened because he knew Yabu was one of the best investigators around.

He gazed in silence at the cigarette Yabu held between his fingers.

"We can go as far as to say that the shot was fired at close range with a rifle. But this brings us to our next problem. Compared with a handgun, a rifle is a pretty bulky object. You can't just carry it around hidden in your jacket pocket or inside a bag. It would at least have to have been something like a golf bag or fishing rod case. I don't think the killer could carry it unless he was in a car."

"A premeditated attack, huh?"

"Most likely. It's hard to imagine some guy out there carrying a rifle around in the trunk of his car on the off chance he might come across a couple of police officers to use as target practice."

"Has it been announced? That it was a rifle?"

"No. It hasn't even been made public that only one shot was fired. All we've said is that the firearm used in the attack is currently being investigated."

"So, it looks as though the killer was waiting for the police officers with the rifle in his car."

Yabu looked at Samejima and replied, "Pretty much. Then again, if a car were parked on that alleyway with someone in it, the officers would take a look inside. Anyone intending to kill a police officer wouldn't pull a stunt as stupid as that."

"Well, maybe he waited for the officers to go past, then pulled the rifle out from the trunk?"

"But what about the range? Even if the guy had rushed out the car, opened the trunk and pulled out the rifle, they would have been a hundred meters away."

"Maybe the rifle was in the car, hidden under some sort of camouflage?".

"It's a possibility, I guess," answered Yabu. But his face suggested something else was on his mind.

Yabu left the Crime Prevention Section and Samejima reached his hand out to the phone. He dialed the number for Agamemnon.

"Yes, this is Agamemnon."

Samejima knew from the voice that Fuyuki had answered.

"It's Samejima."

"Ah, from this afternoon."

Fuyuki replied in a cheerful voice that was higher-pitched than when they'd met at the café terrace.

"I'm leaving the station now. If he shows up, call me at home. If I'm not home, leave a message on my answering machine and let me know the time."

"Okay, understood."

The sound of men singing a karaoke duet carried in the background. The tune was "Shinjuku Born and Bred."

Samejima replaced the receiver and stood up.

The detectives on the case in the Criminal Investigation Headquarters would probably work through the night. The upper echelons of the force were keen to resolve a case involving the murder of police officers, lest a prolonged investigation tarnish their reputation. Perhaps Koda would stay and work late, too.

From what they knew so far, there was a good chance that a radical group was involved in the murders. As a general rule, a handgun indicated the work of a gang; a hunting rifle pointed to extremist organizations. It wasn't entirely unheard of for the *yakuza* to use rifles, but radicals rarely if ever used handguns.

Because a rifle had been used as the murder weapon, HQ regarded as being highly likely the possibility that this was the work of the militant left.

Samejima walked by the side of a room bearing the sign *Special Criminal Investigation Headquarters. Murder of Police Officers Kabukicho*, and left the police station.

Having eaten dinner at a place nearby the Nogata stop, Samejima returned to his apartment.

He opened the door and saw in the darkness the blinking light on his answering machine. He went quickly into the room and pressed the replay button.

Hi, it's Sho. When do you have some free time next? Call me and let me know.

The message ended there, and nothing else had been recorded.

Samejima gave a wry smile. He always told Sho to leave the time with her message, but she never obliged.

There were a number of people in Shinjuku who knew his private number. Some of them called his place at his request to pass on information he was after. Occasionally he received calls asking for his help. It was sometimes difficult to figure out precisely what time the call had been made. He would have a clue, at least, if Sho gave the time either before or after such a call.

He undressed and went into the bathroom. It was a pre-moulded unit too cramped to wash in comfortably. But on his salary, he couldn't afford a place with a bigger bath within thirty minutes of Shinjuku.

Samejima showered, then sat cross-legged on his sofa next to the bed in his six-mat living room. A small-sized, compact refrigerator and TV were positioned within easy reach. There was a mini cassette deck on the TV stand. Lately he hadn't even turned it on other than to listen to Sho's demo tapes. He hadn't said it to her in quite so many words, but Samejima loved listening to Sho's songs. Her voice was good; it had about it an exceptional sensitivity. Combined with her good looks, he knew she could go places if she turned pro.

But he wondered how she'd change. It wouldn't be a problem if she could accept herself as a star. On the other hand, he knew there was a good chance she'd become sick of it.

It's a pain in the ass, she'd probably say, and give it up.

Although she loved singing, she wasn't the type to change her way of life for the sake of it.

Samejima reached out and took a can of beer out of the refrigerator. He turned the TV on and tuned into the nine o'clock news. He thought the chances pretty slim of Kizu showing up at Agamemnon that night. For a start, it wasn't so many days since he'd last been there. Another, major factor was the killing earlier in the day of the police officers.

Kizu had already been to prison twice; for that reason alone he would be particularly wary of the police.

Kizu was a professional criminal. He made his living illegally manufacturing guns. He probably hadn't done anything else for the last ten years.

As with the sale of narcotics, or fraud, or dealing in stolen goods, manufacturing firearms was an illegal activity. Bookmaking at the races was also illegal. The activities always carried with them the risk of arrest. Their perpetrators, however, were a little different from people who were reported to the police for some crime of impulse.

People on the run would as often as not manage to make an honest living by some means or other. Lying about their identity, they would pick up work, say, laboring on a construction site.

A criminal by trade didn't run. He had his own workplace and wouldn't be able to do business if he moved away. As a result, he was susceptible to betrayal. He might shut down his business temporarily in an attempt to remain inconspicuous. To the extent that he couldn't run away, he was more cautious.

Kizu knew full well that Shinjuku was awash with police officers because of the murders. According to Fuyuki, Kizu had shown his face the day before, but his prior visit had been ten days before that. He'd gone to ground while the police were out in strength during the state visit and had reappeared at Agamemnon only afterwards.

Doubtless he wouldn't move for a while now because of the killings.

That was Samejima's take on it at any rate.

The news began.

The murder of the police officers was the top story. It was given wide coverage; however, since there had been very few official announcements by the police, the information was singularly lacking in detail.

It soon became apparent that the announcements had been suppressed at the instigation of Koda and Public Security.

The reporter, broadcasting from the crime scene, let it be known that no eyewitnesses had been found and that only one shot had been heard.

The hotel employee who had heard the gunshot also appeared on screen. He described how he thought for a moment it was a fight between the *yakuza*. But he heard only one shot, and when he went and looked outside, two police officers were lying on the road.

There were dozens of people around at night. Close to the hotel, there would also have been a lot of pimps and prostitutes—both male and female—hoping to attract a customer. The reporter concluded that, given the recent surge in sex workers of Asian descent, there would surely have been eyewitnesses had the shooting occurred at night.

Samejima thought that prostitutes may indeed have witnessed the crime. But they were unlikely to go to the police and report what they'd seen. And it would be even more difficult to track down an eyewitness from among the hotel guests, considering the rapid increase of foreign prostitutes in the area the reporter had mentioned.

Public Security Section Three would undoubtedly be waiting for a statement about the crime from some far-left group. It was at this point that Samejima started to form the vague idea that maybe this wasn't the work of a radical sect.

Surely, if a group like that were to murder a police officer, they would target someone more important than a couple of uniformed officers patrolling the backstreets of Shinjuku. They'd more likely go after a member of the riot police or the Imperial Palace guard.

A left-wing group escalating its struggle to murder would, generally speaking, be acting in the knowledge that its opponent was effectively the state itself. They would consider themselves as soldiers fighting for a cause and the police as "the enemy." Killing hostile troops would be an act of war, not murder, and a surprise attack was a logical strategy to use against an enemy with overwhelming military force.

From that perspective, the murders could be characterised as urban guerrilla warfare. But there had to be some meaning to it other than the initiation of armed struggle; there had to be a specific reason for targeting ordinary police officers. The extremist groups were well acquainted with the police's structure. Perhaps the point of targeting the rank and file was to inject a feeling of malaise and aversion to war amongst the "troops" on the ground; even so, bearing in mind the point of the struggle for such groups, the first attack would have targeted a more appropriate level of police officer. Tactically, too, attacking officers on patrol offered poor chances of success. Police officers going about their patrol duty were alert. Officers assigned to the Shinjuku Station in particular were ready to face the unexpected. If a sniper failed to take out his victims, there'd be a fair chance of an immediate counterattack. The fact that only one shot was fired was also a little odd if this genuinely were an armed struggle.

The camera moved from the scene of the crime back to the studio.

The studio presenter announced that none of the belongings, including the handguns, of the murdered officers had been taken. For the moment, the police would be progressing the investigation on the assumption that this was a grudge killing.

Samejima thought this possible. Compared with other forces, officers assigned to the Shinjuku Station dealt with a much greater volume of trouble and were prone to treating suspects harshly. It was possible that someone could have borne a grudge against Onoue or Saka.

Samejima had known both of them. On balance, Saka was the quieter type, while Onoue, a year older than Saka, was much more aggressive in his behavior and manner of speech.

When questioning a suspect, Saka would begin, *I'm sorry to trouble you, but do you mind...* whereas Onoue had been the opposite. If he saw anyone behaving suspiciously, he instantly got high-handed. Samejima had witnessed this: *Wait a minute, wait—I said wait!*

Then again, Onoue had served with the Shinjuku force longer than Saka, and he was probably just used to acting that way.

Police officers had a strong sense of loyalty toward one another. Consequently, Samejima knew that even if there had been anything at work or in the private lives of Onoue and Saka that had caused someone to feel aggrieved, it wouldn't be easy to get their colleagues to let on.

It wasn't so much that he didn't feel any pain over their deaths, but rather that Samejima felt unconnected with this feeling of loyalty and camaraderie. The reason why police officers possessed this sense of familial relationship was that they felt estranged from society at large. The special nature of their occupation necessarily had the effect of making officers feel a sense of isolation outside of the force. This was probably true, thought Samejima, in any country in any era.

So long as this sense of loyalty persisted within the force, it would be more difficult to detect crimes committed by police officers than the rest of the population. The fact invited the distrust of the general public and perpetuated the feeling of isolation for the police.

Within the police, the disregard and tacit hindrance typically shown to internal informants was fairly rampant. Those who were estranged from the police social structure could not continue as officers except in special cases.

While he knew that the situation wouldn't change, Samejima desperately hoped that it would. But change, if it did come, certainly wouldn't happen as a result of external pressure. For the police to change, he knew it would be necessary for officers like himself to stay in the force.

A good many police officers had a strong sense of justice and felt their role in life was to uphold the law and cause others to do the same. What was necessary was the creation of a police structure that didn't alienate them or confound their hopes.

The Japanese police force had a hell of a long way to go to achieve this. Samejima had two battles to fight: one with the criminals, and another with the warped structure of the force.

The phone rang.

"Are you avoiding me?" Sho's voice sounded from the receiver. "Why didn't you call me?"

"I just got back."

"Liar. From the time it took for you to answer the phone, I can tell you've already showered. Now you're drinking beer and watching TV," Sho accused him.

"You should become a detective."

"No way. I don't want to get killed, not for anybody."

"What's the matter?"

"Nothing in particular. Did you know the two guys who were murdered?"

"Yeah."

"Why were they killed?"

"I guess the Criminal Investigation guys are looking into it."

"Hmph. When are you free next?"

"Friday."

"Four days to go. Can I come over?"

Samejima laughed in spite of himself. "Why are you so keen on coming here?"

"Why can't I come over?"

"Fine. But I can't go out. I'll be waiting for a call."

"That's okay with me. We can cook dinner. If you don't mind."

"Who will?"

"Me, I'll make it. If you don't want to."

"I wouldn't mind if you did cook dinner."

"What time shall I come over?"

"In the evening, before it gets too late."

"I finish my part-time job at five. So how about six?"

"That's good. I'll come and meet you at the Nogata stop."

"So…"

"Yeah?"

"Why were you really stalling on me coming over?"

"I wasn't."

"Liar."

Sho put down the phone. But there was no hint of anger in her voice. If anything she sounded pleased.

Samejima replaced the receiver and looked at the TV screen.

The news had moved on to a different item.

He knew the internal feud within Public Security that he'd gotten caught up in had yet to be resolved. So long as he had possession of that letter, they'd continue to keep a watch on him.

He liked Sho. Right now she was the most precious person in his life. He only hoped the situation would never arise where he'd be faced with trading her for that letter.

If the brass at Public Security learned of Sho…

He was unable to tell himself with any confidence that it would never happen.

That night the phone didn't ring.

6

In the end, he didn't go to Marksman. It was probably more accurate to say he couldn't.

It was gone 10 p.m. by the time he returned home. He bought a hamburger near the station and climbed the steps to his apartment with the bag in his hand.

He disliked eating alone in places where there were lots of other people around.

The hamburger had gone cold in the fifteen minutes it took him to walk from the station. But he didn't mind.

The first thing he did when he went into his room in the apartment was lock the door. The room was neat and tidy. It had a four-and-a-half-mat-sized kitchen area and a six-mat Japanese style room. There was a desk in the Japanese room that he'd used since he was trying to get into college and that he now used also as a dining table.

Having locked the door he went straight over to the desk. He opened the uppermost drawer.

The drawer contained three imitation guns, all in their holsters. The holsters were of different types: a shoulder holster, housing a Smith&Wesson Automatic M39, a pancake holster containing a Colt Roman MkIII 357 Magnum, and a waist holster with a 1910 Model Browning.

To the side were a police-issue pocket book and a pair of handcuffs, and a special police baton.

He stripped off the sweater he'd been wearing. He fastened the shoulder holster over his shirt. Next he stuffed the handcuffs down his back in the waistband of his jeans. He put the pocket book in his hip pocket and put his sweater back on.

Closing the drawer he returned to the entrance hall.

There was a small shoe rack next to the toilet containing a variety of tools. A length of linen tape used for securing packing cases was coiled up in the bottom.

He had brought it home with him from a part-time job he used to have. He cut the tape with a pair of scissors.

The floor of the six-mat room was covered in pink carpet. First he described a human form with the tape on the surface of the carpet. Then he put up a double length of tape, about waist high, across the partition between the six-mat room and the kitchen. Then, standing on the outside of the tape so that he had his back to the furniture, he looked down at the human shape beyond the tape.

He was becoming excited. He could feel himself moving into his "other" world.

An inspection was taking place at the scene of the crime. Strobe lights on cameras flashed, and officers from the Criminal Identification Section moved around collecting fingerprints.

A crowd of onlookers had gathered by the rope, jostling and pushing and craning their necks for a better view.

A uniformed officer stood near the rope wearing gloves—

Ah yes, the gloves, he had forgotten them. He stepped over the tape, opened a different drawer in his desk and took out a pair of white cloth gloves. They were of thin cloth and fastened with a press-stud at the wrist. He casually tucked the gloves into his sweater pocket and moved back outside the tape. He took a few paces back and he could see the onlookers again.

"Don't push. Move back, move back please."

He could hear the voice of the uniformed police officer.

He took a step forward and, noticing him, the uniformed officer quickly saluted.

"Thanks for your hard work," he said before producing his ID from his hip pocket. The onlookers regarded with curiosity this person who did not look like a detective.

Suddenly he strode across the rope. The Criminal Identification Section officers turned around and he nodded toward them.

He took the gloves out from his sweater pocket and pulled them on as he squatted down in front of the human outline on the ground.

"What was the weapon?"

"A handgun. Possibly a Magnum."

He grimaced. "That's bad. What's the estimated time of death?"

"Just thirty minutes ago."

He stood up abruptly and scanned the vicinity. "So he may still be in the neighborhood—the killer."

"We're searching the area at the moment."

"Tell them to take care—watch out for the Magnum."

He stopped talking and produced from his waist a wireless.

"Yes, this is the scene of the crime, Special Investigation team. What is it?"

"We need your help—"

A gunshot rang out in the background and the voice in the radio changed to static.

"I'm on my way!"

His hand whipped out his automatic in a flash. Pulling back the breach block he fed the first round into the chamber and began to run. He crossed the rope in a single bound...

He remembered to keep the muzzle of the gun pointing into the air.

He had repeated this solitary performance over and over again. He would add in variations, but always there would be a gunfight at the end. And always his final words would be: *Call an ambulance.*

It was close to 11 p.m. and he was hungry. The hamburger was where he had left it on top of the desk. He crossed the linen tape with it in his hand.

The detective was having his lunch at the scene of the crime. He knelt down with one knee on the ground and regarded the tape outline of the body while munching on a hamburger.

This was the fourth murder so far. Realizing they wouldn't be able to apprehend the criminal by employing conventional investigation methods, the Criminal Investigation HQ had dispatched him, a special investigator, to the crime scene.

He ate his hamburger and gazed at the corpse in front of him. He had a frown on his face, and only his mouth continued to move.

"Was it a pro?" asked a newly appointed detective nervously.

"Maybe. Whoever it was, he was good," he said and stood up.

He broke off momentarily from his soliloquy and took out a one-liter carton of milk from the refrigerator. He put his mouth to the carton and washed down the hamburger.

With a puff of his cheeks he thought about the murder. Not this one but the one in Shinjuku.

What kind of guy would kill a cop? Killing uniformed cops wasn't the job of a professional hit man. At any rate, he'd more likely kill a detective. Murdering a detective was a ploy often used by crime syndicates forced into a tight corner.

He wondered when he might next come across the scene of a murder. He wasn't bound to encounter one, even if he walked the streets of Shinjuku every day.

The best thing to do was to be in the vicinity of Shinjuku Police Station when a patrol car was dispatched and follow on behind. But he didn't have a car, and he wouldn't know in any case whether the police car was going to the scene of a murder.

He wanted to stand on the other side of the rope, to become a member of the team. Who knew what chances he already may have had to witness a murder scene? It was just that, even though there were dozens of police cars parked there at the station, most crimes were generally carried out inside the home. He wouldn't be able to get in anyway.

He wondered what he would do if he did happen across the scene of a murder investigation again.

There'd been people taking photographs. What about fingerprints and footprints? Were the detectives he saw today carrying guns? If he'd looked carefully at their jackets, he might have been able to tell...

He couldn't bear it any longer; he felt like returning to the scene of the crime.

But the detectives would no longer be there.

It was said that detectives revisited the crime scene a hundred times, but of course that didn't necessarily mean they actually did so.

To begin with, perhaps the murderer was some sort of abnormal personality and had already been arrested.

Serial murder—suddenly the words came to him. If it were a serial murder, then the same detective would certainly be in charge. And if he were there, he could continue his story for real; he'd be able to witness a whole range of scenes.

He knew there was a bunch of guys who monitored police wireless transmissions. But Igawa had told him you could only monitor local transmissions between stations and police patrols, not the bigger cases directed by the Metropolitan Police, who used digitalized wireless communication.

Naturally, in the case of a homicide, detectives from Criminal Investigation First Section would be dispatched. If it were possible to intercept their wireless communications it would be possible to be present not only at the scene of the murder, but also at the scene of the murderer's arrest.

But that would be difficult. According to Igawa, the Metropolitan Police radios didn't use to be digitalized. When the number of radio monitors increased, they switched to digital.

Undoubtedly that wasn't the only reason. The criminals, too, were able to intercept wireless transmissions and get away.

He wanted to see it. He had to see it again.

He wondered what the detectives would think if he showed up at the scene of every major case.

If only he were possessed of some super power which allowed him to foresee major cases...

7

Sho emerged from the station ticket barrier, wearing a gray tanktop, short pants over her jeans and a white vinyl jacket.

She was carrying a large paper bag.

"Here you go."

Samejima took hold of the bag and screwed up his face. "What the hell's in here? It's heavy."

"Kitchen knife, chopping board, salt, pepper, soy sauce, plates, a frying pan and casserole pot," she replied and started walking along.

"But why?"

She stopped and looked back. "Because, I've no idea what you have at your place. I carried that myself all the way to my part-time job, you know."

"I was only asking. I've got a kitchen knife at least."

"It'd be a pain. I'm better using the one I'm used to."

"Well, that's a very grown-up thing to say."

Sho stopped again and almost bumped into Samejima, who was clutching the paper bag and walking right behind her.

"What are you trying to say? That you don't like my cooking?"

"No, that's not what I'm saying. It's not, but—"

"Then be quiet about it, will you?"

Next, Samejima was forced to experience Sho's shopping habits. She selected everything she bought with meticulous care, and she paid for everything.

"I'll pay," he essayed.

"Shut up. I'm making dinner so I'll pay."

Samejima returned to his apartment carrying bags in both hands.

Because he knew Sho was coming, he had at least cleaned the kitchen. Having seen Sho's apartment, he knew that was how she liked it.

Samejima put the bags down on the kitchen floor.

"Right," muttered Sho, removing her jacket.

Samejima stared out of the corner of his eye at her bulging tanktop. Underneath her bare shoulders her cotton shirt protruded quite visibly.

"You've got pretty much everything you need," said Sho, looking in the kitchen utensil cupboard.

"Let's start with a drink," said Samejima, taking two cans of beer out of the refrigerator.

"Go ahead, I've got to prepare the meal," replied Sho, taking the ingredients out of the paper bag one at a time.

"I said come and join me." Samejima pressed the cold can of beer against Sho's inner thigh.

Sho jumped. "You fucking idiot!"

He lifted the can of beer in front of her face. "Here you go."

"All right," Sho pouted and took the beer. She pulled the ring pull and lightly touched Samejima's can with her own.

Just as she took a drink Samejima grabbed her arm and pulled her in toward him.

"Hey, you jerk—"

He chewed on her lip. Sho hoisted the can up high so as not to spill any beer. After a while Sho began to relax, allowing her tongue to entwine with his.

But when Samejima slipped his hand under her tanktop she pulled her mouth away, and said, "What the hell are you thinking?"

"A woman in a kitchen makes a guy want to do her more than when she's lying on top of a bed," said Samejima, fumbling to undo her bra strap.

"Stop it, will you?" Sho protested, sucking in a sharp breath as Samejima's fingers probed towards the pinnacle of her breast. She blushed.

Samejima pressed his mouth against hers again. He set the beer can, which he had transferred to his left hand, down on the draining board and hooked his free hand around her shorts.

"I said, stop it."

Sho moved her mouth away and stared Samejima in the eye.

As she did so, Samejima's hand found its way into her pants. Sho's knees buckled. Samejima caught her and took down her shorts.

"If we take a little exercise first, we'll build up a bigger appetite for your cooking."

"You jerk."

He lifted up Sho's body.

She hooked her arms around his neck and said: "Hurry up and take off your clothes, you dirty-minded cop!"

The meal was sautéed salmon in cream sauce, with diced filet steak for the main course. Sho had brought two bottles of wine with her, and they finished one between them with their meal. The other bottle was put away in the refrigerator.

While Sho began clearing away the dishes, Samejima turned on the TV and tuned in to the news channel. There were three news items, followed by commercials, before the screen went back to the studio announcer.

We have an update on the murder of the police officers that occurred in Shinjuku. According to subsequent police investigations it appears that a rifle was used as the murder weapon. This information was obtained by our own staff following their inquiries and it would appear to be accurate. We now have the following report from an expert on firearms and ballistics.

The screen changed and showed a video recording of a man Samejima had never seen before talking in a small, office-like room.

From the fact that only one shot was fired and from the position of the bodies of the two officers who died—amongst other factors—we can infer that the bullet fired in the attack had an extremely high level of penetrative power.

The man's title, "Firearms Expert," appeared across the bottom of the screen. His appearance, a gentle face and a head of hair shot with gray, gave no hint at all of any connection with guns.

It's difficult to see how this could have been an ordinary bullet. Of course, there are bullets known as KTW bullets that are specially manufactured to enhance the degree of penetration. But they are extremely difficult to obtain in Japan, and even in America they are not common. In the case of a rifle, they are sold under licence for use with hunting guns, so naturally anyone possessing a hunting rifle would be able to buy them.

The screen changed back to the studio.

"The police still haven't made any announcements about the gun used in the crime, have they?"

"That's right. They haven't even publicly stated that the two police officers were killed with one shot."

"It looks like everyone will be expecting the police to make a statement now."

Samejima put a cigarette between his lips. The TV screen suddenly went dark. He turned around to find Sho standing there with the remote in her hand.

"You're not really gonna watch TV are you?"

Under the apron she had brought, she was dressed only in her tanktop and pants.

"Sorry," Samejima lit his cigarette and meekly apologised.

Sho beamed. "I've brought a tape of the new song. Will you look at the lyrics with me?"

"Yeah."

"Good."

She took out the tape and music sheets. Ever since that first time, she had asked Samejima to help her write new songs.

"Oh, we've decided our first single is going to be 'Stay Here.' I'll split the royalties with you."

"You don't need to do that," Samejima objected, looking up from the music sheets. Only the first verse of the lyrics was down on paper, lightly written in pencil so it could easily be erased.

"But why?"

"I'm not doing it for the money."

"That's a bit affected, isn't it? If it's a hit we could be song writers."

Sho sat cross-legged by the sofa Samejima was sitting on.

"You mean quit my day job?"

"If you didn't want to, you wouldn't have to. You could use a pseudonym."

"I don't need one."

"Yes, you do. How about 'Shinjuku Shark'?"

"Give me a break."

"Okay, it could be 'Sleaze Cop.'"

"Do you want the weeklies to carry a story that Who's Honey's lead vocalist is fucking a cop?"

"Now, that would be good. Let's put on sunglasses and sneak to a love hotel in Kabukicho and have our photos taken."

"You can count me out."

Sho pursed her lips.

"Wouldn't you like it if your police friends pinned me up in their lockers?"

"No, I wouldn't."

"What's wrong with that?"

Samejima put down the music sheet he had been reading and looked at Sho. "I want you to sing numbers I like. You're my girl. If you were a pin-up girl, you'd be every guy's girl who liked your songs. Don't you think?"

Sho's face creased with delight. "Yeah. I guess that's right!"

"In which case there'd be no need for me to hang around anymore."

"Would you hate it if I made a song about a cop?"

"A song is just a song."

"How about if I put 'Shark' in the title?"

Samejima stared in silence at Sho.

The phone rang.

"Samejima speaking," he said, picking up the receiver.

"It's Fuyuki. There was a call from someone asking if Kazuo's here tonight. From his voice I think it was him." Fuyuki spoke in a loud and high-pitched voice, struggling not to be drowned out by the high-volume karaoke going on around him.

"Kizu?"

"Yeah, maybe. I took the call."

"What did he say?"

"Like I said, he asked whether Kazuo was here. When I said I hadn't seen him, he asked if he'd been lately."

"And?"

"He said okay, and to let him know if Kazuo showed up or phoned."

Samejima hung up.

Without a word, Sho inserted the cassette tape into the compact cassette player. The tune she had recorded in the studio began to play.

After a lively-paced introduction from the bass guitar, Sho's simple vocals came in and all at once the sound exploded.

"Still not enough impact," said Sho, tapping out the beat with her knee.

Slow down, slow down, carry on like this and we'll burn out... Won't you come here, won't you come here...

Why was Kizu looking for Kazuo, Samejima wondered. Maybe they had quarrelled and Kazuo had run out on him. If he could track Kazuo down, he might be able to find out a lot about Kizu. The fact that he'd called Agamemnon suggested that Kizu didn't know Kazuo's whereabouts. Either that or Kizu needed Kazuo to help him with his work.

"Hey!" said Sho, like she was annoyed. "You're not listening, are you?"

"Sorry. I've got to go out."

For a moment, Sho looked like she was about to explode in a fit of

117

rage. But she controlled it, and instead let out a deep sigh.

"Take me with you."

Samejima looked at her.

"If it won't bother you, take me along."

Sho's eyes welled up with tears.

Samejima was thinking about shadowing Kizu to his apartment. If Kizu showed up at Agamemnon, he could follow him and find out where he lived. Then he could go in there with a search and arrest warrant.

Provided Kizu didn't suspect he was being followed home, it wouldn't be dangerous. He planned on being armed when he made the arrest. If Kizu knew it was Samejima that was coming for him, he would resist arrest, and he was bound to have a customized gun with him. But he wouldn't take it with him to Agamemnon.

"Get your things," Samejima said.

Agamemnon was on the fourth floor of a building facing a one-way road off the Koshu Highway. Samejima took Sho to an all-night coffee shop on the second floor of the building opposite. They sat near the window so they could see the entrance to Agamemnon below.

Samejima called Fuyuki on a pink telephone and gave him the coffee shop's number. He told him to ask for Sho if he were to call the shop; Samejima didn't want to miss Kizu going into Agamemnon. If Kizu showed up, he planned on sending Sho home immediately.

Fuyuki reported that since the earlier contact, he had neither had a call from nor seen Kizu.

"Are you still looking for that guy? The one you were talking about with Tobita?"

"Yeah."

Sho nodded and stuck her spoon into her crème à la mode. "What kind of guy is he?"

"You want to know?"

"Not really. But we've got nothing else to do."

Samejima cast a glance around the interior of the coffee shop. Their seats were the farthest away from the counter where the staff were serving, and the only other customers were a group of four kids who were glued to a coin-operated game. They had no need to worry they'd be overheard.

"He's a guy who's obsessed with guns. He's thirty-five, a year younger than me. He's from Tokyo, somewhere near Kameido."

"Why is he obsessed with guns?"

"I gather it all started when he bought an imitation gun as a junior high student. All boys were into that kind of stuff big time. It developed into a mania with him and he became an apprentice."

"An apprentice?"

"There used to be a notorious illegal gun maker in Ueno. On the surface he earned his living as a tattooist, but behind the scenes he was making guns. Kizu learned from him how to make guns and he also acquired a taste for men."

"He's gay?"

"I hear he sleeps with women, too. But basically he prefers young punks. Members of *bosozoku* gangs, or the bunch they call street kids."

"What happened to the gun maker?"

"He died. Stabbed to death by the mistress of a *yakuza* who'd been killed by one of the guns he'd made. Both the *yakuza* and his mistress knew the gun maker. The *yakuza* had introduced him to the customer in the first place."

"So, as a result of his own introduction, the *yakuza* was murdered by the guy who bought the gun?" asked Sho, covering her crème à la mode in fresh cream and putting the spoon to her mouth.

Samejima nodded. His eyes were fixed on the building opposite.

"That's a horrible story."

"It's a small world for criminals. If you have a run-in with someone you know, they can just as soon become your enemy."

"What happened after the gun maker was murdered?"

"Before the police arrived Kizu cleared everything out of there, the gun maker's tools, the guns he was working on, everything. The woman who had stabbed the gun maker was arrested, but as she was being taken away, Kizu was lying in wait and shot at her."

"Did she die?"

"No. The bullet hit the chest of the detective next to her. Kizu was caught and spent two years in prison. He was twenty-two at the time. But all through the investigation he wouldn't let on where he'd stashed the tools he took away."

On his release from prison, Kizu lost no time in resuming his old trade.

He had attended a technical high school before dropping out and was naturally adept with his hands. Kizu soon surpassed the gun maker in terms of skill. In those days gun smuggling was not so widespread. Even where it happened, many cases were exposed. However, the demand for guns suddenly increased to coincide with a feud that had broken out between rival *yakuza* gangs in the Kansai area. Kizu chose to hide away in Kansai for a while.

Before long, a large number of smuggled guns appeared on the market and the quantity of illegally manufactured guns decreased.

At around that time Kizu returned to Tokyo and started making not only guns, but also customized firearms that could be concealed, rather like a swordstick.

"How do you mean?" interrupted Sho.

"You know, guns made to look like umbrellas. Attaché cases and books that conceal pistols. You can carry them around without attracting attention. *Yakuza* bosses regularly targeted by guns clamored to buy them and arm their bodyguards."

Eventually, one of those guns was used by the bodyguard of a *yakuza* boss, who was being targeted by a rival organization. The person who was shot was the driver of a car that had collided with the car in which the boss and the bodyguard were traveling. The driver died. During the investigation, the bodyguard testified that he thought the driver was a hitman for a rival organization.

The driver had been in the real estate business and he had been driving an expensive, imported car—the cause of the misunderstanding that had resulted in his death.

Samejima, who knew from the bodyguard's confession that Kizu had supplied the weapon, found out where he was hiding out and arrested him. But at the end of last year, Kizu got out of prison after serving his two-year sentence and resumed his business.

"Kizu's workshop wasn't the same place as his apartment. So far he hasn't divulged where that is. Unless we can shut down his workshop, this will be a recurring crime. No matter how many times we arrest him, he'll just be able to go straight back to it again."

Four weeks earlier, two leaders of an Asian prostitution ring had been shot. One had died and the other had sustained serious injuries. The number of foreigners of Asian descent working illegally in Shinjuku increased almost daily, and a number of them were starting to become organized.

Both of the foreigners had been acting as pimps and minders for Asian prostitutes.

Their method of doing business was fairly conspicuous. Inevitably, they got into a confrontation with a Shinjuku gang. It had started off as a petty quarrel with a couple of punks from the gang suffering minor injuries. There were ten or so prostitutes and four minders under the control of the two leaders, none of whom had obtained official work permits.

"The gang involved in the confrontation are the bunch who were chasing your friend."

"Those guys?"

There were close to twenty gangs with territory in Kabukicho and a combined total of nearly two hundred office locations. Some of these belonged to Kansai gangs although they were well outside of their territory.

The gang that had been pursuing Katsuji was the Kanto Mutual Prosperity Association, the Fujino Clan. The main source of their revenue was prostitution and the illicit sale of toluol.

"So, one of those gangsters back in Kichijoji did it?"

"Yeah. The guy who did it turned himself in. He didn't say where the gun had come from, but the Criminal Identification guys believed it to be Kizu's handiwork."

"Which one of them did it?"

"The guy called Makabe."

Sho nodded. "The guy who had the mobile phone."

"That's him. Makabe went alone into the Asian group's hideout and shot them. When he was arrested they found he'd suffered serious stab wounds."

Makabe had driven himself in to the Shinjuku Police Station. The driver's seat was a sea of blood from where he'd been stabbed in the side and back. He had staggered, covered in blood, into reception and said to the desk officer, *I want to see the Shark,* before passing out unconscious.

He was on the verge of dying from loss of blood. Samejima was standing next to his hospital bed when he regained consciousness. Makabe talked freely about the crime he had committed. The only thing he couldn't bring himself to admit was that he had come by the gun from Kizu.

Makabe had used a gun that at first glance looked like a lighter. It was designed to fire two .22 caliber shots from the palm with a squeeze of the hand.

Makabe's first shot pierced the first man's forehead, while his second hit the other in the throat.

He had been frisked when he went into the hideout, but the gun's appearance had failed to arouse suspicion.

"Hello, what's this," Sho said.

A cab entered the one-way street and pulled over.

A thin man wearing a waistcoat and pale sunglasses got out.

He peered up at the building opposite and went into the elevator hall.

"It's him," said Samejima.

8

Ten minutes after Kizu had disappeared into the building the phone in the coffee shop rang.

Samejima stood up.

It was from Fuyuki. His voice sounded tense. "I'm calling about the video…"

"Okay, thanks. You don't need to do anything more." Samejima put down the phone.

"Right. I'll go home."

Samejima turned around and Sho was standing there.

"Is it okay if I come and collect my stuff next time you're free?"

Samejima nodded. Sho nodded back and smiled.

"Your food was delicious."

"Thanks," said Sho, pleased, and then left the coffee shop.

Samejima took out his pocket book and made a note of the taxi company Kizu had used. Even if he lost Kizu tonight, he'd be able to check where the gun maker was picked up. It could give him a clue.

He returned to his seat and looked down again at the entrance to the building.

He hadn't expected Kizu to make his move so quickly. Only four days had passed since the two police officers had been murdered.

Kizu had a driver's license, and when he wasn't in prison he always got around by car. He probably took a cab to avoid the police checks.

Kizu was clearly taking a chance. As Samejima suspected, there had to be something between him and Kazuo.

Perhaps he suspected Agamemnon's staff were shielding Kazuo.

Samejima promised to himself that this time, when he arrested Kizu, he'd make sure to close down his workshop as well.

He looked at his watch. It was a few minutes to midnight. It was Friday, and it would be tricky for a while at this time of night to catch a cab. Samejima decided Kizu would either call a cab to Agamemnon or continue drinking and wait a while until there were more cabs free.

Samejima sipped his tepid coffee. He felt completely sober now. He wondered if he'd be able to appropriate an unmarked patrol car if he went to the police station at that hour. It would certainly be better if he could arrange for someone with time on his hands to drive one over to where he was. However, this was the busiest time, with the Special Investigation HQ in operation, and it being close to midnight. He doubted anyone would have that kind of time to spare.

Samejima stood up and put a call in to the station. Sure enough, all the unmarked cars were out. He regretted not bringing his own car.

Samejima had a second-hand BMW with no optional extras. He kept it in a parking lot close by his apartment. He had decided on a BMW despite the price tag because he wouldn't be suspected of being a cop when he tailed someone.

In any case, he still smelled of alcohol when he left the apartment. He didn't want to drive to Shinjuku and risk losing his job. Samejima called the cab company.

For situations such as this, the police sometimes requested a cab company to make an emergency allocation of vehicles.

Of course, while they couldn't be forced to comply with the request, in practice cab companies tended to voluntarily allocate the next available cab on a priority basis.

He was informed the cab would arrive in about fifteen minutes. If Kizu came out in the meantime then it would all have been for nothing. He would have to take a chance and either ask him to accompany him voluntarily or else make a mental note of the cab he took and try and trace it later to find out where he had been set down.

Unless he had good reason, Kizu wouldn't hang around Shinjuku.

If Kizu came along with Samejima voluntarily, it would only make it more difficult to locate his workshop. In order to pinpoint the workshop, Samejima knew there was no alternative but to continue to watch Kizu's movements.

The cab arrived about a dozen minutes later. Samejima quickly settled his bill and left by the front entrance. The cab driver wasn't aware he had been dispatched at the request of the police. Needless to say, it made no difference that the passenger was a detective and the cab fare would be charged as normal.

Samejima climbed into the cab and produced his police ID. He explained the situation and asked for the driver's cooperation. The driver appeared irritated; he was being forced to run the meter for waiting time only, at the busiest time of night.

"Here, this is for your trouble," said Samejima, handing the driver a 5,000-yen note.

Without a receipt, he wouldn't even be able to get a refund. He would have to use his investigation expenses budget wisely in order to arrest Kizu. He wanted at any cost to locate Kizu's workshop.

Samejima had the driver move the cab closer to the exit of the one-way street. Then he asked him to extinguish all the lights and put the "Not for Hire" sign on.

He climbed out of the cab. He smoked a cigarette then got back in and killed time engaging in small talk with the driver. Having received the 5,000 yen tip, the driver was in a better mood.

Just after 2 a.m. a cab with a yellow "Reserved" light on stopped in front of the building where Agamemnon was located. This was the third cab to pull up there. There were a number of other eating establishments in the same building as Agamemnon, and it looked as if one of those customers had called the cab.

Samejima waited in his. He watched the entrance to the building through the rear view mirror he'd had the driver reposition for him.

He saw a tall, thin figure climb quickly into the waiting cab. Samejima looked back over his shoulder. Illuminated by nearby neon lighting, he could just make out Kizu's face inside the cab.

"Start the engine."

The driver, who had been listening to a late night radio broadcast, with his seat half reclined, sat up in a hurry.

"Don't turn your lights on yet."

Kizu's cab passed them by. Samejiima slid his body down in his seat.

"Okay, follow them."

"At last, sir?"

The driver moved the car forward.

Without answering, Samejima made a note of the other cab's affiliation in his pocket book. There was nothing out of the ordinary about two cabs following one another at night, and he wasn't worried that he might be spotted. Even so, when they pulled up side by side at traffic lights he took care to make sure his face couldn't be seen.

Kizu's cab turned left onto the Koshu Highway. If they continued straight they would come out at the convergence with Shinjuku Street.

"Have you any idea which way they might go, sir?"

"I think they might be headed in the direction of Fukagawa."

"So I guess from Hanzomon they'll go around the Imperial Palace and onto Eitai Street."

Samejima thought about what Fuyuki had said—that Kizu had met Kazuo at a snack bar in Monzen Nakacho.

Kizu was originally from Koto Ward. Professional criminals disliked living in areas they were unfamiliar with; when the heat was on them, they needed the geographical advantage, the friend's house where they could seek refuge. What was more, nobody went out of his way to visit a small snack bar in Monzen Nakacho of all places. The exceptions probably came from the direction of Chiba, somewhere east at any rate.

In fact, Kizu's cab did turn right at Otemachi and join Eitai Street.

There were fewer cars around once they had crossed Eitaibashi bridge and the cab picked up speed.

The road surface on Eitai Street was in a pretty bad state. The fact that they were travelling in excess of 70 km/h must have had something to do with it too. The cab bounced continuously.

"Eitai, it's the worst or maybe the second worst road in the city."

A large truck overtook them with a roar, pushing close to 100 km/h.

"Too many of those monsters breaking the road up."

The cab passed the intersection at Monzen Nakacho and turned right onto the road just before Tomioka Hachiman.

"Take a right and stop. Turn your lights off."

"Aye, aye."

After they'd turned right he wasn't sure how far they should go before pulling over.

Kizu was sure to be on his guard once he was outside the cab.

If another cab went by, he might think it more than mere coincidence.

In that area of Koto Ward were tributaries of the Sumida River; the Oyoko, Sendaibori and the Heikyu connected it with the Arakawa River. The blocks in between were spanned by numerous bridges large and small.

They had just turned right and started to go forward when they saw a small bridge ahead of them. The cab Kizu was riding in had crossed the bridge and turned left. All the roads were narrow and mainly one-way.

"Okay, drive with your lights off."

Although the streetlights were lit and there was no danger of being hit from behind, the driver muttered to himself, "Goddam."

But he did as Samejima told him.

When they came to the bridge Samejima stopped the cab.

On the other side of the bridge, about two hundred yards off to one side, they could see the brake and interior lights of the other cab.

Kizu got out.

He didn't appear to have noticed Samejima's cab. He went straight from there into a building on the right.

Samejima waited a few minutes and then climbed out of his cab. He walked to the building Kizu had gone into: a relatively new condominium containing rental apartments, three stories high and wide across the front. There didn't appear to be an elevator. There were four rooms on each floor and the light was on in the room on the second floor at the extreme left.

Samejima looked at the row of mailboxes in the first floor entrance. Room 204 was the one with the light on. There was no nameplate on the corresponding mailbox.

Having made a note of the condo's name and address, Samejima returned to the waiting cab. He had found Kizu's address. Now he needed to locate the workshop.

9

At last, I'm here, he thought.

Ever since that day, a certain idea had lodged itself in his mind and refused to go away.

He would stand on the inside of the rope gazing at the scene of the crime with the other detectives. He was about to become one of their exclusive number.

There was only one course of action open to him. If all went well, he would be a member of the group from start to finish.

Becoming part of the team, and standing on the inside of the rope, would be proof that he was the same as the detectives and different from all others.

Different. He would no longer be an ordinary person.

He would stand on the same side as the detectives, inside of the rope. He would be a special person, different from the onlookers and TV personnel.

Yes, he was different from the rest. He shouldn't have been on the outside of that rope. He should have realized sooner, much sooner.

As he thought this, everything seemed to open up before him. It was as though he had groped around in the dark for the way out, while now, suddenly, a flight of stairs appeared by his feet.

He would become a member. He would be a colleague of those detectives.

His thoughts accelerated; with alarming speed, plan after plan came into his mind.

First he needed a phone. He would use one of the public phones in Shinjuku station. Ten seconds. More than that and he'd be caught.

He got off the train on the Seibu line at Shinjuku station. Exactly a week had passed since that day. The murderer of the two police officers hadn't been apprehended.

The murders had to be part of a serial killing. Without a doubt, the murderer would attack again. He had used a rifle to shoot the officers— some sort of gun that could kill a person from a distance. The detectives would be paying careful attention to the upper stories of tall buildings and the rooftops of empty buildings.

He stood in front of a public telephone in the eastern exit of Shinjuku station and adjusted his shoulder bag. His fingertips were wet with perspiration.

There were four telephone booths and all were being used.

The call from the booth on the far right looked as though it was coming to an end. A man in a suit who looked like a salesman had closed his electronic palm book and was bowing into the receiver.

His hand went into the shoulder bag. His pair of white gloves were inside. He put a glove on his right hand only and inserted his hand in his trouser pocket. He would look conspicuous wearing gloves at this time of year, and he wished to avoid attention.

The salesman pushed the door of the phone booth open. Pretending not to have noticed, he stood in front of the booth next along. He averted his eyes, anxious not to have his face remembered. Since he didn't make any attempt to go into the booth, the salesman shot him a suspicious glance, but then soon walked away.

In this city people didn't worry about other people. The salesman would quickly forget about it, or so he told himself.

Even then he felt ill at ease.

He turned his head and looked after the salesman. He was just crossing at the lights, and didn't look back.

Withdrawing his right hand from his trouser pocket, he opened the door to the phone booth. He went in as swiftly as he could, with his back facing the street.

Okay. He had cleared the first stage. Nobody could have spotted his white glove.

He groped around in his pocket and fished out a ten-yen coin. Before he inserted it into the phone, he rubbed it several times with the fingertip of his glove. There would be several ten-yen coins in the box. They wouldn't be able to tell which was his. He needn't be overly cautious.

If he were to use a telephone card, it would take time, if only a few seconds, for the card to be ejected once he had put down the receiver. For that reason he decided on using coins.

He dropped two ten-yen coins into the slot. Taking up the receiver, he hunched over the phone. He was sweating profusely.

He pressed the numbers with the finger of his gloved hand. The last four digits were "0110." The number always ended with 0110 for police stations.

As he finished punching in the number he held the receiver slightly away from his ear. He was afraid the police might trace his blood type from his sweat.

"Hello, this is the Shinjuku Police Station," a female operator answered promptly.

He wasn't sure if a ring tone had sounded or not. He caught his breath at the speed with which she had answered.

"Hello, can I help you?"

"Hello," he said at length.

But he needn't worry. Unlike with the emergency number "110," all sorts of people called the police station with a whole variety of queries. They wouldn't suspect him for simply calling the general number. Moreover, the woman at the other end of the line wasn't a detective but an operator.

"This is the Shinjuku Police Station."

"Ah, could you put me through to the Criminal Investigation HQ?"

"Which investigation?"

He swallowed hard. From this point on he couldn't stay on the call very long.

"The one handling the police murders."

"Please hold the line."

There was something in the operator's voice that made him feel she was on her guard.

He could hear the internal ring tone as the call was being transferred. It rang only once.

"Section One," a man's voice answered in a businesslike manner.

He knew he was now speaking to a detective.

"Hello, this is Section One," said the detective.

He inhaled and in one breath said, "Pass this on to Sotoyama. I'll do it again. More police officers will die. I hate the police."

He'd already decided beforehand what he would say. He had rehearsed it over and over again.

"I'm sorry, the line is bad, I can't hear you very well. What did you say? What will you do again?"

He looked at the receiver and started to repeat the same words. Then suddenly he realized there was no way he couldn't be heard. The detective was trying to prolong the conversation to trace his call and get a fix on his location.

"Police officers will die again."

He put down the receiver. He did so with more force than necessary; the sound of the receiver being slammed down reverberated inside the booth. He would need to be quick; he had to get away from there. Hurriedly, he turned toward the door. He almost touched it with his left hand which, flustered, he pulled back.

The door began to close and bumped him on the forehead. Hardly caring, he pushed his way outside.

Two girls aged about eighteen stood by the row of phone booths.

They were looking on in surpise at him for having bumped his head on the way out.

He had his right hand stuffed in his pocket. With a look of indifference he began to walk away.

His whole body was soaked with sweat. He still hadn't taken his glove off. There was still the second stage of his plan.

Kabukicho wasn't all that busy yet.

As he walked in the direction of the Koma Theater, he stuck his right hand into the open zipper of his shoulder bag. His fingertips came into contact with a slender object.

This was the next phase.

As he suspected, the square around the movie house in Kabukicho was thronged with people. They sat or stood around the edges of the flowerbeds. Most of them seemed to be meeting up with others.

He would do it quickly, and then go to Marksman.

In the flowerbed red and yellow flowers were in bloom. People were gathered round about. A loutish man wearing sunglasses sat on the edge with his legs crossed, smoking a cigarette. A group of girls stood off the perimeter.

The incessant cacophony from store announcements and the electronic whir from the arcades knocked around the small square, closed in as it was by buildings on all four sides.

He felt irritated by the heat of the day. It felt as if this place in Shinjuku was especially hot.

A bell sounded, announcing that the movie was about to begin, urging customers to be quick and take their seats.

He sat on the edge of the flowerbed, his right hand still inserted into the shoulder bag.

The man with the sunglasses, who'd been sitting a little distance away, suddenly stood up.

He gave a start.

"You're late."

"Sorry."

"It's already begun."

A heavily made-up woman with strong perfume in a black trouser suit tripped passed him. The man had already turned his back to begin walking toward the movie house at the rear of the square. The woman caught up with him and threaded her arm through his.

He shifted his position and scanned the area around him. The shoulder bag rested on top of his knees. Slowly, he lowered the bag to the side of his right knee. Holding the edge of the bag with his left hand, he gripped the slender object in his right that was still in the bag. He kept his line of vision straight ahead; he made sure he didn't look down at the bag.

He casually turned and looked behind him. Nobody was paying him any attention. The bottom of the bag protruded into the flowerbed some four inches from the edge of the surrounding wall. Below was dark earth and a tangle of shrubbery.

There was a small hole in the bottom of the bag that he'd cut out the night before. He pushed the slender object through the hole. Without a sound, it dropped into the undergrowth below.

He wondered if anyone would find it after he had gone. He'd dropped it in a fairly conspicuous place. It would be no good if it were too obvious. But it would be worse if it were never discovered.

For a while he kept very still.

Two girls, deep in conversation, walked past in front of him. They weren't speaking Japanese. Using his left hand he lifted the bag onto his knees. Inside the bag he removed the glove from his right hand.

His heartbeat was relatively normal.

He'd visit Marksman and chat with Igawa. Then he'd call again. He'd already decided where he would make the call from. And then, he'd come back here.

He had to see his plan played out from start to finish.

10

Samejima was eating dinner at a Chinese restaurant when he discovered that two more police officers had been murdered.

The restaurant was on Eitai Street, close to Kizu's condominium. An hour earlier, Kizu had dined there before returning to his apartment. Samejima figured Kizu wouldn't leave the condo for a while and felt safe enough eating at the same place. Other than to eat or do his shopping, Kizu had not ventured out once these three days. He'd confined himself to his apartment.

Samejima was growing tired of lunch boxes and hamburgers. But he had little choice in the matter, there being no support to take turns in the surveillance.

In order to carry it out, he'd explained the circumstances and arranged to use the foreman's cabin in the storage yard of an ironworks diagonally opposite the condo where Kizu lived.

He discovered that Kizu kept an old Nissan Cedric in an open-air parking lot a short distance away. According to one of the local residents, it was almost always parked there; when it wasn't, it generally returned within a few hours.

The foreman's cabin was a prefabricated building about three mats in area. While it kept the rain out, it turned into a steam bath under the penetrating rays of the sun.

Having been told by the owner that it was a no-smoking area, he couldn't even have a cigarette. All he'd done for the last three days was to watch and wait in the tube chair he'd brought with him.

It was almost 9 p.m. and the Chinese restaurant was closing for the night.

When Samejima came to the restaurant, a middle-aged man in white overalls, who looked like the owner, was taking in the curtain from the entrance.

The owner was friendly and said he could have a seat if he didn't mind having just soup and fried rice. Once he'd served the food, the owner tuned the TV to the NHK news channel and sat in one of the customers' chairs.

Once again, two police officers have been shot in Shinjuku. One is dead and the other is seriously wounded.

The incident was the top news story, the first item the newsreader announced.

Samejima stopped spooning soup from his bowl and stared at the screen.

This latest incident had occurred at 6:40 p.m., just after dark.

A police car from the traffic section of the Shinjuku police had stopped at a light while patrolling the area in north Shinjuku popularly known as "Tax Office Street," when a motorbike approached from behind and pulled up alongside. Moments later there was gunfire.

Two shots were fired. Sergeant Kanai, who was sitting in the driver's seat, was in critical condition after being shot in the head through the window. Officer Hasebe in the passenger seat died instantly when the bullet from the second shot entered from his right shoulder and passed through his left lung.

The killer was wearing a full-face helmet and the bike was a motocross model whose number plate was obscured by mud.

The police are working quickly to analyze the bullet. The case is being viewed with deepening suspicion as a crime committed by the same killer who shot the two police officers last week in the Ni-Chome area of Kabukicho. The police are concentrating all their efforts on arresting the killer.

Wasn't the weapon supposed to be a rifle? thought Samejima, losing his appetite and lowering his spoon. If the killer was not only riding a motorbike but had fired from alongside the police car, it surely couldn't have been a rifle.

The murderer, who fled the scene, was wearing a black sweater and jeans. His face was covered completely by his helmet and couldn't be seen.

The TV screen showed a hospital. The reporter was broadcasting from the front lawn outside the ward.

This is the Tokyo Medical School Hospital where Sergeant Kanai, now in critical condition, was brought. The hospital is close to the scene of the crime and a short distance from the Shinjuku Police Station where Sergeant Kanai is based. The incident happened at around 6:40 p.m. Sergeant Kanai was brought in not by ambulance but by a police car that had arrived promptly at the scene. According to doctors, while the bullet has been removed, the patient is unconscious and it is not certain at this stage whether his condition will improve.

Questions are being asked as to why police officers, and officers assigned to the Shinjuku force in particular, are being singled out and targeted. The police are coming under pressure, in light also of last week's murders, to drastically reappraise the state of their investigation.

The camera returned to the studio.

We now turn to the press conference held earlier at the Special Criminal Investigation Headquarters at Shinjuku Police Station...

"*Systematically targeting and murdering uniformed police officers in the line of duty represents a challenge to the constitutional state, and any activity which endangers the very existence of the law by taking the lives of the police officers whose job it is to uphold the law will under no circumstances be tolerated. The Criminal Investigation Headquarters is increasing its personnel, and we are resolute in our determination to ensure that this crime is not repeated.*"

The spokesperson was an inspector with the Metropolitan Police. His face was flushed; his eyes flashed with ill-concealed anger.

Two consecutive incidents involving the killing of police officers had dealt a crushing blow to the Metropolitan Police's prestige and sullied their reputation.

In the studio, the commentators tried to build up an image of the killer.

"I think it is fair to say first of all that the perpetrator of these crimes has an extreme hatred of the police and police officers. Perhaps he's been involved in some trouble with the police in the past and that forms the basis of the hatred. Because the crime has been repeated in Shinjuku, the trouble also is likely to have occurred there."

"Another possibility is that this could be a so-called act of terrorism, carried out by a guerrilla group with radically anti-establishment views. To them, police officers represent the 'enemy,' and they would be prepared to extort any sacrifice, even taking the lives of officers. No group has issued a statement claiming responsibility, but if they were to do so, we can't rule out the possibility that terrorist activity will escalate in the near future."

Samejima forced down half the fried rice.

The crimes had been carried out exactly one week apart, on Mondays. This was undoubtedly a carefully planned serial killing.

It wasn't uncommon for arson to be carried out on the same day of the week. Arson had an element of what might be termed "a prank crime," where the motive appeared to be summoning a crowd—the attendant commotion—rather than the size of the fire itself.

In such cases, the perpetrator might commit his crime to coincide with a regular event, following the same weekly TV program or a periodic occurrence at the workplace. There were also instances of offenses being repeated on vacation days. The regularity of everyday life tended to give rise to serial crimes.

To an extent, this made the perpetrator easier to apprehend. But there was also another tendency with serial crimes: the longer they went on, the shorter the interval between cases.

For a serial crime, once a week was a relatively short cycle. If the frequency in the current case were escalated, there could be a new strike every three days, or even every day, in which case the chances of an arrest shot up, while Criminal Investigation HQ would be faced with the dilemma that the number of victims would be increasing at the same time.

Samejima also knew that all personnel with the Shinjuku force might be ordered to carry firearms.

He left the Chinese restaurant and returned to the foreman's cabin.

He smoked a cigarette as he walked along. He couldn't use any lights in the cabin at night.

There was one on in the window of Kizu's apartment.

Sitting in his tube chair, Samejima gazed at it out of the small sliding window of the cabin.

Additional personnel for the Criminal Investigation HQ would be culled not just from the Metropolitan Police but from within Shinjuku Station. Inevitably, a request for support would be made to the Guard Section and Crime Prevention.

At the moment, Samejima didn't want to be forced into helping out.

He had found Kizu's apartment; he felt close to discovering the whereabouts of his workshop. If he could smash the workshop, for a while Kizu would be unable to resume his work when he came out of prison. It was for precisely this reason that he kept his workplace separate from his place of residence.

Manufacturing guns required a variety of tools, including a lathe, and guns were no use unless one had bullets. Samejima suspected that Kizu stored quite a number and variety of bullets in his workshop.

Surely he couldn't hold out much longer. Perhaps he could forego alcohol and sex, but Kizu was not someone who could live for any length of time without making guns. He was probably relaxed about not being able to visit the entertainment districts, but not for much longer should he be able to stay away from his workshop—from rolling his sleeves up and getting his hands dirty and feeling his half-finished guns.

Samejima had arrested Kizu not long after being transferred to the Shinjuku Police Station. It was Samejima who discovered his sexual preference. Kizu hadn't realized that he was being investigated.

He was well known among the gangland bosses for his skill in manufacturing firearms, but the bosses couldn't be expected to inform the police about their method of communicating with Kizu, and he himself avoided meeting his clients unless they made contact by special means.

At the instigation of Sub-Section Four, a detective from Crime Prevention had been on the heels of Kizu. Samejima volunteered his assistance to the Ueno Police Station to stake out Kizu.

A number of places run by gays that seemed like the sort Kizu might frequent came up in the investigation. Samejima, whose face wasn't known in the area, continued his surveillance and at length managed to arrest Kizu when he stopped by one of the establishments.

At the time of his arrest, Kizu didn't put up much resistance. It was the second time he'd run into Samejima at that particular hangout. When Kizu found out Samejima was a detective he was deeply shocked.

"I know a cop when I see one—especially a Shinjuku cop. But you, I had no idea at all."

"I'm sorry."

Kizu laughed.

He was handsome, with a slender, fair-skinned face and almond-shaped eyes. He could do well with the ladies if he desired. His narrow-eyed grin, however, was not pleasant.

"A new face?"

"Yup."

While he was being taken under guard in a police car to Shinjuku Station, another detective told him all about Samejima.

Samejima returned in a different car.

As Samejima was passing by the interview room by chance, Kizu, handcuffed and alone, called him over.

"I heard you're an inspector."

Samejima stared at him.

"An inspector without a single man under his command. At least that's what your colleague said."

Samejima tried to walk away without saying anything.

Kizu's voice rose up in a peal of laughter.

Samejima tarried.

"If I ever meet you again," said Kizu, "I'll teach you the taste of men."

"No thanks."

Kizu shook his head. "I will. You know what your colleague said? He said, 'Teach him for me.'"

Kizu's words turned into hysterical laughter as he announced to Samejima how he intended to violate him.

The one who had stirred things up was a detective in the same Crime Prevention Section.

Already at the time, Samejima felt as though he didn't have a single friend in his section.

The detectives assigned to the investigation weren't able to make Kizu divulge the whereabouts of his workshop.

Consequently, though it was his second offense, Kizu's sentence was extremely light.

Samejima hadn't been allowed to take part in the interrogation.

His pager buzzed and he was jerked back into the present.

It was a call from the station. He turned the switch off. He didn't want to be recalled and assigned to Special Investigation HQ. It wasn't that he didn't feel any anger toward the cop killer—just that he didn't think the whole force should be put on one case. There were plenty of criminals out there besides the one responsible for murdering the officers.

It was his revulsion for a police organization that was so worked up to save face that made Samejima unwilling to give up on Kizu. But more than that, Samejima had been the one responsible for sending Kizu to prison. Tomorrow he'd have to show his face at the station but he couldn't afford to let Kizu out of his sight until then.

Come on, make your move, prayed Samejima, gazing up at the light coming from Kizu's apartment window.

"HQ wants you with them," said Momoi, soon after Samejima turned into work the following morning.

"Not interested."

"We're getting trouble. From Officer Saka's father, and from the Metropolitan Police."

"It's nothing to do with me."

"You've been nominated. The Met wants to utilize your talents," said Momoi, staring Samejima in the face. He lowered his voice and added, "They want someone with the experience."

"You mean Superintendent Koda does?"

Momoi declined to say either way.

Under the pretext of reinforcing the investigation, Koda wanted to rein in Samejima and have him at his beck and call.

Samejima stared back at Momoi who, feigning indifference, looked away.

"I found out where Kizu is holed up. I'd like to track down his workshop, too."

"How long have you been watching him?"

"Three days."

"Can't you take him by surprise?" asked Momoi, meaning storm the apartment while Kizu was asleep.

"He won't have his tools with him. They'll definitely be stashed some place else."

Momoi closed his eyes. "If I talk to Public Security, they'll tell me to assign someone else to Kizu."

"Public Security won't catch the killer."

"Why not?"

"Because I don't think he's a leftist activist."

"That's your opinion?" said Momoi. He sounded extremely weary. "I see."

Samejima went back to his desk and finished writing out an application for Kizu's search and arrest warrant. Then he went over to the Criminal Investigation HQ. The morning meeting had just ended and the army of information gatherers filed noisily out of the room.

It looked like Yabu had also been in the meeting. He came out into the corridor.

"Call me later," he said as he brushed past Samejima.

Samejima nodded, and went into the room.

Koda was standing in front of the whiteboard at the back. His hands were thrust into his pockets as he talked in an overbearing manner with the Crime Section Chief.

As Samejima came into the room, the din quietened down. Voices became hushed and several sets of eyes followed his progress into the room.

Koda became aware of him.

"Ah, thanks for coming over. Find yourself a desk and sit down," he said curtly before resuming his conversation with the section chief.

"Superintendent Koda."

"What is it, Inspector Samejima?"

The room went deathly quiet.

"I am declining the request to augment this investigation."

Koda's face was expressionless.

"You mean you're in the middle of an investigation? If that's the case then hand it over to someone else in Crime Prevention."

"I can't do that. I'm handling the case alone."

"Alone? I'm not aware that this police station allows individuals to conduct investigations."

"Superintendent—"

The Crime Section Chief started to speak, but Koda cut him off with a raised hand.

"If I arrange for the station chief to give you a direct order?"

"Do as you see fit," said Samejima, heading for the door.

"Samejima."

Samejima turned around. "What is it?"

"That's no way to speak to me," Koda said, puckering his lips. "No matter. There's nobody at this station who will stick his neck out for you. I gather you are pursuing an illicit gun maker. Well, that isn't what this station is concerned about right now. You don't have an arrest warrant, and we can't afford to let anyone assist you. Tell me, how do you intend to handle it?"

"I wonder."

"Are you looking to get yourself demoted to a uniformed officer?"

"A superintendent from Public Security has the authority to make personnel decisions at Shinjuku Police Station?"

Koda stared fixedly at Samejima. At length, he said in a barely audible voice: "Get out of here."

Samejima left the room without replying.

Samejima returned to Crime Prevention and dialed Yabu's internal number.

Knowing it was Samejima, Yabu answered in a friendly voice: "Fancy an ice coffee?"

Fifteen minutes later, Samejima found himself in the coffee shop of a high-rise hotel in west Shinjuku. The hotel lobby was on the second floor, and the guests generally used the café facilities in the lounge on either the first or second floor. The coffee shop located in the basement was long and narrow and didn't usually attract many customers.

Samejima sat in a seat furthest in the back, facing Yabu.

"Headquarters has an embargo agreement with the press, but there was a threat yesterday."

Yabu downed his ice coffee in one and ordered another.

"The far left?"

"Nope. I've dubbed the tape recording. Care to listen?" He added that in readiness for a call from a radical organization claiming responsibility for the crimes, Criminal Investigation HQ was recording all incoming calls.

"Why are you telling me this?"

For a moment Samejima suspected Koda was using Yabu to pull him in and persuade him to join them. Samejima had caused Koda to lose face in front of the other detectives. Be that as it may, if Koda really wanted Samejima for his investigation team, he'd stop at nothing to bring him in.

"I'll explain later. But first, listen to this."

Samejima took the earphones. After a moment of whispered nothingness, he heard a voice that was obviously from a public phone booth.

Pass this on to Sotoyama… I'll do it again… More police officers will die… I hate the police.

The tape had been edited with the intervals between the replies cut.

Police officers will die again…

Samejima looked at Yabu. While it sounded like the voice of a young man, it could have been the high pitch of a tense middle-aged man.

I called earlier… I put the evidence in a flowerbed in Kabukicho… Go and see for yourselves…right in the middle of the biggest flowerbed… You won't catch me…

The recording ended there.

"The communication about the flowerbed came one hour after the first call. 3:18 p.m. and 4:20 p.m. They were both made from public phone booths and we weren't able to trace either. We compared the voices. Although it's the same guy, he was slightly more relaxed during the second call."

"Is this the first time we've had this kind of call?"

"No, not exactly. The news agencies and TV stations have received a number of calls. The majority seem to be hoaxes."

"But it mentions Chief Sotoyama by name, huh?"

"And there's something else. After the second call, a patrol car went to the square in Kabukicho and found some spent rifle cartridges in the flowerbed."

"What caliber?"

"5.56mm."

"Do they match?"

Yabu shook his head. "The same type of bullet was used in both cases, a 30-06. That's 7.62mm, much bigger than a 5.56. The U.S. Army's standard rifle uses 5.56s. The souvenir stores around Yokosuka Base sell those by the bucket load as key ring holders."

"It sounds like a hoax to me."

"Because Sotoyama was referred to by name, things are a little more complicated. There's also the timing issue. Usually we receive the most prank calls the day after the crime is committed, and the number declines as the days pass. The only call we had yesterday, was that one."

Samejima knew how HQ would deal with this: basically as a hoax, but also as a possible attempt by the killer to throw the investigation into a state of confusion.

"So, what is it you want to talk to me about?"

"There were no cartridges found at the scene of the crime yesterday."

Samejima looked at Yabu.

"The 30-06 is a rifle round," Yabu pointed out, "but it wouldn't have been possible to carry out yesterday's shooting with a rifle. The shooter was on a bike. Even if he'd slung the rifle across his shoulder as he approached, shooting with such a long barrel from the side of the car isn't easy. Both the eyewitnesses in the area and the officers in the car would have noticed him taking aim. There are no eyewitness reports that suggest he had a gun of any length."

"How about if he'd cut down the barrel?"

"That was my first thought. It's common in America to shorten the barrel of a shotgun. The gunshot disperses widely, and at close range there's hardly any need to take aim. The bullets spray out like a shower, you see. But I've hardly ever come across the same with a rifle. I touched on this the other day. When you shorten the barrel, the base of the round oscillates and the rate of accuracy drops significantly."

"Maybe the killer doesn't know much about firearms. He might have just lopped a piece off with a hacksaw to make it easier to carry."

"But the reason I don't think so is the cartridges," argued Yabu, softly.

"As I'm sure you know, a rifle with a large caliber, over 7mm, would be bolt action. Actually, whether it's a bolt action or automatic, it still has to eject the cartridge or you can't fire the next round. It doesn't work the same way as a revolver."

À bullet is made up of a cartridge and a bullet head. The latter is the lump of metal that hurtles through the air, while the cartridge is long and cylindrical, contains gunpowder, and has a base fitted with a percussion cap to detonate the round. When the trigger is squeezed, the spring-loaded percussion pin strikes the percussion cap, which causes a small explosion and detonates the gunpowder inside the cartridge. The energy produced by the explosion discharges the bullet head. Naturally, once the bullet has been fired, the spent cartridge is no longer of any use. There is usually only one chamber in a gun to deal with the explosion. An exception to this, the revolver, has a lotus-shaped cylinder magazine that is capable of housing a number of rounds; another exception is the side-by-side shotgun, which has two chambers. All other types of firearm, including automatic pistols and rifles, have only chamber. Accordingly, once the bullet has been fired, the cartridge remains as an obstruction in the chamber of the gun. An automatic weapon ejects the cartridge by using the gas produced by the combusted gunpowder. With a bolt action that doesn't happen; instead, the spent cartridge is ejected by manually moving a bolt backwards and forwards after each shot is fired.

In either case, in order to fire two shots from a rifle, the shooter needed to eject the cartridge from the first shot to be able to fire the second. Yabu was saying that the cartridge from the first shot had not been found.

"The traffic at the scene of the crime is pretty heavy. It's conceivable that the ejected cartridge struck a passing vehicle and spun away further down the street. At any rate, it doesn't seem as though it was a bolt action.

Eyewitnesses said the killer fired two rounds in rapid succession."

"You think it was a fairly sophisticated customized weapon?"

"Rather than simply customized, it sounds like a completely different type of gun. It would be about the same size as a handgun but would fire rifle ammo. It would have multiple chambers and there'd be no need to eject the spent cartridges."

"Is there a handgun that fires rifle bullets?"

"There is, in the States. But it's a single-shot bolt-action job. Generally speaking, there's no point in having a handgun that fires rifle bullets. If it's stopping power you're after, you go with a Magnum. It holds plenty of rounds and it's not as difficult to use as a rifle. The Magnum bullet originated, actually, from the idea of shortening a rifle cartridge."

"The question is, why did the killer make such a gun?"

Yabu looked at Samejima. "That's right. If firepower was what he needed, why do you think?"

"In America, you wouldn't need to use a rifle bullet in a handgun, since there's a powerful bullet you could use. But in Japan—"

Samejima stopped mid-sentence. Kizu suddenly came to mind.

Yabu said, "A powerful handgun and bullets of that kind aren't easily obtainable in Japan. On the other hand, it's relatively easy to get hold of rifle bullets. And if you could come by the bullets, you could manufacture a handgun to match them."

"But there aren't too many people around who possess that kind of skill."

"That's right. If the gun the killer used were a multi-chambered handgun, it would be like no other gun. It wouldn't be easy to manufacture a handgun with multiple chambers for rifle bullets."

"That's it, then?"

"That's it," nodded Yabu.

11

Kizu made his move on the evening of the sixth day of surveillance.

He didn't go out for his evening meal on that day. Instead, at around 3 p.m., he bought a large quantity of groceries from a convenience store.

Samejima's evening meals always coincided with Kizu's. He didn't leave the foreman's cabin until Kizu went out for dinner. Having made sure that Kizu had gone in the restaurant, Samejima would dash into the nearest store and buy a prepacked meal or something else handy.

He tried to take his meals in the same cycle as Kizu. If Kizu took his evening meal at 7 p.m. and didn't go to bed until after 1 a.m., he'd surely be a little hungry. If he stayed up past that time, it meant he had some instant food he had bought in. Otherwise he'd have to go out during the night for a bite.

To understand the rhythm of his life was to grasp his mindset.

Clearly, Kizu was in hiding. He appeared to be in a state of heightened awareness, taking care not to make any unnecessary movements. Nobody fitting Kazuo's description had visited Kizu's condominium.

Samejima refrained from making inquiries of Kizu's neighbors. If he started poking his nose around, a cautious pro like Kizu would sense the subtle change in his environment. He'd likely guess he was being watched and not go anywhere near his workshop.

Kizu's daily routine was simple. He left the condo at about 10 a.m. and ate a set breakfast in a nearby coffee shop. He didn't have a newspaper delivered and instead cast his eye over one there.

Then he briefly returned to his room before going out again around 3 p.m. He took a quick meal at a noodle vendor or some such place and whiled away the time in a pachinko parlor or video rental store.

Around 7 p.m. he went out for dinner, then returned to his apartment without venturing out again.

Kizu wasn't short of money. He had accumulated savings from the sales of his guns. It was known that the leaders of a certain gang had paid almost a million yen for a specially ordered customized gun.

Kizu's guns—guns that didn't appear to be such but could be relied upon for self-defense—commanded very high prices.

On the day he didn't go out for dinner, Kizu left the condo at a little after 9 p.m. He was dressed as usual in a polo shirt and trousers. The only thing that wasn't customary was the large paper bag he carried with him.

Kizu walked to Monzen Nakacho and entered a snack bar.

This was the first time during the surveillance operation that Kizu had gone to this place. It was in the basement of a building just off Eitai Street.

Perhaps he had gotten to know Kazuo there.

Samejima had called Fuyuki several times in the last five days. Fuyuki told him that since the last visit, Kizu called every other day to check if Kazuo was in.

It seemed the day he visited Agamemnon, too, he had asked persistently after Kazuo.

Samejima watched Kizu disappear into the snack bar and decided to continue his surveillance from across the street.

Before a quarter-hour was up, Kizu climbed back up the steps and reappeared on the street. Having assumed he wouldn't come out for a while, Samejima stood up in a hurry.

Kizu crossed Eitai Street at the lights. He started to go back in the direction of the condo but showed no sign of calling it a day and walked briskly on.

Kizu must have stopped by the snack bar to find out Kazuo's

whereabouts. It was still early and there were quite a few people about. Even so, Samejima followed him from a discreet distance.

Kizu walked in a southerly direction. With his back to Eitai Street, he was headed in the direction of the reclaimed land.

Reclaimed land though it was, the residential district was densely populated.

Since leaving Eitai Street, Kizu had crossed over two bridges. Wherever his destination lay, he certainly wasn't headed toward any eating establishments.

Samejima was tense.

He would never have guessed the workshop to be in such a neighborhood. He had assumed that if Kizu were to go to his workshop, he'd do so by car.

Kizu turned left. Samejima stopped walking.

It was an alleyway by one of the tributaries to the Heikyu River. The tributary was held in check a short distance in front of the buildings as if it were a canal constructed for the benefit of the shipping agents and pleasure boat operators that lined the alleyway.

The flow of water on the opposite side converged with the Heikyu River and slipped along into the Shiomi and Toyosu canals before eventually joining the Arakawa River and pouring into Tokyo Bay.

Kizu had gone into one of the shipping agents' buildings. The edifice had a name on its front: Tomikawa.

Although he waited a while, there was no sign of Kizu coming out.

Samejima smoked a cigarette.

A banner on the shipping agent building advertised: *sillaginoid, flathead, goby fish tempura.* It looked as though they rented out fishing craft and houseboats.

Before long there was a great rush of water. Samejima looked around. A houseboat, almost as wide as the narrow channel, had entered the waterway from downstream.

The boat, with a roof like that of a house, was bedecked with dozens of small bright lanterns. As it nosed its way forward, the small fishing boats and motor launches moored on the near side of the channel were hit by a bow wave and rocked about violently in the swell.

The houseboat belonged to Tomikawa. It came alongside the timber wharf that had been constructed in front of the store. The passengers disembarked one after the other to the accompaniment of the boatman's voice in the background. There were as many as fifty passengers.

Having had their fill of tempura and *saké* while enjoying the evening breeze on Tokyo Bay, the passengers streamed off the boat in high spirits.

Samejima mixed into the crowd and approached the edge of the channel. Several boatmen, wearing *happi* coats decorated with the store livery, began clearing up on deck.

"Oi! You've a customer," boomed a voice from the store.

One of the boatmen looked up. "Ah, it's been a while," he said in a crisp voice, recognizing Kizu standing in front of the store.

The man standing next to Kizu looked as though he was the ageing owner of Tomikawa.

"Sorry to trouble you. Do you mind?" said Kizu, within Samejima's earshot.

"No problem. Why don't we go inside and have beer while they finish clearing up out here," replied the boatman.

The flow of inebriated passengers had by now abated, and Samejima moved away from the edge of the wharf. As far as he could make out from their conversation, Kizu and the boatman seemed to be on fairly familiar terms. They looked about the same age too. Samejima thought they were perhaps former classmates.

Did Kizu plan on boarding a boat now?

Samejima chewed on his lip. If Kizu used the channel to go to and from his workshop, there'd be no means of following him.

He wanted to raid the workshop while Kizu was there.

Kizu's arrest warrant hadn't been issued yet. The evidence to be submitted to the court was already assembled. All that was left to be done was to obtain Momoi's approval and make a formal request. But in all likelihood Momoi would need to get the permission of the deputy station chief in turn, and Samejima wondered what would happen at that point.

He looked up at the high-pitched noise of an engine starting and the sound of churning water.

Kizu and the boatman were sitting in a four-man motorboat that was moored alongside the houseboat. The boatman was skilfully manipulating the rudder and steering the motorboat through the narrow gap between the channel wall and the houseboat. Samejima broke into a run, looking all the while at the channel on his right side.

He had virtually memorized the layout of the whole area during the stakeout. This channel was unbroken as far as the convergence with the Heikyu River. From that point it split into three: the Toyosu Canal to the west, straight on to the Shiomi Canal to the south, or east to the Shiohama Canal.

He just needed to know which route they would take.

The motorboat quickly picked up speed once it was clear of the houseboat. There was now no longer any way to keep up. Any time now they'd arrive at the Nakasu waterway "crossroads."

Samejima lifted his knees and ran as if his life depended on it. The sound of the motorboat's engine went up a further notch. He ran as fast as he could along the road that followed parallel with the channel. The channel was several feet lower than the road and there was no danger that he'd be seen and recognized.

He began to pour with sweat. This was the chance to put the results of his daily jogging to the test. He spurred himself on.

He could see a bridge straight ahead, cutting across the channel. It was Tsuribune Bridge, between the two "crossroads" of Ettchujima and Furuishiba.

Beyond that point the channels soon converged. If he could get to the top of the bridge he would be able to see which direction the motorboat was headed.

The sound of the motorboat cutting through the water overtook Samejima. He clenched his teeth and pumped his arms and legs.

At length he reached the bridge. The white wake bubbled on the surface of the channel.

Samejima leaned against the handrail breathing heavily and followed the motorboat with his gaze. The boat was proceeding under Shirasuna Bridge, which linked the road to the reclaimed land at Shiohama.

They had gone south. They were sailing straight down the Heikyu. Eventually they would pass under the Hamasaki Bridge and enter the Shiomi Canal. From there, they would either continue south on the Shiomi Canal or go as far as the Shinnome Canal. In any case, Samejima couldn't see that far from his present position.

He brushed his hair back and his hand came away soaked with sweat. He leaned back against the rail, regained his composure, and lit a cigarette.

Without a warrant, he could only arrest Kizu in the act of committing a crime. In order to do that, he had to find Kizu's workshop.

It was thirty minutes later that the motorboat returned to Tomikawa. The only person aboard was the boatman. There was no sign of Kizu.

Had Kizu located his workshop in a place only accessible by motorboat?

It was possible that the use of the boat was simply a means of shaking off a tail.

While Samejima doubted Kizu had become aware that he was being watched, perhaps the gun maker had gone by boat to a remote location where he could land and continue on to his workshop by train or taxi. If Kizu always took such pains going to and from his workshop, it would be quite tough to locate.

It was a roundabout way of doing things, but Samejima was sure Kizu would go quite far for the sake of concealing his workshop.

Samejima waited for the boatman to come back out of Tomikawa and followed him. The boatman, who had changed into an Aloha shirt and jeans, looked about thirty-five, more or less the same age as Kizu.

He wore leather-soled sandals on his bare feet. He walked a short distance and entered a detached house. It was a small two-story house. It had a garage, and beside a stationary four-wheel drive vehicle was a child's three-wheeled bicycle. The house's nameplate read "Tomikawa." This boatman, then, was working for his father.

Samejima decided to return to the police station. If Tomikawa ever went out in a boat to pick up Kizu, it would mean the workshop was in a place accessible only by boat.

He would interrogate Tomikawa, and if the arrangement was indeed for Tomikawa to pick up Kizu, Samejima would force the man to take him along and march straight into the workshop. Once Samejima came into contact with Tomikawa, there could be no delay in making the arrest. The stronger the relationship between Tomikawa and Kizu, the greater the risk that Tomikawa would give out a warning.

There was an even chance that Tomikawa knew the whereabouts of Kizu's workshop. If he ferried him there in full knowledge of what was going on, it was a fairly safe bet that he was being paid for his troubles, in which case he would try and protect Kizu. Judging from his residence, it seemed he had been acquainted with Kizu for some time. At any rate, they had probably been classmates at junior high or senior high. He had to be helping Kizu out of friendship, not simply for the money.

It was close to midnight by the time Samejima returned to the station. There were still a large number of people in the Criminal Investigation Headquarters.

He wondered whether Yabu had told the investigation meeting that it was highly likely that the gun used by the murderer had been manufactured by Kizu. He probably hadn't. The only person who could be persuaded of that was Samejima—the only one who understood Yabu and his imagination.

In all probability, Yabu hadn't told anyone other than Samejima.

Samejima headed for the armory. Detectives normally didn't bother to pack heat, but sure enough, most of the guns had been taken out. All that was left, other than handguns belonging to officers on vacation, were his gun and that belonging to Momoi.

The New Nambu model, used by detectives, was a two-inch short-barrelled revolver manufactured by Shin Chuo Industries and based on the American Smith&Wesson 38mm M3 Revolver. It housed five rounds and used a 38mm special bullet. It had a strong recoil for a small gun and wasn't particularly accurate.

Samejima housed the gun in the holster on the right side of his belt and climbed into his BMW in the station's car park. He had brought his car there soon after he'd discovered Kizu's hideout. With the creation of the Criminal Investigation Headquarters, the car park was working at full capacity to accommodate the vehicles used by the investigators. By bringing his car in earlier, he had managed to secure a parking space. Since the number of personnel had been augmented, even the contract parking lots in the neighborhood, normally used for impounding illegally parked cars, overflowed with force cars.

If the Tomikawa establishment also arranged fishing trips, its mornings would begin very early. If Samejima were to question the boatman, there was no time to return to his Nogata apartment for a rest.

Samejima drove his BMW to Monzen Nakacho. He decided to park on a one-way street close to the channel facing Tomikawa and took a nap in his car.

Samejima woke at 4 a.m. It wasn't yet daybreak.

He got out of his BMW, flexed his body and shook the stiffness out of his limbs. Today would be a gamble. If he failed, not only would Kizu be allowed to escape, but Samejima himself would be in some danger. He drank down a can of coffee he had bought from a vending machine and walked over to Tomikawa's house.

His revolver was concealed by the jacket he wore over his polo shirt.

The eastern sky was heavy with cloud. It didn't look as though the weather would improve.

In another hour, those customers who liked to go fishing early would show up at the pleasure boat operators.

Already, a light was on in Tomikawa's house. As expected, Tomikawa was an early riser. For an instant, Samejima, who knew nothing about the Tomikawa family, felt a shudder of guilt as he pressed the doorbell at the entrance.

He had already checked around the house, in case Tomikawa should make a run for it. There was no rear exit. One could only enter and leave through the front door. Even if he left by the window, there was barely space between the sides of the house and the walls of the neighboring properties for a person to slip by, except perhaps a child with a pliable body.

The only light came from the latticed window of what appeared to be the kitchen on the first floor. It was just to the left of the entrance hall.

"Coming. Who is it?" the suspicious voice of a woman replied a moment later.

All of a sudden the window opened and a woman in her thirties wearing an apron over her tracksuit stared out at him. She wasn't wearing makeup and her hair was cut short.

The smell of *miso* soup drifted out from the window.

"I'm sorry to disturb you so early in the morning."

Samejima bowed and showed her his police ID.

"I'm Samejima from the Shinjuku Police Station. Is your husband home?"

The woman stared in bewilderment at Samejima from the latticed window. At length she turned around and called out, "There's someone to see you."

Tomikawa came to the window wearing a faded black jersey.

"What is it?"

His voice was tense. His hair was cut short and his suntanned, dauntless face was somewhat pallid, perhaps on account of having just awoken.

Samejima tilted his head again. "I'm sorry to disturb you. I wonder if you could spare a few minutes to talk about a man called Kaname Kizu."

Tomikawa stood bolt upright, staring at Samejima. It was barely perceptible, but he seemed to turn a shade paler.

He knows, thought Samejima. *This man knows what Kizu's up to.*

"I'm eating breakfast right now. Then I have to go straight out to work," Tomikawa stated bluntly.

"I won't take up much of your time. Last night you saw Kizu, didn't you?"

As if he were about to be struck, Tomikawa jerked his head backwards. His eyes were wide open and staring.

"What is it? What's wrong?" the voice of his wife sounded from behind.

Samejima nodded and indicated the door with his eye. "I'd just like a quiet word."

"What's the matter?"

"Be quiet," said Tomikawa impatiently, turning his back on the window.

Before long Samejima heard the sound of the door being unlocked. On his guard, he took a step back. While he thought it unlikely that Tomikawa would put up any resistance, if the man was taking Kizu to his workshop with full knowledge of his work, it was to be assumed that he regarded Samejima with hostility.

Tomikawa stood in the doorframe of the entrance. He was dressed in a black jersey with an orange line across the middle.

"I'm very sorry to trouble you so early in the morning."

Samejima bowed once again. Standing face to face, Tomikawa was about the same height as he was. His build, too, was compact.

"Kizu's a friend of mine. I've known him since junior high,"

159

Tomikawa divulged vaguely.

"Do you know what he does for a living?"

Tomikawa stared at Samejima. Then he turned around to face his house and shouted, "Hey, I'm just going out for a while."

He slipped on his leather-soled sandals and gestured toward the channel with his jaw.

Samejima nodded. He understood that Tomikawa didn't want his family to know about Kizu.

Content to have him walk ahead, Samejima followed toward the channel fronting the Tomikawa building.

As he walked, the boatman gazed out at the eastern sky. He seemed troubled by the weather.

When they were far enough out to look down on the channel, Tomikawa stopped and looked around at Samejima.

"You came from Shinjuku?"

Samejima nodded.

Tomikawa took a cigarette from the pocket of his jersey and lit it. It had already been partially smoked. He spat as if a strand of tobacco had come away in his mouth.

"Are you going to arrest him?"

"Some more people have died by the guns he made."

Tomikawa's face was devoid of emotion as Samejima's tone changed.

"Yesterday, you took him somewhere by motorboat, didn't you?"

Tomikawa glanced up at Samejima but didn't say anything.

"How far did you take him?"

Tomikawa averted his eyes and looked over at the houseboats and motorboats moored at the wharf. He took a drag on his cigarette, dropped it to the ground and stomped it out with the sole of his leather sandal.

"What's your name?"

"Samejima. I'm with the Crime Prevention Section of Shinjuku police."

Tomikawa was looking down and his facial expression wasn't visible.

"Where is Kizu," Samejima said quietly.

Tomikawa exhaled. He probed his gums with the tip of his tongue and gazed out in the direction of the channel. He blew air into his cheeks.

"If he goes to prison this time, he won't come out again for a while, I suppose?" Tomikawa said without looking around at Samejima.

"That depends on him."

"He's sick. If he weren't, he wouldn't be such a bad guy. He's persistent, and clever. We've hung around since we were kids."

"Are you indebted to him?"

"Not really."

Tomikawa looked for the first time at Samejima.

"Once, I got into trouble gambling and nearly had my boat taken away from me. It was some dodgy mahjong saloon backed by a *yakuza* clan. Kizu had a word with them and resolved it all without me losing my boat."

"Which clan was it?"

"What's that got to do with it?"

"Which clan?"

Tomikawa clicked his tongue.

"The Arao family, from Shinjuku."

The clan boss was a client of Kizu's.

"Was it Kizu who invited you to the saloon in the first place?"

"Like I said, what's that got to do with it?" Tomikawa demanded.

Samejima didn't reply. Tomikawa didn't seem to realize that Kizu had ensnared him.

"I'll see to it you don't get mixed up in this. Take me to Kizu."

"He's a friend. Are you telling me to betray him?"

Samejima was sure of it now. Tomikawa had taken Kizu all the way to his workshop.

"If I let it go, you'll face a charge as well. You've got a family."

"Don't try and blackmail me!"

Tomikawa's facial expression changed; Samejima gripped him by his collar.

"Kizu likes to make friends with murderers. It's one thing for *yakuza* to go around killing each other. What if a stray bullet hits a woman or a child? Because of the guns he's made, several people are now dead. How would you feel if one of the victims was your own?"

Tomikawa glared at Samejima.

"Take a look!"

Samejima opened the front of his jacket. Tomikawa's eyes fastened themselves on his revolver.

"My own life's at risk. If he isn't arrested, more people will be killed."

Tomikawa's body stiffened.

"Take me to where Kizu's hiding out."

"Are you going alone?"

"Yeah."

"Heavens, you're not going to blow him away."

"No, nothing like that. I intend to put the cuffs on him and send him to court."

"He said he couldn't go to prison again. The first and second time he was locked up, he was forced to do it with some pretty hideous guys."

"Do you think I care?"

"But he's not like that with me. He's a friend, that's all."

Samejima took out a cigarette. He smoked it in silence. Tomikawa was lost to his own thoughts.

After he'd smoked it, Samejima asked, "Will you take me?"

Tomikawa breathed out a long sigh. "Climb aboard, Mr. Detective."

12

As the motorboat picked up speed, a variety of scents combined with the smell of the canal and invigorated Samejima's senses. The smell, which was both like the fragrance of the tide, and the odor of exhaust fumes, seemed to be contained in each droplet of water in the spray that now assaulted the boat.

It was sticky and hot on the canal. Even without the spray, their clothing seemed to soak up the humidity and weigh them down.

The cloud-filled sky was reflected darkly on the water surface and made the channel look deeper than it actually was. Curiously, only the white bubbles rising out of the water churned by the screw propeller gave Samejima a sense of being on water. There were few rough waves and the boat proceeded without encountering any resistance.

Samejima had the odd feeling he was traveling faster than he would have in a car on the expressway higher above ground. The outlines of the buildings receding from his vision on either side of the boat differed from the Tokyo he knew.

Here and there were a number of small jetties constructed with steps cut into the seawall so that people could climb up to the road and buildings above.

The motorboat passed under a fourth bridge, the Shirasagi-bashi. Another bridge spanned ahead of them.

"How far are we going?" shouted Samejima, looking at his watch. It was five in the morning.

"Once we clear Edagawa Bridge, we join the Towun East Canal. Kizu is in the building on the right as we come out from under the Shuto Expressway," Tomikawa shouted back.

This was their first exchange since the boat had set off.

"How long have you been ferrying Kizu around?"

"Since a year before he went inside."

"Has it always been the same place?"

Tomikawa was silent.

The boat, which had continued straight on for a while since coming under Edagawa Bridge, slowed down as it reached the point where the canals converged. Before long the rudder moved to the left and the prow of the boat nosed into a canal that was much wider than the ones they had travelled on so far.

It was the Towun East Canal.

Ahead, the Shuto Expressway was large and imposing as it crossed the canal.

"When we get closer, cut the engine," said Samejima.

He didn't want Kizu to be alerted by the sound of the boat. If Kizu put up any resistance, Tomikawa might get caught up.

The boatman cut back the throttle just before the Shuto Expressway. The engine noise died down and eventually stopped. The boat continued to move forward under its own inertia.

"Where are we?" asked Samejima, now speaking more quietly.

"It's the junction of the Shiomi and Tatsumi Canals. There are timber yards ahead."

"Which building is Kizu in?"

Tomikawa pointed toward a row of warehouses along the right side of the Tatsumi Canal. Amongst the buildings was a small warehouse standing on a pile of dull brick foundation stones.

A set of stone steps faced the canal and led up to a steel door. The lower steps were submerged beneath the water.

"Is that the building?"

"The Miyama Transport warehouse."

Samejima looked at Tomikawa. Miyama Transport was a business controlled by one of the largest, most influential gangs in western Japan. It looked as though Kizu had made the connection while he was in the Kansai area and secured a safe place from where to carry on his business.

It had been a mistake to assume he was not affiliated with any organization. Perhaps Kizu wasn't actually allied with any one group, but he had undoubtedly been making guns to the special requirements of the Kansai overlords.

The widely influential gang that had taken Miyama Transport under its wing had clearly not made inroads into Tokyo by agreement with the local Kanto organizations. As a result, the warehouse hadn't appeared on the police's radar.

"Have you ever been inside?" asked Samejima, scrutinizing Tomikawa's face.

Tomikawa shook his head. "Kizu doesn't allow anyone in. He doesn't even let the warehouse people in there. On the other side of that door there's a basement. The only way in and out is through that door."

That was the reason it hadn't been found. Had this been a room in an apartment, the police would have steam-rollered their way in and caught him red-handed a long time ago.

The motorboat nosed slowly toward the stone steps.

"When were you to come and collect him?"

"Tomorrow night. The same as yesterday—once the houseboat had returned."

Samejima nodded.

"What about me? What shall I do?"

Samejima's reply was to stare at the door. It was a steel door covered in red rust that didn't look as though it was in use. There was an external bolt across the door.

"Is there a key to the door?"

"I don't know."

"What happens when he goes in?"

If it had been constructed as a basement room in a warehouse, there would be no need to lock it from the inside. It could be locked from the outside by securing the bolt with a padlock.

"Come to think of it, when it's not in use, he puts a chain and padlock on the bolt."

Even if it didn't have one originally, it was possible that Kizu had fitted a bolt inside the door once he started using the place as his workshop.

There were no windows close to the door.

"Is there a phone inside?"

"No, although he said there's electricity."

If Kizu couldn't be made to open the door, he might barricade himself in. Although there was no danger of him slipping away undetected, it would be a nuisance to wait around.

"Take me back."

"What?" Surprised, Tomikawa transferred his gaze to Samejima.

"Take me back."

"What do you have in mind?"

"We can't break down that door from the outside. I'll arrest him when you come to meet him, tomorrow night."

Tomikawa stared hard at Samejima.

"You've got work, don't you?"

"Aren't you worried I'll warn Kizu?"

"Is there anyone else besides you at Tomikawa who knows about this?"

"Nobody."

"Ah," said Samejima, looking once again at the door.

Without taking his eyes off Samejima, Tomikawa started the engine and maneuvered the boat into a sharp U-turn.

"What'll happen to me?" Tomikawa asked when they returned to the jetty.

Samejima smoked a cigarette in silence. Then, jumping onto the steps, he said, "Nothing's going to happen. I'm only after Kizu."

Tomikawa looked up, dumbfounded, with the mooring rope clasped in his hand.

"I'll be back tomorrow night."

Spitting out the words, Samejima began to walk away.

13

Having been beside himself with joy, he was now uneasy. And then, his hopes as well as his frustration swelled out of proportion.

Why didn't the police make a move? What he'd done hadn't been announced either in the newspapers or on TV.

He had watched as the spent cartridges had been retrieved from the shrubbery in the flowerbed at the square in Kabukicho.

As he had hoped, detectives had appeared at the scene and scoured the flowerbed, disgorging all manner of unrelated items—cigarette butts, discarded gum, empty cans.

A rope had been put in place and men wearing gloves moved around the place.

And yet, there was something missing, something not quite right.

Perhaps it was the small number of detectives present.

Within minutes of his second call from a public phone box close to Marksman, uniformed police officers arrived at the square. There were four of them.

They divided the work amongst them and began searching through the shrubbery. Before long they had discovered the M16 cartridges. One of the police officers, a middle-aged man, made a report with the mic of a portable transmitter he wore on his shoulder.

He watched the scene unfold from the front of a hamburger store a short distance away.

A few minutes later, a number of police cars, sirens wailing, and a

Criminal Identification Section truck, came rushing to the square. It was a truly thrilling moment.

As the onlookers began to gather, he lost no time in making his way to the very front of the crowd. He was a little afraid. What if someone said he had placed the cartridges there? What if the police started asking people if they knew of anyone who had been present, and someone pointed at him and said: *He was—he was here!*

Standing in the front row thinking these things required a good deal of courage.

The cartridges were immediately placed in a plastic bag by the gloved hand of a detective. Most of the onlookers didn't even know what had happened.

The only ones who knew were the detectives, and himself.

The thought caused a shiver of delight to run through him. Even though he was on the outside of the rope, his mind was on the inside. He fought back the urge to smile. To avoid the detectives' notice, he placed the straw to his cup in his mouth several times.

But the reason he felt there was something missing was that the detectives he had come to know best were not there. None of Hamura, or Sub-Section Chief Sotoyama, or the important man with the spectacles, had shown up.

As he feared, had they viewed it as a hoax after all?

He had returned to his room and, full of hope, turned on the TV. Maybe they'd announce the discovery of the cartridges and the fact that he had called. The cartridges had been key rings he had bought several years ago from a general store in Shibuya. He had removed the key ring using a workbench; the store had since gone out of business.

He wasn't anxious that his voice might be broadcast on TV. One's voice was always strange on the phone, even more so played from a recording. No one ought to recognize the voice as his. He knew for sure his call would have been recorded. If he were a member of the Criminal Investigation Headquarters, he would definitely record any outside calls.

A guy who killed cops would undoubtedly make a dramatic statement about the crime.

The news began, and his hopes were shattered in an instant. The real killer had struck again.

"It's not true!" he screamed in spite of himself.

This time, two police officers in a patrol car had been shot. One had died and the other was in serious condition.

His sense of dissatisfaction began to escalate from that point. The news program didn't touch on the cartridges or his call at all. It was almost as if the announcer were singularly unaware of the issue.

Why don't they announce it?

It could be interpreted in one of two ways. Either they considered it to be an irresponsible prank and were ignoring it, or they thought he was indeed the real killer and were progressing their investigations in secret, suppressing news reports.

Nobody would think it a mere coincidence if the second crime had been carried out on the day of his warning.

It was exactly a week since the first murder. He was stunned. The killer thought the same way he had. He had given his warning for a Monday. The killer had repeated his crime on the same day. He was a fiend who chose to kill on Mondays. It wasn't a chance happening. The killer was bound to murder a police officer in Shinjuku next Monday, too.

As he thought about this, he felt a surge of delight.

"I did it. I did it!"

He felt in tune with the killer. He had crossed over to the other side of that rope. There was no doubt about it, the police thought he was the killer.

In which case—

Now he felt uneasy. If they really did think he was the killer, then surely they would continue investigating the discarded cartridges and the phone calls he had made.

He continually flicked between the news programs. He wanted to find out what kind of weapon the killer had used. He had learned that it was a rifle from last Friday's news program. It had been on TV when he got back from his part-time job; he had decided to take a part-time job that paid by the day for a while and showed up for work every other day. It was a job that involved cleaning offices and directing traffic on construction sites.

A firearms expert had said it was a rifle on the news program that had begun at ten on Friday night.

The first thing that came to mind when he heard the word "rifle" was an M16 assault rifle.

It was the standard armament used by the U.S. Army—a 5.56mm capable of both semi-automatic and automatic firing.

Since then, the police had not made any announcements at all concerning the type of firearm. It appeared that the question had been asked during the press conference but brushed off with a "still under investigation."

It was also unclear as to whether the killer was a member of a leftist faction or simply an abnormal person who hated the police.

Did the killer use an M16?

He had to find out somehow. If it was a 5.56mm weapon, he was completely in sync with the killer. He might even be able to search out the killer himself.

Unless he talked to the detectives—if he weren't there—they probably wouldn't be able to arrest the killer. He had to steer them in the right direction and lead them to the killer.

At the moment he knew the killer better than anyone else. It proved he was a special person.

What was important was leading the police to the real killer by allowing them to think he was the killer. Once the true killer was caught, he wouldn't mind turning himself in.

Everyone would be so surprised.

"How did you know who the killer was?"

"I understood him—understood what made him tick."

That was what he'd say.

An ordinary person couldn't understand. It was because he had the talent to be a detective; it was something he'd been born with. This stuff only happened to someone who was destined in life to become a hero.

The world of his imagination began to bloom.

Good. I'll enjoy this world for a while. And then, when I'm tired of it, I'll close in on the killer.

A true special investigator, who didn't have to leave his room, was on the perp's trail. If the perp knew, he would be dismayed.

14

In the Crime Prevention Section, as always, half the personnel were out.

Shinjo had been asked to cooperate with the Criminal Investigation HQ and, delighted, had transferred over there taking a number of subordinates along with him.

A large number of personnel had come in not just from the station but from Mobile Investigation and Metropolitan Police.

Momoi was, as usual, sitting stooped over his desk. Samejima thought he'd probably stay that way until he retired from the force. If this were a business, he would doubtless be taken to task. But here, it simply served to demonstrate that the police was simply another bureaucracy. Yet, even this man once pursued criminals out of a belief in the just and righteous cause.

Samejima stood in front of the man's desk, and Momoi looked up over the top of his glasses.

"About the application for Kizu's search and arrest warrant."

Momoi removed his glasses and placed them on top of the pile of investigation reports he was halfway through reading. He looked like he'd been up all night and rubbed his tired eyes.

"I read it," Momoi replied aloofly, as if he'd just been pressed as to whether he'd read the morning paper, on a slow news day at that.

Samejima waited in silence.

Momoi looked surprised that Samejima seemed to be expecting a more detailed answer.

"The senior guys are busy right now. It doesn't look as if approval has been given yet."

He looked back at his paperwork. His expression made it clear the conversation had come to an end.

"I'm going to get Kizu," said Samejima.

Momoi raised his eyes again.

"If I catch him in the act, I don't need a warrant."

Momoi stared at Samejima. "So, it's urgent?" It looked as if Momoi's interest was just about aroused.

"Will you listen to what I have to say?"

Momoi stuck out his chin and looked around at the deserted desks in the section. Samejima thought he looked like a teacher who'd come to class on a day when school was cancelled.

Rising, Momoi said, "It's a little early, but how about lunch? It won't be that busy right now."

They headed over toward the station canteen. Just as Momoi had predicted, the place was virtually empty.

Momoi didn't appear to have developed any interest in Samejima until now. While Momoi, unlike Shinjo, hadn't displayed any open hostility, he hadn't tried to understand the maverick either. Momoi treated Samejima simply as another member of the section. Neither love nor hatred, just indifference.

"There's something I'd just like to say first," said Momoi as he sat down opposite Samejima. The tables around them were unoccupied. "I know what people say about me in the station. And I know what they say about you, too. You stand alone. It's inevitable. With the police, there are only two structures. Vertical and horizontal. And a police officer, well, he lives within that framework and clings to it for all he's worth. The structure means nothing outside of it, but if a cop doesn't stick with it, he has nothing at all to hold onto in life. The crooks hate him. The public eschews him. That's what it means to be a cop. But you, you've ignored that structure. You can't do that. It doesn't matter how good you are. Regardless of what you want, the police, as an organization, doesn't want people around with your values."

"I know," said Samejima.

"I'm not done. I haven't harbored any malice toward you, so far. That's because I, too, find the structure disagreeable and have avoided being drawn into it. I'm not saying I'm minded to join forces with you, but as one outsider to another: there's no need for us to lock horns. I've come to realize that these last ten days."

Samejima stared at Momoi's face.

It was devoid of emotion. He spoke in a disinterested manner, almost as if there were nobody there in front of him.

"The reason I don't quit the force is that I think the police's job is important. It's not that I think it's a really masculine thing to do; in fact, looking from the inside, there's quite an unmanly side to it. But even so, I think it is a really fine job.

"Those police officers—the way they were killed one after the other. And all from the same station. All the victims were young. They had fine careers ahead of them. I want the killer caught as quickly as possible because, emotionally, and rationally, we are all in this together as fellow officers. But you—and you probably have your reasons—you turned down a secondment to the Investigation Headquarters. I know that Kizu is a criminal you simply have to catch. But I think it's unfortunate that, as a fellow officer, you regard that as more important than arresting the killer of those police officers."

Samejima inhaled slowly. It was understandable that Momoi felt that way. At the Special Investigation Headquarters, several hundred detectives were wearing themselves out physically and mentally for the sake of tracking down perhaps just one killer. Whereas he was pitted alone against one criminal.

If Momoi felt that was egotistical, Samejima couldn't argue against it.

"It may be a bit timid of me to put it this way, but I'll say it anyway.

175

Compared to me, you are by far the superior detective. That's what Shinjo disliked most about you. You follow a career officer path, and with hardly any practical experience in the job, you manage to be the smartest detective in the section. There's no reason why you should be liked. Deep down, everyone feels you've never actually rolled your sleeves up and gotten your hands dirty. There's no need for someone as useless as me to join the ranks in battle. But I wish you would help them."

"I heard you were an excellent cop."

"I'd rather not talk about it," said Momoi, coolly. "I'm not talking about myself at the moment, I'm talking about you. This might sound a little cowardly, but I don't intend to change my view."

"I understand."

"Okay, now speak to me."

Samejima began to explain the course of events so far in his investigation of Kizu. What was important wasn't so much that he had discovered the whereabouts of Kizu's workshop but that he may be able to close it down for good this time. He conveyed the possibility that the cop killer had used a weapon manufactured by Kizu.

While listening to this explanation, Momoi kept his eyes trained on the dull wall of the station canteen. Even when the explanation had come to an end, his gaze stayed there for a while.

Finally, he looked at Samejima. "When did you say it was that Kizu made an appearance at Agamemnon?"

"Last Friday. Exactly one week ago."

"You were off duty, weren't you?"

Samejima nodded.

"Might it have been Kizu who killed the police officers?"

"If it was a serial killing by the same murderer, then it's not possible. I was watching him constantly at the time of the second killing."

"Kizu is lying low. That's what you think."

"Yes."

"Why did Kizu show up at Agamemnon? Even if he'd fallen out with his lover and had gone there to patch things up, it would have been an extremely dangerous time for Kizu to be in Shinjuku."

"I think it's because he had to contact Kazuo at any cost."

Momoi nodded. He pointed out aloofly: "It was that Friday that TV disclosed the murder weapon was a rifle."

Samejima stared at Momoi. A commentator had appeared on the program and reasoned that the murder weapon had been a rifle. Up until then, the media had not made that assumption, since HQ had refrained from making any announcements. The popular news show in question had presented its own homespun views about the murder weapon. It was the following day that HQ acknowledged to the press that the weapon indeed seemed to be a rifle. But still nothing was divulged about the caliber.

"And so, Kizu saw that and became concerned?" asked Samejima.

It was a possibility. It was immediately after that news program that Fuyuki called to report that a man sounding like Kizu had just called.

"Assuming Kizu's lover, Kazuo, had taken possession of the customized gun that used rifle bullets—it would hardly be surprising if Kizu heard on the TV news that the weapon was a rifle and started to get worried."

Momoi spoke with an even tone.

"The killer was either Kazuo," Samejima rejoindered, "or possibly someone who had received the gun from Kazuo."

"That has to be right."

"Can I get a warrant?"

"We can probably get one if we explain this to the station chief and to the Criminal Investigation Headquarters. But at that point, Kizu is no longer just your responsibility."

"That's fine with me," said Samejima, decisively.

Suddenly Samejima heard Koda's voice.

"Oh, what's this? You guys in Crime Prevention seem to have a lot of time on your hands. You two detectives have been chewing the fat since before lunchtime."

Koda was sitting himself down at a table a short distance away, holding a tray in his hands. He had two detectives with him—obvious at a glance that they belonged to Public Security.

Samejima ignored them. Momoi glanced over in their direction, and asked casually, "He was the same intake as you, wasn't he?"

Samejima nodded and calmly noted, "HQ still hasn't managed to get hold of any evidence identifying the killer."

Koda spoke again: "You must be having a nice time. While your colleagues are being whacked, and we're drafting in outside support, you're here having a nice friendly chat over lunch."

"The food here at the Shinjuku Station's really bad," complained one of the detectives with him.

"I bet you miss the food over at HQ?" said Koda with a chuckle.

Momoi looked over and forced a smile.

Koda had a look of contempt in his eyes.

Momoi turned his head back and said, in a low voice so only Samejima could hear: "We've got to snag the perp before they do."

At a little before 9 p.m., Samejima stood outside the storefront of Tomikawa. The houseboat had not yet returned.

It came back at just after 10 p.m. It was probably because it was a Friday, but the boat was nearly full, with nearly eighty passengers on board.

Samejima waited for all the passengers to disembark and then approached the waterway.

Dressed in a *happi* coat, Tomikawa looked up and noticed Samejima.

"Please wait a little," he said.

Then he issued crisp instructions to the young boatmen to clear things away. With the mooring rope in his hand he balanced one leg on the prow of the boat and the other on the jetty.

At length, with the tidying up finished, Tomikawa nodded in Samejima's direction. He couldn't read Tomikawa's expression in the dark.

Samejima came down the stone steps and stood on the jetty.

"It's all right now, you can come aboard," said Tomikawa, jumping directly from the houseboat to the motorboat.

Samejima climbed onto the vessel.

Tomikawa looked as though he was completely resigned to the situation. Since yesterday, he'd probably been torn about whether or not to warn Kizu, although there wasn't the slightest indication that he had been.

He threw his cigarette into the waterway and said, "All right, let's go."

Samejima sat down and nodded. Tomikawa started the boat's engine.

As they passed the first bridge, Tsuribune-bashi, Tomikawa yelled, "I didn't think you'd come here alone again."

"If we attacked in force, Kizu would barricade himself into the basement. Then we wouldn't be able to do anything for days."

"I thought detectives went around in teams of two?"

"Usually that's the case."

The boat passed under two more bridges, Shirosuna-bashi and Hamazaki-bashi, and then slowed down to negotiate the convergence with the Shiomi Canal.

"You aren't usual?"

"That's a good question."

"Ah, you wear your hair long. Detectives are always clean cut. Like we are."

Samejima felt anxious. Tomikawa was talking too much—possibly so that Samejima wouldn't notice he was tense about something.

"How old were you when you first got to know Kizu?"

Tomikawa was momentarily stuck for words.

"Second grade in junior high."

"And you used to hang around a lot?"

Samejima fingered the bulge on his waist with his right hand. He could be walking into a trap.

"Yeah, you could say that. We used to skip class and go to the pachinko parlor and stuff."

"What kind of guy was he?"

"He was one determined son of a bitch. One time, he was surrounded and beaten up by a bunch of senior high school punks. No matter how much it hurt, he didn't cry out once. He just kept quiet and glared at them. As stubborn as a mule. He had some of those replica guns with him, and the only time he cried out was when it looked like he was going to have them taken off him. He screamed like a warrior, he really did. Then they beat the crap out of him again."

They passed under the Shirosagi and Edagawa Bridges. Then they took a diagonal left into the convergence of the Towun North Canal and East Canal. Ahead they could see the No. 9 Shuto Expressway, a band of light suspended in mid-air.

"How does Kizu usually wait for you?"

"When I pull the boat alongside and turn the interior cabin light off, he comes out. I wrap a chain around the metal door and he transfers from the stone steps onto the boat."

He had to get in there before Kizu closed the metal door. If he noticed Samejima he might throw the key to the bolt into the canal.

Just short of the expressway, Samejima had Tomikawa cut the engine. The noise of the traffic overhead bore down on them.

Thanks to the lights from the expressway above, there was no trouble maneuvering the boat along the canal, but the surface of the water was as black as could be.

"When I jump onto the stone steps, I want you to move away a short distance. When I give you the signal, start the engine," said Samejima, staring at the approaching stone steps. The surface was covered in moss and appeared slippery.

There wasn't so much as a sliver of light coming from inside the metal door.

"Mr. Detective," said Tomikawa.

Samejima turned around. It was due in part to the lamp, but Tomikawa's face appeared pale.

"Take care of yourself," he said in a rather timorous tone.

Samejima thought that perhaps he was regretting setting a trap. But then there was no turning back for Samejima either.

Samejima leapt onto the stone steps, then heard the sound of the boat's side making contact with the wall. As he suspected, the steps were slippery with wet moss and he almost lost his balance. He clung to the steps with both hands and legs and barely kept himself from falling backwards into the water.

He looked behind him to see the boat, pushed back by the recoil from his jump, drifting about three feet away. Tomikawa stared intently from the helm.

Altogether there were seven steps above the water level. Samejima pulled out his revolver while he climbed the steps, taking care not to make a noise. His gun was loaded with live rounds. Afraid it would slow him down, he had decided not to wear a bulletproof vest.

The metal door was constructed so as to slide open. The uppermost step opened out into a wider area like a theater apron. It was probably a space used by barges to unload goods.

Samejima stood on the handle side of the door and waved a hand at Tomikawa. Seeing his signal, Tomikawa started the engine. The high-pitched noise of the engine as the propeller churned the water reverberated all around. He was going to push his way in the instant Kizu opened the door from the inside. A damp wind blew over Samejima's body.

Suddenly he heard the grating sound of a latch being opened from the inside. A gap, no wider than a hair's breadth, appeared in the door. In that instant, Samejima pushed the door open with both hands and dashed inside.

A strong light shone in his eyes. To his front was a supporting pillar, constructed from what appeared to be a steel scaffold. Fixed to the middle of the scaffold were a number of spotlights. One of them had been trained directly at the entrance and Samejima's eyes were dazzled.

Just as he tried to change direction, there was a deafening roar at the base of his right ear and Samejima was knocked to the ground. The shock felt as if he'd been struck on the right side of the head with a hot iron hammer.

He rolled onto his back in agony. The space opened out beyond the metal door, and steel shelving appeared to have been placed at right angles to the wall facing the canal. The shelving contained cardboard boxes of various sizes. A number of iron plates had been placed parallel with the floor at intervals of about a foot and a half. Kizu's form appeared behind the iron plates.

Kizu had used the shelving as a makeshift barricade and had been waiting behind it for Samejima. From a gap three or four plates up from the bottom, four steel pipes protruding from a long narrow box—it looked like some form of gun—pointed in Samejima's direction. A bullet from one of those pipes had grazed Samejima's head. The acute pain he felt in his ear transferred to his entire head; it was so bad he couldn't open his eyes. He clenched his teeth, forced his eyes open and aimed the gun in his right hand at Kizu.

From somewhere in the depths of his subconscious, an ounce of reason caused him to lower his arm. *I mustn't kill him.* He tried to aim below Kizu's waist.

From behind his customized gun, Kizu stared down wide-eyed at Samejima.

Samejima didn't have a chance to take aim again. The pain exploded inside his head and carried him off into unconsciousness.

15

When Samejima came to, he found his hands were cuffed behind his back. The chain of the cuffs had been passed through the steel scaffold that stood in the middle of the room. He was only able to move around the scaffold. Even after he had regained consciousness, the acute pain in his right ear and head refused to go away. Slowly, Samejima looked around the workshop.

It was more or less a square-shaped room. It must have been about one tenth the total area of the warehouse. In each of the four corners, and the middle of the room, were steel scaffolds, supporting the ceiling. There being no windows, the lighting was provided by spotlights affixed to the scaffolding. There were three spotlights: one facing the entrance, and the other two illuminating the areas to the left and right.

The iron door was situated in the middle of the wall facing the canal. Besides the steel shelving that Kizu had used to shield himself with, there were two more sets against the wall to the right coming through the door. Just in front of the shelving was a rectangular workbench measuring approximately six feet long by three feet wide.

Different types of gas cylinders used for welding and a variety of hacksaws were laid out on the shelving. Attached to the workbench were heavy-duty tools including a vise and lathe.

On the opposite side of the central supporting pillar, along the wall to the left, metal pipes of varying degrees of thickness and length and other metal components were arranged neatly and stacked in piles. Beyond that, toward the back of the wall, there was a tube bed, a small refrigerator and a portable toilet. Wooden shelves were fixed to the wall by the bedstead, on top of which were arranged boxes of gunpowder and a number of finished products. Amongst them was the four-barrelled gun that had been used earlier to shoot at Samejima, and also his revolver. The floor was bare concrete.

There was no sign of Kizu.

Samejima fought against the pain and struggled to recall what had happened.

He looked around toward the door.

The steel shelving that Kizu had used as a shield was stacked three shelves high from the bottom with cardboard boxes. Several long, thin umbrella boxes were stacked on the bottom shelf, while on the shelf above it lay a variety of small and medium-sized boxes, all of which were empty. Amongst the smaller boxes were boxes for videotapes, while a larger one had the letters "NTT" printed on them—the privatized telecom corporation. Beyond the shelving was an old bed mattress that had been jammed into a wooden frame. It had been fastened to the wall so that it was fixed opposite the workbench. Samejima noticed that the mattress was peppered with holes. An experimental gun would be held firm in the vise and test fired into the mattress—that much seemed certain. At night, there would be no need to worry about anyone hearing the gunfire. Even if the sound escaped, the din of traffic from the expressway near the warehouse probably drowned it out.

There was a mark in the concrete wall where the bullet had embedded itself, in line with the position of Samejima's body when he had collapsed to the left of the entrance.

The bullet had been fired not more than three feet away from Samejima's ear. Had he been a little slower turning around, it would undoubtedly have struck him in the temple.

When he moved, the chain to the handcuffs made a grating noise as it rubbed against the scaffold. He couldn't hear anything with his right ear.

He didn't know whether this was the effect of the sound of the gunshot, or the shock of the bullet as it grazed his head. In any case, he could hardly hear at all.

With his hands behind him, Samejima gripped the scaffold and levered himself into an upright position. The key for the cuffs was on a key ring that had been in his left-hand pocket, but it had been removed. He leaned against the scaffold and closed his eyes. His head was splitting and he felt nauseous.

Had Kizu made a getaway?

Surely he wouldn't escape leaving so many finished items behind.

He must have returned briefly with Tomikawa. As Samejima had suspected, Tomikawa had tipped him off.

His naivety had brought this upon himself. He slithered down the scaffold and collapsed again into a sitting position.

Kizu intended to return, and not only that; the fact that he'd been confined here meant that Kizu would dispose of him later. At any rate, it would be one, maybe two, nights. He would keep Samejima locked up and, once he was weakened, move in for the kill. It wouldn't be two nights, thought Samejima, absentmindedly. Kizu would probably return tonight.

Before daybreak, Kizu would remove everything he needed, put a bullet in Samejima's head, and seal up the door. Provided he could stop Tomikawa from blabbing, what had gone on here would remain a secret forever.

Samejima hadn't notified Momoi of the exact location of the warehouse. Even if the lack of any communication from Samejima started to concern Momoi, it would be the next morning before he did anything about it.

Samejima looked at his watch. It was about three minutes to midnight. He had been unconscious for not quite twenty minutes.

Perhaps Kizu had gone back to collect a truck. He would park it in front of Tomikawa and then return here to remove his things.

In which case, he would be back within the hour.

Samejima turned his head and searched for any tool within reach that he could use to remove the handcuffs.

There was nothing. There was nothing at all within three feet of the scaffold. Even when he stretched his arms out as far as possible, there wasn't anything he could hook his nails on.

The irony of his predicament struck him.

This place was equipped with all kinds of tools from acetylene torches to hacksaws and pliers. Yet they were all positioned out of his reach.

Of course, Kizu had to know that. He could almost hear Kizu's mocking laughter.

He wondered what Momoi would do when he realized communication had been severed. Samejima pondered the possibilities.

The man who was nicknamed "cadaver" wasn't likely to go out of his way to try to persuade Criminal Investigation Headquarters.

Even if he did, Koda and his cronies wouldn't easily believe him.

Either they would believe him or they wouldn't, and in either case Momoi would be dealt with severely. He was responsible for Samejima continuing a solo pursuit without reporting an important clue in a major investigation involving the participation of several hundred personnel.

He certainly wouldn't be the head of Crime Prevention when he retired.

Unless Momoi acted, there would be no investigators at Shinjuku Police Station who would search for him. In fact, there would be none at any station.

By the time Momoi did something about it, it would be gone afternoon the next day, well after Kizu had made good his escape.

Samejima's fate looked beyond hope.

At eight minutes past midnight, he thought he heard the low drone of a boat engine coming from the other side of the iron door. Samejima turned his left ear in that direction.

The sound of the chain being unfastened and the bolt drawn back followed.

Samejima stood up, took a deep breath and faced the door. Blood stained his wrists—the result of his frantic efforts to remove the handcuffs.

The iron door opened. The pitch of the boat engine, receding into the distance, went up a notch.

Kizu's figure appeared in the doorway.

He wore jeans and a work jacket. He came in and quickly closed the door, securing the latch behind him.

He squared off against Samejima.

Close up, Kizu looked as fair as ever, the handsome man with an air of cool indifference.

There was an element of brutality about his lips, nose and eyes.

He stared at Samejima with his almond-shaped eyes opened wide. He fixed his eyes on Samejima for an unnaturally long time.

"Long time no see," said Samejima, his voice hoarse.

Kizu remained silent and stared at Samejima all the more.

Then he thrust his hand into the pocket of his jacket. He pulled out a pair of cotton army gloves and put them on.

"You made the gun that fired the 30-06 rifle bullet, didn't you?"

Without replying, Kizu looked away and started to move off. First, he went over toward the wooden shelves by the bed. He stuffed the boxes of bullets that had been on the shelf into a carrier bag. There were several hundred rounds of different varieties for use with rifles, shotguns, and handguns. When the bag was full he sealed it with tape and hefted it with both hands over by the door.

Then he applied spray oil from a can to each of the finished guns and began wrapping them painstakingly in cooking wrap.

He wrapped each one precisely and laid them on the bed. There were as many as thirty guns, both large and small.

Kizu rolled up the bed sheet and used it like a carrying cloth to wrap the bundled weapons, tying the edges securely together. He went to place it by the iron door.

The only item left on the shelving was Samejima's New Nambu. Kizu picked it up, freed the latch and pushed out the cylinder. He saw it was fully loaded and shot a glance at Samejima before stuffing the gun in his hip pocket.

Then, using a towel, he began meticulously to wipe every part of the interior of the room. He seemed intent on removing any fingerprints.

Samejima kept a close watch in silence.

Kizu's movements were scrupulous, a study in economy and thoroughness. Even the refrigerator, the bottom of which it seemed he had overlooked, was turned on its side and scrubbed.

He wiped the floor surface, and each and every one of the steel pipes.

It was extremely humid, and Kizu was drenched in sweat as a result of his exertions in the stuffy confines of the workshop.

He ignored the sweat dripping from his brow and continued wiping furiously.

He didn't say a word. He even wiped up the droplets of sweat.

When he had finished wiping, Kizu flung the towel on top of the things he was taking away and stood right in front of Samejima. His whole being was dripping with sweat, and the T-shirt under his jacket was stuck to his body. He undid the fastener on his jacket, pulled his arms out and flung it in the corner of the room. Next he peeled off his T-shirt and threw that away too.

Sweat glistened on his pale body. On his left shoulder was a red scorpion, its poisonous tail raised in the air. The tattoo was elaborate, three-dimensional, appearing almost alive from a slight distance.

Kizu stood facing Samejima, his damp chest heaving up and down with his erratic breathing. He removed a glove from his right hand and, using his palm, wiped the sweat from his chest. Then he grabbed hold of Samejima's cheek with the same hand. The stench of perspiration hit Samejima's nose. Kizu wiped more sweat off with his hand and rubbed it into Samejima's neck and cheeks. Samejima's face was wet through. All the while he was doing this, Kizu gazed intently into his eyes.

At length, Kizu took a step back and scrutinized Samejima, looking him up and down.

"It's all your fault."

Kizu had spoken for the first time. His voice was unique—hoarse, and yet, not at all low.

"Because of you I have to leave this place."

"It's no use. Both you and Tomikawa will soon be caught."

Kizu had a broad smile on his face. "No one will come. I know how it is. You're a lone wolf cop."

He went over to the workbench and picked up a large cutting knife. With the knife in his left hand, he drew the revolver with his right. The gun hammer cocked with a click as the chamber rotated.

Kizu took aim at Samejima between his eyes. Extending his left arm, which held the cutting knife, he laid its thin edge against the collar of Samejima's polo shirt. He held the knife downwards so its tip was a V and applied some strength.

"Good job. Your belly doesn't stick out," said Kizu.

"No," said Samejima, as he stared down the barrel of the gun. His head moved back involuntarily.

"I don't like fat guys."

Then Kizu ran the cutting knife all the way down in a single stroke. Startled, Samejima gulped hard.

A sharp pain shot across his mid-section near his navel. His polo shirt had been cleaved in two down the front.

Kizu stared at Samejima's naked torso. Samejima looked down to see what he was staring at. His skin had been split in a line from just above his solar plexus to his navel. The blood, which had begun to run thinly, was now dripping.

Kizu smiled. "Shall I lick it off for you?"

"You needn't trouble yourself."

"It's no trouble. You want me to lick it?"

Samejima didn't answer. Kizu raised the gun in his right hand again.

"You want me to lick it?"

Samejima blinked. The sweat from his brow mixed with the tears in his eyes and blurred his vision. "Yeah."

"Oh, what's this?" said Kizu, delightedly. "Well, I'm not going to. That's your punishment."

Samejima sighed with relief.

"You've got a great physique. Do you go to the gym?"

Samejima swallowed spittle and shook his head.

"So, how do you keep your body in such good shape?"

"I run."

"Every day?"

"If I'm not—working early in the morning."

"That's splendid. It's really great. Do you remember what I promised you all that time ago?"

"I—don't remember."

"I said I'd teach you the taste of men."

Samejima closed his eyes. "You have no time for that. Everyone knows police officers were killed with the gun that Kazuo took off with."

"Is that right? But it doesn't mean I killed them. The only cop I want to kill is Inspector Samejima."

Kizu's cutting knife touched the belt of Samejima's trousers. He applied force and the belt cut in two.

"I'll have a great time with you and then kill you."

Kizu brandished the New Nambu in front of Samejima.

"This is a terrible gun. If you are going to copy something, then you should copy it properly. The New Nambu's a piece of junk."

"If you think so then I'll have it back."

Kizu roared with laughter. "You're really something, you know that, Inspector Samejima? All right. I'll return it. I'd just like to borrow one shot, then I'll give it back to you."

Samejima exhaled. Despair spread through him like poison and robbed him of his strength. His knees wobbled and were going limp. "Tell me about the gun Kazuo carried away. Or did you give it to him as a present?"

"He made off with it. It looks as though there's going to be another turf war in Osaka. I was asked to make a gun that would pierce a truck. It's quite popular to ram trucks and dumper trucks into the side of a rival gang's office. In the west of Japan at any rate."

"So you made a gun that fires rifle bullets?"

"That's right. It's the same construction as a double-barrel shotgun. It breaks in the middle and holds two bullets. But it doesn't look anything like a gun."

That was why there hadn't been cartridges. With a side-by-side shotgun, unless you broke the barrel, the cartridges weren't ejected. Samejima's breathing became heavy. "How many bullets are there?"

"I made ten to order. The gun and the bullets were a set and Kazuo made off with the lot."

"Did you fall out with him?"

"I scolded him for doing something he shouldn't have. So he ran away with the gun."

"'Something he shouldn't have'?"

"He's light-fingered. Occasionally he'd take money from my wallet."

"Isn't your customer in Kansai angry that his order won't be delivered on time?"

"It's all right. I'm going straight to Osaka from here."

"You'll be stopped at the checkpoints."

"I'll go by boat as far as Yokohama. Then I'll hire a rental car. You don't need to worry. The checkpoints are only in Tokyo."

"What about Kazuo? Is Kazuo the serial cop killer?"

"I wonder. It'd be better if that jerk were gunned down. By the police."

"Who are you kidding? You saw the news and, worried, you rushed over to Agamemnon."

"You're well informed."

This time Kizu began to cut Samejima's trousers off with the cutting knife.

"It's pathetic—you're all shrivelled up. But don't worry, I'll soon make it big for you."

"Is Kazuo the killer?"

"No." Kizu looked up at the ceiling, as if he couldn't stand any more questions. "The kid doesn't have the nerve to do anything like that. He probably wanted to get rid of it and ended up selling it to someone."

"Do you know who?"

"If I knew, I'd have it back by now. Bastard can't go nuts with my work."

"You have to cooperate. Unless you do, you'll be arrested as an accessory to murder."

Kizu raised his face from Samejima's crotch. The cold cutting edge of the knife was resting on his inner thigh.

"That type always self-destructs. He'll end up being pursued and gunned down. The cops would love to shoot him. He killed their own, after all."

"How about Kazuo? I know you're having trouble contacting him."

"I'll find a replacement. Lots of cute kids in Osaka, too. I won't have Kazuo hanging around me all the time."

Samejima groaned. A sharp pain shot through his crotch.

Kizu smirked. "Don't worry, it's still attached. But it won't be much longer."

Samejima closed his eyes. Tears welled up as he felt pain, despair and then fear.

"When I've gotten rid of this for you and you're all neat and tidy, I'll stick mine up you. Then I'll stuff your brain too—with a piece of lead."

"No thanks," said Samejima, his tone nasal.

"You can't refuse. Your customer's picked you."

Kizu looked behind him. It looked as though he had caught a sound that Samejima hadn't heard. Kizu looked at his watch.

"Damn it. It's time to go."

"Hurry up and go."

"Relax."

"Hurry up and go!" screamed Samejima.

Kizu swallowed. Wide-eyed, he looked at Samejima. A grin settled on his face.

"I can get him to wait. This is the chance I've been waiting for. Tomikawa will wait for me. It'll only take me ten minutes."

Samejima turned his left ear toward the iron door. He could definitely hear the noise of a boat engine.

Kizu inserted the New Nambu in his hip pocket and approached the door.

"Who is it?"

"It's me," came Tomikawa's reply.

Kizu lifted the latch and opened the iron door. He looked outside and suddenly his back stiffened.

"Fuck you!" he shouted.

His right hand went to his hip pocket and drew out the New Nambu. He stuck the barrel of the gun through the gap in the door while at the same time trying to close it against some force from outside.

The loud report of two shots fired in succession came from the New Nambu. Kizu was firing at someone right outside the door. He withdrew the barrel and used all his strength in an effort to close the iron door. As the gap narrowed to within just an inch of closing, there was a crack of gunfire—this time from outside.

Kizu's head moved backwards with a jerk. He collapsed onto his back, looking up at Samejima.

Samejima looked down at his body. A bullet had scored a direct hit on Kizu's elegant nose, the impact causing it to implode. An instant later blood began to spurt out from the hole.

Fingers were inserted through the gap in the iron door, and slowly it was opened.

Momoi stood there, gun in hand. The right shoulder of his jacket had been torn open. He stood in the entrance and looked at Samejima. His expression didn't alter when he saw Samejima's bloody, naked figure.

"So you're alive."

Samejima nodded. His knees were shaking with relief.

Momoi came closer and checked over Samejima's wounds. He didn't so much as glance at Kizu's collapsed form.

"You saved me," said Samejima, his voice trembling.

Momoi looked Samejima quickly in the eye and then looked around the interior of the workshop.

"One cadaver per section is enough."

16

The "Monday Cop Killings" were no longer restricted to Mondays.

On Saturday, when he came home from his part-time job, the news reported that yet another police officer had been murdered.

Listening to the news had become his daily routine. He recorded programs from all the channels, editing them on his twin deck player as he collected segments connected with the killings.

The previous evening he'd watched the popular news program that had argued that last week's murder had involved a rifle. The program was televised every week from Monday to Friday at 10 p.m. The newscaster had concluded:

When we see you again next Monday, we sincerely hope that the top story will not be the news of another police officer killing.

Monday had already become known throughout Japan as the day of the cop killings. Citizens interviewed on the streets of Shinjuku had given their views:

"I'm afraid of being hit by a stray bullet, so I don't come here on Mondays."

"My heart's in my mouth every time I see a police officer up close. I'm scared he's going to be shot at from somewhere."

"I find it kind of amusing. I'll be coming to Shinjuku every Monday."

"I don't have a choice. I work here, you see. I want him to be arrested quickly. Even the police look so much on edge."

Yet it was he who had been the first to figure out that the murderer would kill on Mondays. He felt sure that, with the exception of the murderer, he had been the first person in Japan to realize that the murderer would strike again.

Naturally, the police would also have been in a state of high alert on the third Monday. But the murderer had outwitted them.

At around 3:40 a.m. today Officers Takashi Morio (24) and Michio Hayami (26), both of the Kabukicho Police Box, responded to an emergency call reporting that a woman had collapsed in Okubo Park in Shinjuku Ward, Kabukicho, Ni-Chome, and, having rushed to the park, were suddenly shot by a man who had been hiding in the park's public conveniences. Officer Morio was hit in the neck and died, while Officer Hayami is in critical condition having been shot in the left shoulder. It appears that Officer Hayami faced his assailant and fired one round from his firearm without hitting his attacker. The police are carrying out their investigation on the basis that the assailant is the same man responsible for the serial killings. In the murders that took place on Monday of last week and this week, three officers were killed, with a fourth officer remaining in critical condition. Today's incident brings the total number of dead police officers to four. Although seriously injured, Officer Hayami remained conscious and told investigators that the killer was a tall man who wore a motorcycle helmet. The crime scene was in a corner of the hotel district facing the former site of the Okubo Metropolitan Hospital, where few people pass by in the early hours of the morning. Because the serial killings had occurred on Mondays, the Criminal Investigation Headquarters had just decided to enter a state of high alert beginning next Monday.

"Damn it," he muttered, in spite of himself.

Why hadn't he given them advance notice of the crime again? His credibility with the Investigation HQ was bound to suffer as a result of this.

Moreover, this time the killer had left behind a victim who could talk. He would have to be quick about contacting the HQ and advising them of the results of his investigation to date. He looked at his watch. It had just turned 9 p.m.

If he didn't go now to Shinjuku and make the call…

Yes, he would have to call from Shinjuku. If, by some chance, they managed to trace the call, if he were calling from Shinjuku they wouldn't figure out where he was living.

There was another factor. Shinjuku being as busy as it was, once he had moved away from the call box, police who rushed to the scene wouldn't be able to tell who had made the call.

He changed in a hurry. If it were just a matter of making the call and coming back again, he could make the return trip in about an hour. He left his room and quickly headed over to the station. He felt impatient. There were few Shinjuku-bound trains at this time of day. Eventually the train came, and he arrived at Shinjuku station at 9:42 p.m. He had already decided from where to make the call: a red phone near the JR ticket office in the underground shopping mall at the east exit. It was always teeming with people; once he had finished the call, he would be able to lose himself in the crowds.

He hurried to the east exit. He felt there were fewer people than usual for a Saturday, but it was still pretty busy.

This time he had decided against wearing conspicuous gloves, opting for a handkerchief instead. He pretended to wipe away sweat and picked up the receiver, punching in the number with the handkerchief.

"Hello. This is Shinjuku Police Station."

This time, it was a man's voice that answered.

"Please put me through to Sub-Section Chief Sotoyama," he said without hesitation. It probably sounded to the person making a call next to him like an ordinary conversation a company worker might have.

"Do you mean Sotoyama of the Criminal Investigation Section?" asked the man.

"Yes, of HQ," he said, keeping a watchful eye about him.

He didn't feel any of the apprehension or fear that had assailed him that first time. It was because he was now a colleague of the detectives. He spoke confidently, without hesitation.

The call had been put through and someone was hollering, "Sotoyama-san…!" A lot of phones were ringing in the background and he could hear people shouting. The morning's incident must have turned the place upside down.

"What? He isn't in? Oh, I see… Hello? Who is it please?"

"A friend of Sotoyama," he said, somewhat disappointed.

"What does your call relate to? Shall I leave a message for you?"

He thought for a moment. "Is there someone more important than Sotoyama I could speak to?"

"More important? How do you mean?" The voice of the detective who'd taken the call grew lower.

"I'm the one who dropped something the other day in the square at Kabukicho."

The line suddenly went quiet. He stared at the second hand of his watch. He wouldn't be able to talk for much longer.

When suddenly the detective spoke again, his voice was harsh. "So you thought that was a clever prank?"

"Don't be absurd," he said, genuinely surprised. He'd never intended it as a prank.

"Where did you come by Sotoyama-san's name?"

"Oh, he's a very famous detective."

"You asshole!"

Then somebody said, "Wait a minute," and he had the feeling the receiver was being passed over to someone else.

"Hello, the call has been transferred. Go ahead and speak to me please."

It was a man's voice, a little haughty and important sounding.

"Who are you?"

"Koda, Metropolitan Police superintendent."

I've done it, he thought. Maybe he was the man with the glasses, who arrived late at the first crime scene.

"Mr. Koda. I see. I'll call you again afterwards. Please stay where you are."

"What is this in connection with?"

"I'd like to talk to you about myself."

He pressed down on the hook and rang off.

17

"He hung up," said Koda, putting down the phone.

"We couldn't trace it," said another detective, replacing a separate phone.

"He's lying," said Samejima.

He had shown up at the Criminal Investigation HQ for a briefing some two hours earlier. Momoi and Yabu were also there.

"How do you know? From the sound of that asshole's voice, he was really enjoying himself. Is there any reason you can say with certainty that it wasn't Kazuo or a friend of his?" Koda turned his bloodshot eyes on Samejima and thrust his finger at him. "Well?" Making no attempt to conceal his anger he continued, "Without any approval from your superiors you please yourself and rush the scene of important evidence of the weapon. What's more, you end up with a dead body on your hands. As for your superior, he sends in a subordinate without an arrest warrant, and to make matters worse, he follows on behind and personally guns down the suspect. How are we going to announce that?"

He loosened his tie. His shirt, with its rolled-up sleeves, was all creased. He had dark shadows under his eyes from lack of sleep.

The Criminal Investigation Headquarters fell completely silent.

"If we make it known that Kizu is dead, the killer might take off. At any rate, Kazuo is bound to make a run for it. And if that happens, we'll lose all chance of obtaining clues as to the killer's whereabouts," Samejima remarked quietly.

Visibly disgusted, Koda turned to the head of the Metropolitan Police Crime Department, who was present and listening.

"Commissioner..."

Commissioner Fujimaru had observed the exchange in silence. His rank was three levels more senior than that of superintendent.

Koda stated to Fujimaru, "I am here as the representative of the Public Security Department. Even if the killer is not a left-wing extremist, I cannot let pass an incident that affects the police force as a whole. And I won't tolerate loose cannons."

"Samejima," Fujimaru said.

Samejima looked at the man, who was fifty-one and was said to be next or perhaps next but one in line to become Chief Commissioner. Fujimaru hadn't made clear which side he would take in Public Security's internecine power struggle. He was reputed to be an able tactician.

"I understand that you were eager to arrest Kizu. But you ought to have informed us as soon as you realized he was connected with the serial killings. The responsibility also lies with Inspector Momoi."

Koda inserted a finger in the waistcoat pocket of his three-piece suit. *I told you so.*

"With regard to the shooting of Kizu, we are waiting for the findings of the inquiry commission. However, I would like to conclude for now that, while it seems clear that there was some recklessness in the course of events, so far as I can see from reading the report, the outcome was unavoidable."

"Thank you very much," said Momoi, without altering his expression in the slightest.

"It seems that, on a personal level too, Kizu bore a grudge against Inspector Samejima. Judging from the wounds inflicted on Inspector Samejima, Kizu was probably not in a normal psychological state of mind. As a police officer, I am inclined also to agree with the actions Inspector Momoi took in summarily compelling Tomikawa to take him to the Miyama Transport warehouse."

Momoi stood upright with his head bowed down.

Fujimaru turned to face Koda. "As far as we are concerned, it cannot have been desirable for Inspector Samejima to have been murdered by Kizu. We would have lost yet another officer. I'm sure you agree?"

"Yes," Koda replied in a non-committal tone.

Samejima had been discharged from hospital after just a few hours. Besides the cuts inflicted by the cutter knife, he had also suffered concussion and a perforated right eardrum. The diagnosis was that it would take three weeks to make a full recovery. The perforated eardrum would possibly take longer.

It had been Samejima, of course, who insisted on leaving the hospital.

An inspection of Kizu's workshop was carried out during the early hours of the morning.

Fujimaru had declared there would be no press announcement.

Samejima and Momoi were told to submit reports. Their punishment was yet to be decided.

"They're back."

Four detectives, under the command of Sub-Section Chief Sotoyama, appeared in the entrance to the HQ with three people in tow.

Fuyuki, from Agamemnon, was one of them.

One of the other two was a slim man in his mid-thirties whose short hair stood up straight. The other was young like Fuyuki.

All three had on primary-colored sari-like costumes and wore a light application of makeup.

"What's going on?" the slim man said, grabbing hold of Sotoyama's arm.

Fuyuki noticed Samejima. "What's this all about?"

Koda walked over towards them.

"Now be quiet," said Sotoyama.

"Don't be kidding me. You come bursting into my place without a warrant, and while I'm open for business, too. What am I suspected of doing?"

"I'm Koda of the Metropolitan Police. I'd be grateful for your cooperation."

"Quit fooling around," said the one who appeared to be the mama.

Koda looked like he'd been slapped. "Who do you think are, homo?" he yelled all of a sudden.

But the mama wouldn't be outdone. "Oh, so sorry I'm a 'homo.' You think I don't know the police force is full of us? If you don't behave, I'll write to the papers. This is discrimination."

"Superintendent Koda," Fujimaru spoke up.

"Oh! Are you a superintendent? You must be very important. Well, I'm not afraid of you. You throw around your authority as police and come down hard on anybody who's different."

Momoi shot a glance at Samejima.

"Fuyuki," called Samejima.

"Yes."

Fuyuki answered as if frightened. The mama fell silent, surprised.

"Would you come over here for a minute and listen to a tape recording? I'd like you to tell me whether or not you think it's Kazuo's voice. That's all."

Fuyuki glanced at the mama's face. It was full of caution and suspicion. The mama gazed at Samejima.

"That's all it is, honestly," said Samejima, with a nod.

"You. Who are you?"

"I'm Samejima, of Crime Prevention."

Fuyuki whispered something in the mama's ear. The words "Mama Force" could be heard.

"Are you a customer of Mama Force?" the mama asked Samejima.

"For a good few years now."

The mama stared intently at Samejima and said, "I see. They choose their customers carefully over there. I think I might be able to trust you."

Koda looked around him as if to say, *You can't be having this kind of conversation here.* But nobody laughed.

"Please," said Samejima, softly.

The mama exhaled forcibly and nodded, "It's okay. You can go with him."

With this, Fuyuki approached the table in front of Samejima.

Koda's breathing became erratic and he left the room. Flustered, the other Public Security detectives followed after him.

Having shown the three of them to seats, Yabu played back the tape-recorded phone message.

The voice began to play on the tape.

"It's not him."

"It's someone else."

"I agree."

All three gave the same verdict at once.

Yabu nodded and changed the cassette. The other voices the Criminal Investigation HQ had recorded—voices of informers and those purporting to take responsibility for the crimes—flowed from the tape.

But the three men shook their heads each time.

"Thank you," said Samejima, adding, "Do you know where Kazuo is at the moment?"

"I don't. Until a little while ago it seems he was living with a customer called Kizu."

"We know."

Kizu's Monzen Nakacho condominium had also been subjected to an investigation earlier that day, but nothing had been found indicating Kazuo's whereabouts.

"What on earth is going on?"

The mama looked up at Samejima as he stood in front of her. Samejima had a gauze on his right ear and a bandage wrapped around his head. He still had a headache, but the nausea had abated.

"Kizu used to customize guns. A gun that Kazuo stole from Kizu was used to murder the police officers."

"Oh my God!"

The mama was astounded. Fuyuki turned pale.

"Are you saying the murderer is Kazuo?"

"We don't know. But even if he isn't, it's possible he knows the killer. We're searching for Kazuo at the moment."

"Well, in that case…maybe Kazuo's been murdered?"

"Maybe."

"That's terrible…"

"Would you have any idea who?"

The mama looked at the other two young men and said, "Who would do a thing like that?"

"Where did Kazuo live before he was with Kizu?"

"A one-room condo over in Sasazuka. But I think he's cleared out of there."

"Do you have his address?"

"I can get it if I go back to the bar."

"Okay. Do you know anything else? Where's his home town?"

"He said it was Sakura in Chiba Prefecture. I don't know where in Sakura though."

"I heard he used to be a member of a bike gang."

Samejima looked at Fuyuki. Fuyuki nodded.

"What was the name of the gang?"

"Kyosakkai. You spell it with the characters for 'brutal,' 'murder' and 'world.'"

Samejima wrote it down and showed it to Fuyuki. Fuyuki nodded.

One of the detectives took up the receiver. Samejima passed over his notebook.

"Give me the Chiba Prefecture Traffic Section please."

The detective who had taken hold of the notebook issued his instructions to the switchboard and looked at the three slim men. He asked, "What's Kazuo's full name?"

"Miyauchi. Kazuo Miyauchi," said the mama.

The traffic section and highway patrol of each prefectural police force compiled lists of arrests and records of juvenile offences of bike gang members.

When he was put through to the traffic section of Chiba police, the detective began making inquiries about Kazuo. If they had any relevant data, it would be faxed over immediately.

"Did he hang around with anyone else besides Kizu? Any women? After he arrived in Tokyo?" Samejima asked.

"I'm pretty sure Kazuo came to the city after dropping out of high school. He attended a hair-styling school, but it didn't suit him. He was working part-time at a convenience store when he saw our ad."

"Was your place his first time working in the bar business?"

"I heard he worked in a coffee shop or someplace like that once."

"Was Kazuo straight? I mean, originally."

"Far from it! He's as gay as they come. By the time he found my place he'd already had some experience."

"Did he have a steady lover before he came to work at Agamemnon?"

"It's possible I guess. It seems like Kizu was the only one he made out with at my place. It was just a game with our other customers."

The mama looked to the other two for confirmation.

"They've got something!"

The detective who had been talking with the Chiba police turned toward Fujimaru and shouted.

"It looks like they've got fingerprints as well."

"Have them send photographs, too. And quickly."

Fujimaru rattled off orders in quick succession.

"Squad Four, over to his family home. And request the assistance of the Chiba police."

Eight detectives rushed out of the Criminal Investigation Headquarters. The atmosphere in the HQ changed.

"What about Kazuo's friends in Tokyo?" asked Samejima.

The three exchanged glances.

"To be honest, Kazuo didn't really fit in at my place. He was hardcore."

Samejima looked at the ceiling.

Fujimaru spoke: "I want you to hand over the follow-up inquiries to someone else. It will be too much for you in your present physical condition."

"I'm all right," said Samejima.

Fujimaru countered unequivocally, "I am the one in charge here. As long as I am here, you will obey my instructions."

"Yes, sir."

Samejima had no choice. At Fujimaru's order, Sotoyama accompanied the three men to a separate room. This time the mama from Agamemnon complied.

Fujimaru called over Samejima and Momoi. He lowered his voice so that only the two of them could hear him.

"Your punishment hasn't been decided yet. I do understand that it wasn't to win promotions that you conducted the investigation the way you did. It remains the case that the suspect is dead. The shooting of a suspect is contrary to the policy of the Metropolitan Police, you understand, Inspector Momoi?"

"Yes sir," said Momoi, straightening himself.

"Effective from today's date, I am formally transferring Inspector Samejima of the Crime Prevention Section to the Special Criminal Investigation Headquarters relating to the serial murders of police officers attached to Shinjuku Police Station. Have you any objections?"

"If the detective in question has no objections, then neither have I," said Momoi.

Fujimaru looked at Samejima. "Well?"

"I accept my appointment," replied Samejima.

"Good. Inspector Momoi can return to the Crime Prevention Section. You can go now."

Momoi looked at Samejima, and Samejima noticed that his face had gone back to assuming its lifeless expression. He now carried the burden of another spirit besides his son.

When Momoi had come to the hospital to collect Samejima, he had let slip, *There's another mortuary tablet in my Buddhist altar.*

The name Kaname Kizu would have been on that tablet.

As Momoi left the Criminal Investigation HQ, Fujimaru looked up at Samejima and said, "I've heard about you."

"And I know about the Commissioner."

"Is that right? I'm not inclined right now to make issues out of your past. What is important is that we arrest this killer. The interval between the killings has shrunk and it worries me. I don't particularly wish for him to be caught in the act of committing an offense. If you see what I mean."

Of course, Fujimaru meant apprehending him in the act of carrying out his fourth round of murder. Public assessment of the police's investigative abilities would depend on whether the criminal was arrested in the act of committing the offense or at other times, for instance at home. If the criminal were arrested while committing the offense, it was liable to be credited at least partially to luck. An arrest made in the home gave the impression that the police had closed the net on the suspect and made their arrest. Fujimaru was referring to this difference.

"I understand."

"Good. I'd like you to go home now, rest up for the whole of tomorrow, then come back the day after and give this investigation your all."

Just then, a detective who had answered the phone shouted: "It's for Superintendent Koda. Our friend is on the line."

18

Koda was in the police station dining hall.

Having been summoned to the phone, he took up the receiver without so much as saying a word to the other investigators.

Yabu operated the monitor and broadcast the caller's voice throughout the HQ.

"First of all, tell me your name. I told you who I am, and I'd like you to tell me your name," said Koda.

It was standard procedure.

The man on the other end of the line fell silent for a while. Then he said, "Ed."

"Ed, is it? Okay. Can you talk to me, Ed?"

Koda had his emotions under perfect control; there was no trace in his voice of the resentment and anger that had gripped him earlier.

"I don't hate police officers—no, not at all. Or at least, I didn't."

"Oh really? In that case, why do you murder them? Why do you kill them when they are still young, when they have parents, brothers and sisters, lovers and wives, and children?"

"Something happened, and I came to hate them."

"Something? Won't you tell me about it?"

"I can't tell you right now."

"Why don't you stop playing games?"

"What are you trying to suggest?"

Samejima took out a notepad, wrote down the words "How did you get the gun?" and showed it to Koda.

Koda ignored it.

"Won't you meet me just once so we can talk about it?"

"I'm afraid I can't. I don't want to die."

"The police won't kill you."

"Really? Cop killing is a serious crime in any country. Police officers lose their cool when their colleagues are murdered."

"Did you have a bad time at the hands of the police?"

"I'll tell you about that some other time. I'm of two minds at the moment—whether to kill a cop next or somebody else."

Koda's expression changed. "But I thought you hated police officers?"

"I'll call again."

"Wait. The cartridges you indicated to us the other day—were they used in a murder?"

"I'll call again."

The phone went dead.

"It came from a public phone box in the neighborhood of Shinjuku train station," a detective who contacted the operating room straight after the call reported.

Without even looking at him, Koda bawled, "Too slow!"

"Are we narrowing down the location?" Fujimaru asked.

"That's as far as they got with it."

"Perhaps he always calls from a public phone around Shinjuku station," said Samejima.

Yabu said, to Samejima, "Those 5.56mm cartridges did come from the U.S. Army. They're Korean-made and it's been several years since they were fired."

Samejima nodded.

Koda came over to them and said in a hushed voice, "Why are you still here? You're done with your briefing, aren't you? Keeping the homos company or what?"

"I'm just about to leave," Samejima said coldly.

Their questioning having come to an end, the three men from Agamemnon came out of the other room and walked toward the exit.

"I'll drive you back," said Samejima, coming toward them.

"In a patrol car? I'll have to turn down your offer. It would be embarrassing turning up at my place like that."

"I'll take you in my car. It's not a patrol car."

The mama thought for a moment and turned to Samejima. "All right, let's go."

When they pulled up by Agamemon, Samejima said, "Can I stop off for a drink? I'll pay."

"You're going to drink and drive?"

Samejima shrugged his shoulders. "I can leave the car here. They'll overlook the illegal parking."

"Are you sure it's okay with all those injuries?"

"I can manage a beer, I guess."

"Normally we don't admit straight guys," said the mama, sighing, "but I guess it's okay. It's not like we're going to do any business tonight anyhow. I was really shocked by all this, you know?"

"Thanks."

Samejima went into Agamemnon. The bar was perhaps 350 square feet in area and was brighter than Samejima had imagined. It felt clean and tidy.

Samejima sat himself down at the marble counter. The mama moved to the middle of the counter and lined up some beer glasses. The glasses were so cold beads of moisture had formed on the outside.

Fuyuki took out a bottle each of Heineken and Guinness from the refrigerator.

"Mama, half and half?"

"Yeah, why not."

Samejima watched as Fuyuki mixed the drinks, pouring half a

Heineken and half a Guinness into the glass. Samejima had the same.

"Cheers. Thank you very much for your help."

They clinked glasses.

"I'm tired out," said the mama.

When he had first seen her, he thought she was in her mid-thirties, but close up it was obvious she was over forty.

"Bureaucrats are all the same, aren't they? Arrogant and overbearing."

"Have you had a run-in with them before?"

"No."

The mama took out a cigarette and lit it. She had long fingers and her nails were polished and shiny.

"A long time ago, I was in the Self-Defense Forces. Airborne Brigade."

Jolted, Samejima looked up.

"I'm not the one, okay? When the last killing happened I was here all the time in the bar—I have several witnesses."

The mama, sensing Samejima's surprise, talked quickly. "But marksmanship with a rifle was one of my fortes. Everyone in Airborne was good."

"The weapon that Kizu made was a customized gun that could fire two rifle bullets. He said it didn't look like a gun at all."

Officer Hayami, who had been shot in Okubo Park, hadn't seen the attacker's gun. With the shooting that occurred on the street in north Shinjuku, there was testimony from the driver of a car that had stopped alongside that the motorbike rider had something resembling a black bag slung over his shoulder. Whatever it was, thought Samejima, it didn't look like a gun.

"What happened to Kizu?"

"I can't say right now," said Samejima, shaking his head.

"Do your injuries have something to do with him?"

Samejima nodded. "Yeah, something to do with him."

"Come to think of it, didn't you help out a young guy called Miyuki in the Shin-Okubo sauna? A slim guy, but well-hung."

Samejima recalled the young man who was being tormented by a cop.

"You fit the description of the guy Miyuki told me about. Hair long at the back, a bit of a loose cannon."

"I remember him."

"Afterwards, Miyuki came by and asked if you were here. He didn't realize you were straight. Seems like he really fell for you. Oh, wait a minute"—the mama's large eyes opened even wider—"wasn't it a cop too who was giving him a hard time? I'm sure he was a superintendent type, like that guy, what was his name? The guy we met today."

"I wonder."

"There are young guys who like straight men, you see? They like to come on to straight guys, seduce them, make them their own."

"Kazuo was good at that game," said Fuyuki, sitting down next to Samejima.

"Oh? How do you mean?" asked the mama.

"He would tell his customers that he only worked here as a part-timer and that he was straight. He enjoyed the attentions of middle-aged men who thought they were seducing a straight kid."

"So this is like pretending to be a virgin?"

"You could say that," said the mama, laughing. "I wonder if he pretended it hurt."

"Wasn't there an older guy who used to be really hot for him?" said one of the youths, called Tsunemi.

"There was! He was loaded and was always giving Kazuo presents and things. He hasn't been in recently."

"Isn't that because Kazuo quit?"

"He was coming on to Kazuo?" asked Samejima.

"Yes. But I'm not sure if they did it."

"Oh, they didn't. My guess is, they didn't, and that's why the guy was so desperate," said Tsunemi.

"What was he, this guy?"

"I think he was a dentist. He'd divorced. He had a pile of money."

"What was his name?"

The mama pursed her mouth, wavering. Tsunemi and Fuyuki were also silent, trying to read their boss.

"Hara. Doctor Hara." The mama exhaled, resigned. "Works in a clinic in Kawasaki."

The color left Sho's face.

It was the afternoon of the following day. Her part-time job had ended early, and she had gone to Samejima's apartment.

"What the hell happened?"

"A huge firework exploded just by my ear," said Samejima. But he couldn't fool her.

"So, when you said you'd taken a vacation, what you really meant was you'd arrested that guy Kizu, I bet. Is that how you picked up those injuries?"

"Yeah, that's right."

The night before, when he had slept in his own bed after such a long absence from it, he had been woken again and again. Kizu had appeared several times in his dreams with the cutter knife in his hands. The stench of Kizu's sweat lingered deep within him.

When Sho came into his room, she sat on his bed and said something. Samejima turned his left ear toward her, and Sho seemed to understand then what had happened.

"Is that your only injury?"

"Apart from a few bruises here and there."

"Tell me!"

"I was cut with a cutter knife. Down my stomach, and my inner thigh. It wasn't bad enough to have stitches though."

"Fuck you," said Sho quietly.

Samejima recalled those same words, screamed by Kizu an instant before he was gunned down.

Having averted her eyes from Samejima, Sho was gazing out of the window in the direction of the No. 7 Highway looproad.

Her face in profile conveyed annoyance.

Samejima thought she had extremely lonely eyes. Why was that, he wondered.

"What happened to Kizu?"

"Do you really want to know?"

"Not if you don't want to talk about it," said Sho without looking around. Tears welled up in her eyes.

"He's dead."

Sho suddenly turned toward him, tears rolling down her face from the abrupt movement.

"There was nothing in the newspapers."

"Huh, so you do read the papers?"

"Is that wrong?" Sho screamed. "I was worried sick that your frigging name would be in there. With all those Shinjuku cops getting shot at, I was concerned. That's all. Is that so bad?" She was really angry.

"I'm sorry."

"It's too late for that. I'm going home." Saying so, she stood up.

"Wait a minute, will you?"

Samejima grabbed hold of her arm. Sho shook herself free. "You're just a stupid cop after all. Acting the man of justice who charges ahead no matter how badly he gets hurt or beaten up, the oh-so-weighty burden of the law on his shoulders that no one else will bear! Dying is your highest hope. You probably think it's cool?"

Samejima sucked in a deep breath. "That's not true. I was scared. I almost got killed."

"You liar. 'Go ahead and do it. Go ahead, shoot.' You chose to cut a figure."

"No!" Samejima yelled, and Sho fell silent. "I was really scared. Kizu meant to murder me. He was going to torture me to death. He said he was going to lop bits off me with a cutter knife and then blow my brains out with my own gun."

"What happened to your ear?"

"I was shot without warning from the side. The bullet grazed my head."

"You can't hear with it?"

Samejima nodded. Sho cleared her throat with a gulp. Fear replaced her anger. Samejima knew that the idea of losing her hearing was unbearable for Sho.

"But your song plays inside my head," Samejima said.

"That's a lie."

"No, really. I can hear you singing 'But stay here...'"

"You were almost killed?"

"Yeah. He said he was going to castrate me and then rape me. And while he was raping me, he was going to blow my brains out."

Sho shook her head. "Wow, that's no fun."

"No fun at all. I wanted to quit being a cop when he said that."

"But you're going to stay?"

"Yeah, that's right."

"Even though it's the pits?"

"A core of darkness."

Sho tried her best to force a smile.

"You're a jerk," she sobbed, softly, and then flung herself at Samejima.

Samejima caught her in his arms. "Hey," he groaned, "be gentle with me."

"You nearly missed death and you ask for more?" said Sho, pressing her lips against Samejima's. She smothered him in kisses—not just his lips, but on his eyes and nose also.

"It's because I did, that I want you to be gentle."

Samejima's hand found its way into Sho's miniskirt.

"Hey!"

She glared at Samejima, but didn't stop him.

A little while later Sho said, "Are there any gay cops?"

"I wonder."

"You were very nearly the first."

Samejima stared at Sho with a straight face and said, "Maybe it wouldn't have been all that bad."

Sho bit Samejima's forearm as hard as she could. Samejima screamed for real.

While Sho was preparing dinner, Samejima played her demo tape. It contained a number of stage-recorded songs, including "Stay Here." The same collection was on sale at live concert halls and in record stores dealing in Indies music. The number of Who's Honey fans had increased steadily and the first release tapes had all sold out.

"When's the live concert?"

"Next week. We're not performing any new songs, so everyone in the band's pretty relaxed."

"What about the recording of your debut song?"

"We're meeting the guy from the company after the live concert. But it won't go on sale until the fall apparently."

Samejima nodded.

"Will you catch the cop killer by next week?"

"I don't know. What day is the concert on?"

"Saturday. It's at the TEC Hall, same as last time. The tickets are all sold out." Sho turned from her pot of *miso* soup and made a "too bad" face at Samejima.

"I can't get in?"

"I'm sure they'd let you in if you flashed your police ID."

"Oh, I see. And I might just bring the Juvenile Sub-Section Chief along with me, and see what he manages to find. I'm sure there'd be a huge commotion with all the underage drinking and smoking. I bet that's not all he'd find, either."

"Go ahead and try it. I'll poke a drumstick into your other ear."

"Okay, you win. I'll have more bad dreams if you do that."

Sho carried a plate over and stared at Samejima. Her face was serious.

"Did you have a nightmare last night?"

"Yeah."

"You'll be fine tonight," she said confidently. "If you have a bad dream, I'll sing to you, by your ear."

19

The whereabouts of Kazuo Miyauchi proved extremely difficult to fathom. The investigators who went to his family home discovered he hadn't been back once in the last three years; he'd phoned them about two years ago and that was it.

He had washed his hands of the friends he once had, including his companions in the bike gang. Nobody knew where he was.

While in the bike gang, Kazuo had been arrested for driving cars and motorcycles without a licence. Kazuo measured 5'4", which could hardly be described as tall.

He was the same height as Officer Hayami. When a detective of about the same height stood in Okubo Park with a helmet, Hayami said he thought the killer had been taller.

If the killer wasn't Kazuo, it was possible that he had been murdered by the killer. There were calls within the HQ for a public search and arrest on the grounds that Kazuo was an important witness. But Fujimaru suppressed such demands, fearful that it would serve no purpose other than to provoke the killer unnecessarily.

There had been no further calls from the man who gave his name as "Ed."

Four days had gone by. Tension at the HQ heightened with the passing of each day as the killer's crime cycle threatened to become more frequent.

The investigation pursued other lines besides that of Kazuo Miyauchi.

Acting on a report from a passenger, the railway police arrested a man in possession of a reproduction gun in Shinjuku station. The man said he'd wanted to confront the serial killer had he come across him.

One of the TV stations received a statement admitting responsibility for the crimes from an organization named "Flames on the Horizon." The caller warned that a crime would be carried out in two days' time, but it failed to materialize.

The HQ compared the voice of the man who'd given the warning with the tape-recorded voice of "Ed" and concluded that it was a different person.

The only clue of any significance was Kazuo Miyauchi.

Following the second killings, the HQ had set up a phone to take calls from the general public. The strategy was used by the Public Security Department to uncover extremist hideouts and had produced results in the past.

On a busy day the phone, the establishment of which had been Koda's proposal, received in excess of thirty calls a day. It soon became obvious that the majority of them were hoaxes, but the investigators had to run around checking each and every one of them.

It emerged that "Flames on the Horizon" had sent threatening letters to a number of department stores with branches in Shinjuku. The letters threatened that if money was not paid, customers would be murdered in the stores.

One store responded to the blackmailing. A criminal investigator lying in wait arrested a forty-eight-year-old man who'd come to collect the money.

The man was a lone operator, a former racketeer who, after the Commercial Code reforms, had been unable to make a living and had been arrested a number of times. A thorough questioning revealed that it had been an opportunist crime.

There were countless anonymous reports and statements purporting to claim responsibility. After they'd all been sifted through, the only significant one left was "Ed."

Samejima was in Miyamae-daira in Kawasaki.

There were a handful of dentists in Kawasaki called "Hara" but none fit the description given by the mama of Agamemnon.

Samejima made inquiries of the Kawasaki Association of Dental Specialists and started looking for dentists called Hara who hadn't opened their own practice.

On that day, he was making a visit to a dental clinic in operation in Miyamae-daira for many years. The director of the clinic was an elderly man who, because he had no children, requisitioned the services of two dentists, who didn't have clinics of their own, to work three days a week each. One of the dentists was called Hara.

The ink calligraphy signboard on the building read "Toyoma Dental Clinic." A coral tree hedge surrounded a two-story reinforced concrete house that had probably been white at one time. Judging from the construction of the porch in front of the entrance hall, it was a fairly old building. It looked as though the second floor housed the living quarters while the clinic was on the ground floor. The wooden door, once painted white, had lost its paint here and there and only the brass doorknob, which glittered in the light, appeared to have been replaced recently.

Samejima turned the doorknob and went inside. The consultation times were 1:00 p.m. until 6:00 p.m., and it was just after two in the afternoon.

The waiting room was immediately past the entrance. Two period sofas were arranged against the wall and a large charcoal brazier stood in one corner of the room. It looked as though it hadn't been used in a long while and had been deposited out of the way.

The interior of the waiting room was dark. There was no sign of patients.

"Is this your first visit?" a middle-aged woman in a white coat called to Samejima from the reception window that separated the waiting room from the consultation room.

Samejima took out his police ID and showed it to her. The woman's expression didn't change. From close up, she wasn't middle-aged at all, but closer to seventy.

"May I see Doctor Hara?"

"Doctor Hara is in on Wednesdays, Fridays and Saturdays," the woman stated in an unfriendly manner as she glared at Samejima over the rim of her thick glasses. "What is it you want?"

From inside the consultation room came the high-pitched metallic sound associated with dental clinics.

"Is it possible to see Doctor Hara tomorrow?"

"Yes, but what is this concerning?"

"It's something I'd like to talk to Doctor Hara about in person. Is Doctor Hara married?"

The woman pulled in her chin and regarded Samejima with distrust. "I'm afraid I don't know about the doctor's private life."

Samejima sighed quietly to himself.

The metallic sound stopped.

"What is it?"

A man in his mid-thirties wearing a white coat and mask opened the door of the consulting room. He held a pair of tweezers in his left hand. An absorbent cotton swab stained with liquid medicine was held between the tweezers.

Samejima produced his police ID again.

"I'd like to ask you some questions about Doctor Hara."

"Hara? We graduated from the same university. Is there a problem?" the dentist asked suspiciously.

"Is Doctor Hara single?"

"Yes. He was married once, but got divorced."

Samejima exhaled.

"I'd like to meet with him. Can you tell me where I can find him? It's nothing serious. My name is Samejima, of the Shinjuku police."

"Has Hara—"

"No, not at all. There's been a minor case in Shinjuku, a trivial argument, that's all. I'd like to ask Doctor Hara whether or not he saw it."

In gathering the sort of information he needed, it was standard to withhold from any but the concerned party the real reason for the questioning.

"I gather Hara does go into Shinjuku from time to time. But he's away on vacation at the moment."

"Whereabouts?"

"Hawaii, I think. He said he was going before it got too crowded with the summer vacation. He's been gone for a while, actually. Two weeks or so. I'm planning on taking the same amount of time off. We cover for each other here."

"When is he due to return?"

"I think it was Saturday. He's a bachelor, so he can please himself that way."

"Have you heard of a young man by the name of Kazuo Miyauchi?"

"Have I? No, I haven't," said the dentist, staring at Samejima.

"Has Doctor Hara ever mentioned to you a bar in Shinjuku called Agamemnon?"

"No, he hasn't. He's pretty strange about things like that. He won't introduce you to bars he knows in Tokyo even if you ask him to."

"When did he leave on vacation?"

"Hmm. He said he was going for a full twenty days, so that would have made it Monday two weeks ago I guess."

"He went alone, I suppose?"

"I don't know. I didn't ask anything as inappropriate as that."

"Doctor?" the receptionist cut into the conversation.

"Ah, yes, all right. Was there anything else?"

"Yes. Thank you for sparing your time. Just one last question. I wonder if you could give me Doctor Hara's home address?"

"Please inquire at the Department of Dentistry at the Saint Francesca

Medical University. They'll be able to tell you."

The dentist waved his tweezers and disappeared through the door.

Samejima apologized for interrupting and, with the receptionist's icy glare on him, left the dental clinic.

Samejima managed to get hold of Yoshiaki Hara's home address and record of legal domicile from Saint Francesca Medical University, where Hara also worked. His house was in Musashikosugi in Kawasaki.

To be sure, there was no sign that he'd returned to his apartment near the Tokyu line railway station during the last two weeks.

Monday of the week before last was the day the first of the murders had occurred.

Samejima returned to Shinjuku Police Station. He requested all the airline companies with flights from Narita to Hawaii to sift through their passenger lists on the day in question for the name "Yoshiaki Hara."

The passenger lists were all managed by computer and the replies came back promptly from the airline companies.

On the day in question, two different companies had flights to Hawaii, each of which carried a passenger by the name "Y. Hara." On one of those flights, the passenger sitting next to "Y. Hara" was "K. Miyauchi."

"It seems likely that, having fled Kizu's hideout and having nowhere to go, Kazuo made contact with Hara, who had once been very fond of him. In any case Kazuo seems pretty thick-skinned, like a woman who enjoys toying with middle-aged men, leading them around by the nose. Hara, who apparently tried but failed to seduce Kazuo in the past, was probably delighted that Kazuo made contact and took him with him on vacation."

At Samejima's report at the Criminal Investigation meeting the following morning, there were more than a hundred investigators in attendance. The meeting had begun early in the morning.

"I understand he's a bachelor with no apparent financial worries, but would Hara really take off on a twenty-day vacation with someone who'd contacted him that day, or the day before?" queried Crime Section Chief Yonai. He was an inspector, the same rank as Samejima and Momoi. All eyes fell on Samejima.

"According to the travel agent who processed the tickets for the airline, it appears that Hara was originally scheduled to stay in Hawaii alone. Already at that point, however, the resort hotel in Hawaii didn't have any single rooms available and so he took a double. In other words, even if Kazuo Miyauchi traveled with him, there would be no change to the hotel price, just an increase in the cost of the flight and meals. Hara had booked a round on a golf course—at the time of the reservation for one person. Just before departure, the reservation was changed to two people."

"Supposing for the moment that Kazuo Miyauchi was with Yoshiaki Hara—how did the gun Kazuo steal from Kizu end up in the hands of the killer?"

The question came from Superintendent Tonezaki of Section One of the Metropolitan Police, who was presiding over the meeting.

"I don't believe that Kazuo Miyauchi departed on vacation with Hara on the same day that he fled Kizu's hideout. I think he would have turned up unexpectedly at a close friend's house while he collected his thoughts; then, fearful that Kizu would track him down, he contacted Hara. Invited by Hara to go together on vacation to Hawaii, and knowing he couldn't take Kizu's customized gun with him, he deposited it somewhere or else disposed of it."

"And right now, where is Kazuo Miyauchi?" asked Fujimaru, seated next to Tonezaki. The commissioner was keeping a close watch over the meeting.

"Assuming he is with Hara, that would be the Hilton Hawaiian Village on Oahu Island. Up until yesterday local time, he was staying at the Makaha Sheraton."

"And he returns tomorrow, Saturday?"

"According to the travel agency, both 'Y. Hara' and 'K. Miyauchi' have reconfirmed their flight. It will be landing at Narita at 2:00 p.m. tomorrow."

"Good," Fujimaru said. "Let's pick up Miyauchi at Narita. Get him to tell us what he did with the gun before the press get wind of this. Request the assistance of the airport police and carry out your initial inquiries in the airport building. If he divulges the whereabouts of the gun, we'll dispatch a separate unit from here straighaway. Until then, we need to completely shut out the press." Looking at Samejima, Fujimaru continued, "At the moment, Kazuo Miyauchi is an important thread. A thread that will hopefully lead us to the killer."

Samejima nodded.

Following this, Koda stood up. Toying with a paperclip, he made as though he hadn't been paying any attention to Samejima's report. It was said he'd objected bitterly to Fujimaru about Samejima's sudden secondment to the Criminal Investigation HQ.

No one at HQ was surprised that Samejima had cornered Kizu. There was, on the other hand, a general feeling of amazement that Momoi, nicknamed "cadaver," had gunned down a suspect to save Samejima. There was a subtle change in the attitude of the detectives who hitherto had looked on Momoi with ill-concealed contempt.

Momoi didn't show the slightest interest in this change. His cadaverous presence remained lodged in the Crime Prevention Section Chief seat just as before the saving of Samejima. Shinjo, currently of Criminal Investigation HQ, was clearly becoming impatient and had started to align himself with Koda. The younger detectives who thought Shinjo's behavior shameful came to Samejima and pointed this out, but he refused to have anything to do with it. When the time came for the HQ to be disbanded, Samejima, Shinjo, and the young detectives would all return to Crime Prevention.

Samejima had no interest in the section's factionalism.

"You will each have been distributed a psychologist's analysis based on the recording of the suspect known as 'Ed,' who has for some time now been calling the Criminal Investigation HQ and claiming responsibility for the killings. If I could ask you to read the document, you will appreciate the finer points of the analysis."

As Koda explained, the detectives began to open the materials that had been circulated. These had been handed out at the entrance before the meeting by one of Koda's subordinates.

"Inspector Samejima. It appears you aren't interested in my report," Koda said suddenly. Samejima alone did not have the report in hand. "If you are not interested, perhaps you'd be good enough to leave the room."

Samejima, his face expressionless, looked at the detective who had distributed the materials. The detective cleared his throat and looked away. The materials had been distributed to everyone except Samejima.

Fujimaru looked searchingly at Samejima. Just as Tonezaki was about to say something, Koda continued:

"Excuse me, let me go ahead then. According to this analysis, 'Ed' is a young man in his twenties who has been to a university or technical college and is highly educated. His physique is either extremely thin or quite stocky. He is weak at sports, prefers his own company and is obsessive. He is likely to be the target of intimidation in busy areas of the city, and it is possible he commits petty crimes such as shoplifting. He has little interest in clothes, and in that sense he is different from most young people today. In addition, he has a strong interest in the police organization and crime, and also firearms; in the event he carried out a crime like those we have been experiencing, his psychological makeup would compel him to boast about it. In ideological terms, he is either apolitical, or conservative. His walking speed is either extremely quick or extremely slow. In other words, when he is focused on the present object of his interest, nothing else will distract him. Conversely, when he is not focused, he becomes restless and inconsistent in his behavior. Furthermore, the analysis finds that he is sexually immature—it is very unlikely that he leads a married life. For reasons associated with his character already referred to, he probably has only a handful of friends and acquaintances."

Koda stopped talking momentarily and scanned the faces of the detectives present. His eyes came into contact with Samejima's but his expression remained the same.

"Now, when we consider the motive behind his crimes from this point of reference, it is conceivable that he was questioned in the past by a police officer at this station—and furthermore, that he developed a grudge due to a perception of unjust treatment. Assuming he had been the recipient of persistent questioning—so persistent that he harbored a grudge against those responsible—there ought to exist within the station a record made at that time by the outside duty officer. I think it would make sense to carry out our inquiries along these lines. Even if 'Ed' is not the killer, the killer's hatred of police officers could well have come about as a result of such experiences."

"That's a logical opinion," agreed Fujimaru, looking in Koda's direction. "I would like Superintendent Koda to lead that investigation. Assistant Inspector Shinjo, you will be his deputy."

"Yes, sir."

"I would also like Superintendent Koda to be ready, in this station, to deal with calls from 'Ed.' Thanks to the cooperation of NTT's Yodobashi business office we expect the time required to trace a call to be reduced."

"Is there anything else?" Tonezaki looked around the meeting room. "If there is nothing else, may you all focus your attention anew on arresting the killer and carrying out your investigations to the best of your abilities, always with due regard for your own safety. Furthermore, while the killer is a vicious criminal and has firearms in his possession, and while each of you carry firearms in order to counter that threat, I would urge you to use your weapons with discretion. That's all!"

The noise of the detectives pulling back their chairs and standing up all at once echoed around the crowded room. Yabu, of the Identification Section, was also there. He had been attending the meeting in the capacity of adviser to answer specialist questions relating to firearms and had also given a report on matters such as Kizu's workshop.

Samejima called over to him.

Yabu was on his way out of the room, but stopped and grinned. "Your adversary was pretty outspoken today. How's your ear doing?" Yabu was referring to Koda's snub.

"It's a schoolboy quarrel. It's not hurting that bad."

Yabu shook his head. Side by side, they left the HQ together.

"Those guys who pass the upper exams have seen nothing of real life. Even the way they pick a fight is childish." Needless to say, Yabu said this knowing full well that Samejima, too, was a career police officer.

"More to the point, the psychological profile of 'Ed' in Superintendent Koda's report is exactly you, don't you think? It's just your age that's different," Samejima said as he walked along on Yabu's right.

"I guess that's right. Under different circumstances, maybe I'd be a notorious gun maker like Kizu," Yabu said, unruffled.

"By the way, did you find anything in Kizu's workshop?"

"Plenty. What do you want to know?"

"What sort of work went into the gun that Kazuo made off with?"

"Oh, I see. Well, why don't I invite you along to my lab."

"You won't make me drink coffee from a beaker?"

"Don't worry, I have a special cup reserved for visitors."

The special cup was a china mug in the shape of a hand grenade.

Yabu poured into it a diet sweetener from a bottle marked "Maru Ex." Maru Ex was the argot for Molotov cocktail.

The Criminal Identification Section room was full of Kizu's things. Each gun on the table was tagged with bullet type and capability. All of the items from Kizu's workshop along the canal had been confiscated.

"Have you checked them all out?"

Samejima took the coffee Yabu had made for him and stood in front of the table where the guns were laid out.

"Not yet. I've just had a quick look. My next job is to look at them all carefully, including the unfinished ones. If HQ doesn't take them away first, that is."

"What do you think?"

"About Kizu? He was a genius. He really understood guns. He'd divide them into two categories and manufacture them according to his customers' requirements: guns that had to have precision accuracy and those that didn't."

"I suppose his guns were expensive."

"Yeah, I'd think so. Take this one for example. You probably don't want to look at it. It's the weapon that almost blew your head off."

Samejima groaned. The weapon Yabu had pointed to was the gun with the four barrels mounted in a box.

"This comes as a set, with an under and over double-barrelled gun, each with two different types of barrel. Viewed from the shooter, the double barrels on the right are from a 222 Remington rifle, while the barrels on the left are from a 12-gauge shotgun. There are two triggers, on the left and on the right. In other words, it's designed so that when you fire, the percussion pin strikes top to bottom, top to bottom. The gun that shot you was the upper right barrel of the 222 Remington. Had he used the shotgun, everything above your neck would have disappeared completely. Perhaps the reason he didn't was that he was attached to the place. He didn't want to defile his sacred workshop by splattering your brains all over it."

"Well excuse me!"

"Since you didn't die with the first shot, he decided to change tactics. Now, check out this gun."

Yabu pointed to a box that looked to the casual observer like a videotape case. A sticker of Charlie Chaplin's *Limelight* was stuck on the front.

"This really is like one of those devices used in spy movies. When you open the lid, a .22-caliber bullet shoots out of it. The muzzle is this little hole, located just above the joint of the case."

"How does the mechanism work?"

"The thing is like a fairly complicated safety pin. It has a spring, and a clasp to hold it down, and a hook to release it. All you need is a nail to use as a percussion pin. Kizu's guns aren't made to fire hundreds of rounds. Basically you use it and dispose of it. That's why he was able to experiment with a number of different ideas."

"How accurate are they?"

"That depends on the barrel and the shape of the gun. The barrel, of course, is the part the bullet passes through. With regard to the rotation of the bullet, as I mentioned the other day, as long as the barrel doesn't cause the bullet to travel unevenly, even with a short-barrelled gun the rate of accuracy isn't all that bad. Provided it's a minimum length."

"But the other day you said the rate of accuracy declines with a gun barrel that has been shortened."

"That's true where you shorten the barrel of a rifle that's already on the market. I knew it as soon as I saw Kizu's guns. He doesn't just cut down the gun barrel. He loved guns. You might say he was obsessed by their appeal and destructive power. He had a policy when it came to the products he made. Even if it was a customized gun, since it was a gun it had to be beautiful."

Samejima remembered how Kizu had reviled his New Nambu calling it a useless piece of junk.

"And another thing, when an amateur cuts down the barrel of a gun that he buys on the market, he scratches the rifling grooves on the inside of the barrel, leaving metal filings on the surface of the muzzle. If the bullet so much as touched the metal filings it would go off course. The condition of the barrel surface is almost as important as the rifling to the accuracy of the bullet. But Kizu paid particular attention to that, whether it was a short-barrelled gun, a pistol or a rifle."

"You also mentioned the shape of the gun."

"That's about absorbing the recoil."

Yabu pointed at the New Nambu at Samejima's waist.

"The energy produced inside the cartridge by the explosion only has one way out—in short, it travels down the barrel and pushes the bullet out. But it doesn't simply dissipate with that, and there is recoil from the back of the chamber, in other words, in the direction of the shooter. If a gun had to be built into something like a lighter that's small and light, Kizu would use a .22-caliber bullet. With a gun that was ensconced in something big and heavy, like an attaché case, he'd use shotgun rounds, a .45 round, or a rifle bullet. If you think about it, while it's possible to make a small gun that will fire a large caliber bullet, generally they're not made."

"Because unless you hold on to it very tightly, you wouldn't hit your target?"

"That's not the only reason. There are certain shapes that are easy to hold. You could make a gun fit into a stuffed toy, but it would be soft and difficult to hold, not suited for aiming. A good number of Kizu's guns were housed in umbrellas, although, as you would imagine, they didn't use large caliber rounds. Umbrellas are fairly easy to take aim with, and you can grip them with both hands. So, why do you think?"

Yabu looked at Samejima.

Samejima shook his head. "I've no idea."

"It's the weight. In other words, the impact on the shooter depends on how much of the recoil the gun's own weight absorbs before it's transmitted to the shooter. Moreover, if the weapon is light, the shooter will have assumed a less than adequate shooting stance."

"So the ideal is something easy to take aim with but substantial in terms of weight?"

"That's right. Large caliber guns are relatively heavy for that reason. With a light casing, the recoil would run out of control in the shooter's hand. Conversely, if it's heavy, even a gun with a fairly large caliber won't recoil so badly that the shooter's arm jumps."

"How about a 30-06?"

"Of course it has to be heavy or it's no good. Kizu even considered the possibility that some of his customers might never have fired a gun before and factored that into the functions of his guns. He was a master craftsman."

"An abnormal one at that," muttered Samejima.

"All I can say with certainty is this: the gun the killer has could be in any form, but it'll be heavy enough to do the job, and it'll be a shape that's easy for the shooter to hold."

"And it will be something that doesn't look like a gun at all. What, do you think?"

Yabu stared fixedly at Samejima's face, then shook his head. "I don't know. There were no weapons using a type 30-06 bullet amongst the guns we confiscated. If you were talking about a suit of clothes, you'd say the killer had a one-off item."

20

Samejima was with Sotoyama in the special examination room of Customs at Narita Airport. The room was about ten mats in size with a single door and no windows. A long mirror was fixed horizontally on the back wall at about chest height.

In the middle of the room was a table and chairs for four people, and a bench had been placed in the corner.

The plan was for the airport police to ask Kazuo Miyauchi, who ought by now to have cleared the entry inspection, to accompany them of his own accord. The door had been left open. In the corridor outside, agents known as handlers walked around with their narcotics tracker dogs. Using the tracker dogs, the handlers checked the luggage as soon as it came out of the baggage hold of the passenger plane. The dogs moved nimbly about on top of the vertical luggage carousel trying to sniff out narcotics.

At twenty minutes past two, four uniformed police officers came walking along the corridor accompanying a young man who was dressed in short pants and a yachting jacket. Confirmation that it was Kazuo Miyauchi had been received several minutes earlier by portable wireless receiver.

Samejima took the earphone for the receiver out of his left ear. Since he was unable to hear with his right ear, he couldn't carry on a conversation while wearing the earphone.

On the other side of the mirror, six investigators including detectives from Section One were on stand by.

Two of the uniformed officers left after they had escorted the young man into the room, while the remaining two stood in front of the door and waited for instructions.

Kazuo Miyauchi was heavily sun-tanned and a pair of sunglasses hung from his neck by a cord. He wore a colorful tanktop beneath his yachting jacket.

The hairs on his body were fine and his body was smooth with a well-built torso and muscular limbs.

"His traveling companion is in a separate room. Room 2," said one of the police officers. He wore the insignia of a police sergeant.

"Good work. Please keep one of your men posted in that room," said Samejima as he closed the door.

Kazuo Miyauchi, now alone, showed no emotion. He was tense, but he didn't appear to be afraid. When he blinked, his eyelashes, which seemed disproportionately long, moved up and down.

With Sotoyama's approval, Samejima took the lead in asking the questions.

"Sit down. I'm Samejima from the Shinjuku Station, and this is Mr. Sotoyama. Your name is Kazuo. You used to work at Agamemnon, right?"

Kazuo slowly let out the breath he'd been holding in. He looked from Samejima to Sotoyama guiltily. His demeanor turned obsequious.

"Please sit down," urged Samejima.

Kazuo pulled up a chair and sat himself down with a thud.

"How was Hawaii?" asked Samejima.

Kazuo stared at him in silence.

"Did you have a good time?"

Kazuo nodded.

"How long were you there?"

"Twenty days," said Kazuo, his voice quiet.

Samejima turned his good ear in his direction.

"I'm sorry, but could I ask you to speak a little louder? As you can see,

I hurt my ear."

"I said twenty days."

"Really? A few things have happened in Japan while you were away. Did you know?"

Kazuo shook his head. It seemed he'd decided to feign ignorance.

"Do you know Kaname Kizu? The man you lived with once?"

Kazuo stopped blinking. "I don't know him."

"Is that right. There are a lot of people who say they know you and Kizu used to hang out together."

"I don't know him. I'm telling you I don't."

"If you're afraid of having to deal with him afterwards, don't worry. Kizu is dead," Samejima showed his hand.

Kazuo's eyes opened wider still. But other than that he didn't exhibit any change.

"So we don't need to concern ourselves with Kizu for a while. Won't you tell me what you were doing before you went to Hawaii?"

"Why?"

"Tell me."

Kazuo thought about it. His eyes started to rove around the room, darting toward the ceiling, then the floor and the mirror, incessantly flitting from one thing to another.

"I was with Mr. Hara."

"From when?"

"The beginning of last month."

"What day?"

"I don't know. Thursday or Friday."

Samejima took out a calendar from his pocket book.

"You departed Japan with Mr. Hara on the thirteenth of last month. That would be a Monday. We're asking Mr. Hara the same questions right now so we'll know soon enough if you're telling the truth."

Kazuo blinked furiously. "It was a Saturday."

"It was the eleventh, right? And where were you before that?"

"At a friend's house."

"Won't you tell me who it was—your friend?"

"Why? Why are you asking me stuff?"

"I want to check with your friend."

"I haven't done anything wrong. Not especially."

"I know that. But we need to get your friend to confirm you were there."

"What for?"

"Well, let's assume, for example, there was an incident that Friday, and we need to prove that Kizu was involved but that you had nothing to do with it. That's why I'm asking who you were with."

"On the Friday?"

Samejima nodded.

"I was at a friend's house. I used to work at a part-time job with him years ago. I—I don't want to get him into any trouble."

"We won't make any trouble for him."

"But, if I tell you, I want you to let me call him first."

"That's fine if you tell us."

Kazuo hesitated.

"You'd better tell me. Otherwise things might get difficult for you."

"Difficult? What do you mean?"

"People, have died."

"Where?"

Without answering, Samejima stared at Kazuo.

Kazuo was probably afraid he'd be charged with stealing the gun from Kizu.

It really did seem like he knew nothing of the serial killings, Samejima thought.

"Sunagami. Koichi Sunagami."

"How do you write his name?"

Samejima took out his notebook. Kazuo wrote it down.

Samejima double-checked aloud, as if to confirm with Kazuo, but in truth so that the detectives on the other side of the mirror could hear him.

"Where does he live?"

"Nakano."

"I see. That's one stop on the Tozai subway line from Monzen Nakacho."

Kazuo raised his eyes.

"Can you tell me the telephone number?"

"I don't have my address book with me at the moment."

"In that case, you can't make a call either," said Samejima, looking at his watch. "What does he do?"

"This and that."

"This and that?"

"First, he worked as a regular employee at a company. But he found it boring and quit and went through part-time jobs."

"And now?"

"I don't know. Is it okay if I smoke?"

Samejima nodded.

Kazuo took out a Virginia Slim Menthol from his jacket pocket and lit it.

"Have you known him long—Sunagami?"

"Three, maybe four years."

"Was it Thursday or Friday that you stayed in his house?"

"Friday night."

"And until then, you were in Monzen Nakacho?"

Reluctantly, Kazuo nodded.

"About what time did you leave Monzen Nakacho?"

"About three o'clock."

That was when Kizu went out for lunch. Kazuo probably went to his place while he was out and took the gun.

"Did you go straight to Sunagami's house?"

Kazuo nodded again.

"Was Sunagami home?"

Kazuo shook his head.

"What did you do?"

"I know where he keeps the key, so I just went in."

"Is it an apartment?"

"Yeah."

"So, knowing that your friend keeps his key somewhere like the milk bottle holder, you used it to go into his apartment."

"Yeah."

"And then when did you contact Doctor Hara?"

"Friday night."

"Was Sunagami back by then?"

"No, he wasn't. He got home late that night."

"About what time?"

"About 11:00 p.m."

"That was pretty late. Had he gone drinking?"

"I'm pretty sure he had a few drinks. He also got into a fight. He was covered in blood."

"A fight?"

"I don't know the details. When he gets drunk he quickly gets bad-tempered. He told me he'd let a good number of trains go past before he finally got on one."

"Because he was drunk? Or because he'd been beaten up and wasn't feeling too good?"

Kazuo shook his head. "I don't know."

"How old is your friend?"

"Twenty-four."

Samejima leaned against the chair and put a cigarette in his mouth.

It was a signal to the detectives waiting in the other room that they should contact Tokyo and search for a young man by the name of Koichi Sunagami, who lived in Nakano.

Kazuo was silent. Samejima sensed that a particular resolve had lodged itself in the young man.

"Was Koichi Sunagami your lover? In the past?"

Kazuo stared at Samejima. There was a look of fierce defiance in his eyes. It was a stare that probed a cop for prejudice against gays.

"He's a friend, that's all," Kazuo spoke, perhaps not having sensed any such bias in Samejima.

"Why did you contact Doctor Hara instead of staying with Sunagami?"

Kazuo stared at the surface of the table.

"Was Sunagami kind to you? Or is it that you were afraid of him?"

"He was kind, but I was afraid."

"When were you afraid?"

"When I acted gay."

"You mean, he didn't like it when you were all over him?"

Kazuo nodded.

"Do you like him?"

Kazuo's eyes fixed themselves on a spot on the tabletop and didn't move.

"Is Sunagami well-built?"

"He's tall, he's got long legs. He looks good."

"Is he strong?"

"Yeah."

"Does he get into fights?"

"Sometimes."

"So, even though he's strong and well-built, he gets himself beaten up?"

"He said they were *yakuza*. He thought he was fighting with just one, then he realized there were lots of them."

"So I guess he was pretty mad about it?"

"Maybe."

"Is Sunagami the type of guy to get even?"

"He said it was the first time he'd been beaten up as bad as that."

"Where was he beaten up?"

"I don't know. I think it was in Shinjuku. He said it was on his way back from listening to some music over in Kabukicho."

"Music? You mean a concert?"

"Yeah. Koichi often goes to concerts of singers he likes."

"What sort of singers?"

"I don't know. He's got CDs and tapes, but he gets annoyed if you touch them."

"So, on the Friday evening, you left Kizu's condo and went to Sunagami's apartment. What time did you arrive there?"

"Four, maybe four-thirty."

"And were you in his apartment the whole time until Sunagami returned?"

"Yeah, I was."

"What did you do about dinner?"

"I was hungry, so I went and bought some bread."

"So you went out?"

"There's a store nearby the apartment. I bought some bread there and came straight back again."

"Wasn't it boring?"

"Not especially. I watched TV, things like that."

"So Sunagami returned home around 11:00 p.m. He was drunk, and moreover, he'd lost a fight, was covered in blood and in a bad mood. When he saw you what did he do?"

"He said, *What is this? Why are you here?*"

"And what did you say?"

"I said I'd be leaving soon and would it be okay to stay one night."

"Did you really intend to leave soon?"

"When I called Doctor Hara, he asked me if I'd like to go to Hawaii and I said I'd like to think it over."

"In other words, really you wanted to be with Sunagami?"

"I liked him from a long time back."

"Before you became friendly with Kizu?"

Kazuo nodded.

"But because Sunagami is straight he wouldn't accept you."

"Yeah. I thought I'd get on his nerves if I were there for a long time, so I arranged to meet Doctor Hara on Saturday."

"Did you go straight to Doctor Hara's house?"

Kazuo shook his head.

"We ate dinner and drank some *saké*. Then we went by car to the Bay Bridge."

"Yokohama Bay Bridge? Does Doctor Hara have a car?"

"He's got a Saab."

"About what time was it when you left Sunagami's apartment?"

"About 5:00 p.m. I'd arranged to meet Doctor Hara at seven."

"Where?"

"Shibuya."

"Where in Shibuya?"

"At a coffee shop called Acuras."

"And then you went for dinner?"

"Yeah."

"What was Sunagami doing when you left his place?"

"Sleeping."

"He wasn't feeling too good?"

"That's right."

"Did you stop off anywhere on the way to Shibuya?"

Kazuo shook his head.

"Did you have a lot of luggage when you left Kizu's condo?"

"A little."

"A little?"

"Clothes."

"What else?"

"What else? What do you mean?"

Kazuo looked at Samejima.

"Were the things you took just your belongings?"

"Yeah."

"Are you sure?"

Samejima lit another cigarette. Kazuo's face had become tense.

"What sort of person is Sunagami?"

Kazuo looked a little surprised.

"He likes you, so he must be a decent guy. Or is he just a little weird?"

"He's kind to me, but I'm afraid of him."

"They're all like that, aren't they? When they're in a good mood, they're kind, but when they're angry, it's scary."

"No. He's really gentle with animals—birds and cats and those. Once, he looked after a kitten that had been hit by a car and abandoned. But people… It's scary when he gets angry at people. He's kind to animals, but he doesn't care one bit for humans."

"Does he hate people?"

"Maybe."

"When does he become angry at people?"

"He hates arrogant, conceited people."

"So he hates the *yakuza*, true?"

"Yeah. And cops," said Kazuo, looking from Samejima to Sotoyama.

"He hates cops too because they like to throw their weight around?"

"He said they're bullies and don't serve any purpose. When they're out on the street they're so bossy—if you do the slightest thing wrong, they call you over, *Hey you, come here now*—but if the *yakuza* are around, they don't do anything. He says the Shinjuku cops are afraid of *yakuza*."

"Is that because when Sunagami was beaten up, the police didn't come and help him?"

"That might be."

Samejima slowly inhaled. He looked at Sotoyama with a severe expression.

Friday the tenth. There had definitely been a heavy police presence in Shinjuku. They had been detailed to guard the garden party at the

Imperial Gardens.

"What else did you take with you from Kizu's condo, besides clothes?"

Kazuo took in a sharp breath.

"What did you take?"

"Nothing."

"Oh really? Kizu said you took a certain something with you."

"That's a lie."

"You think so?"

Samejima gazed intently at Kazuo. Kazuo's eyes fixed themselves once again on the tabletop.

"Did you take all your luggage with you when you met Doctor Hara?"

Kazuo was silent.

There was a knock at the door. Sotoyama stood up and opened it a fraction. A piece of paper was handed to him. He read it and passed it to Samejima, then sat down.

Koichi Sunagami. Address: Nakano Ward, Yayoimachi, Ichome X-X, Daini Co-op, Room 203. Telephone: 385-XXXX. Criminal record: No record of arrest. A search warrant has been issued for his suspected violation of the Firearms Possession Law. No attempt has been made to telephone home address to confirm whereabouts. The 3rd, 8th and 13th Squads have been dispatched.

Samejima folded the note up and put it in his breast pocket. Then he touched Kazuo on the shoulder. For the first time Kazuo looked afraid.

"We know that you stole something from Kizu's place. Something that he made. You quarrelled and, annoyed, no doubt you thought you'd cause him a good deal of trouble. But, afterwards, you became afraid that Kizu would come after you, so either you disposed of the item or hid it. Didn't you?"

"I don't know. I didn't take anything with me."

"I told you already, didn't I? Kizu's dead. There's nothing to be afraid of."

Kazuo opened his eyes wide and stared at Samejima. "Will I be charged with an offense?"

"That depends entirely on you."

"Are you threatening me? I won't talk."

"Very well. Let me explain to you what happened. On the day you left for Hawaii, two police officers were murdered in Shinjuku. The following week, another officer was killed and another admitted to hospital. Having been on the verge of death, he just about pulled through. At the end of the same week—in other words, Saturday of last week—another police officer was killed and his colleague seriously wounded. All of these incidents took place in Shinjuku, and all the victims were police officers on the Shinjuku force. Four officers are dead, and two have been critically injured. All of them were shot with the same gun. A gun that Kizu said you stole from him."

Kazuo's eyes bulged out of their sockets. His look of innocence disappeared, and the tone of his voice was different. "You're lying. Don't fuck with me!"

"I'm not. The gun you stole was used to kill those police officers."

"I don't know anything about it. I don't know, I'm telling you. It's all a pack of lies."

"Kazuo, tell me the truth. You're in big trouble right now. If you gave that gun to Sunagami so even that Friday he could get—"

"I didn't. I didn't!" screamed Kazuo, rising from his seat. "I just left it there, that's all. I didn't know what to do. I thought it was dangerous to keep it with me, so I left it at Koichi's place, that's all. Oh please you gotta be kidding."

"Did you tell Sunagami that it was a gun?"

Kazuo fell silent. He began blinking furiously again.

"Did you tell him?"

"I might have mentioned it. When I asked him to look after it."

"What did you intend to do?"

"Once I got back from vacation, I was going to give it to a friend in the mob and get him to sell it for me."

"How did you put it to Sunagami?"

"I said if I made any money out of it, I'd split it with him. I asked him to look after it until then. When he asked me what it was, I told him it was like a pistol."

"What did Sunagami say?"

"He said, *Is it really?* and got out of bed. But it was wrapped in paper and tied with a cord and I told him he mustn't touch it."

"What did it look like?"

"I don't know. It was about this big. It was in a paper bag, double-wrapped in oiled paper and gift wrap." Kazuo held his hands up and made a square shape about a foot wide.

"How heavy was it?"

"About three kilos. It was heavy."

"Damn it!" spat Samejima.

Sotoyama stood up and nodded. There was a knock at the door.

Samejima went over and opened it.

It was the detective who had questioned Hara. "We've finished our interrogation."

Samejima looked back at Kazuo, who was trembling. He looked at Samejima and said, "I need the toilet. Please let me go to the toilet."

A uniformed police officer, who had been standing on the other side of the door, accompanied Kazuo.

"Let's prepare the statement of evidence," Sotoyama said.

Samejima nodded. He called in the clerk and when Kazuo returned from the bathroom, began to take down the statement.

Kazuo was afraid of being indicted as Sunagami's accomplice. He signed and sealed his statement, the contents of which were virtually identical to what he had told Samejima. When the statement was completed, a detective from Section One who had been in the room next door came in.

"The police went into Sunagami's apartment and we understand that five cartridges were found. However, Sunagami wasn't there. The officers were unable to locate the gun or the remaining bullets. Someone in the room next door said he heard a noise like someone going out, just after midday."

"Let's go back to Tokyo," Samejima said. "Sunagami might strike again."

21

It was close to five in the afternoon when they arrived at the Shinjuku Police Station via Shibuya's congested streets.

In order to avoid the crowds of journalists, Kazuo was taken into the police station in a separate car by the rear entrance.

At HQ, Fujimaru was waiting to receive them. The report had already arrived, but Samejima repeated the outline. A meeting of the Criminal Investigation Section was called immediately, with all personnel attending save the detectives of the three squads who were staking out Sunagami's apartment.

The meeting started at 5:20 p.m.

Sho's live concert would begin at seven. It looked as though he wouldn't be able to make it this time either.

Sunagami's photograph had already been received by HQ. It had been taken when he had been in full-time employment and showed him with short hair and wearing a tie. Kazuo looked at the photo and said that he was a little slimmer now and that his hair was longer.

The photograph was distributed to the meeting attendees. When he saw it, Samejima thought: *Such dark eyes...* It was an unsettling, mysterious darkness. They were eyes that gave off a sense of danger, of, not quite madness, but despair. At the same time there was also a strong feeling of self-adulation playing about his lips.

He looked away from the photograph and put a cigarette in his mouth. Then, a feeling of horror and shock raced through his mind like a bright light obscuring his vision.

He looked again at the photograph.

The meeting had begun, and the important points in the case were being examined. The fact that the gun had not been discovered in his home meant that Sunagami might be walking around with it on his person. It suggested that this could be the fourth day of the serial killings.

There was no mistake about it. Samejima knew Sunagami. He was the man who was being beaten up by those punks from the Hanaigumi gang on the street the night he'd gone from the sauna in Shin-Okubo to meet Sho at the TEC Hall. Three gangsters had surrounded the young man as he crouched on the ground. One of them had held his collar, while the other two took turns aiming kicks at him.

People stopped, but no one intervened to break it up or attempt to help him. Once they realized the attackers were *yakuza,* the onlookers lingered for a moment and moved quickly on.

Samejima himself had thought it, too.

You stupid…

The thought was directed not at the young punks who were administering the beating, but at the young man who was being beaten. It wasn't sympathy he felt, but scorn—the sense of contempt one felt for a young guy who'd run afoul of the tacit rules of the game in Shinjuku.

"Shut up! Fuck off and leave me alone! Dammit!"

The words spoken by the young man seemed to echo in his ears. Had someone intervened a few minutes earlier—before the young man had lost the will to fight—he may not have uttered those words. He wouldn't have been incensed by the city that had abandoned him, the passersby who had deserted him, the police who had left him to his fate.

That day surely saw Sunagami germinate seeds of hatred for police officers on patrol from Shinjuku Police Station.

The sense of shock Samejima felt soon changed to regret. The man had felt anger at being beaten up by the gangsters and having nobody to turn to for help. His anger turned, not toward his attackers, but rather toward those who hadn't saved him, the cops.

His was the wrath of a citizen who hadn't received the protection of the police, when so many officers had been on duty that night. Despite the massive police presence in Shinjuku, he was beaten, thrown to the ground and kicked until a bloody mess. Nobody so much as raised the alarm or rushed off to find a police officer.

Had not the pain and humiliation turned first into anger and disappointment, and then into hatred?

Samejima hadn't informed the injured young man that he was a detective. When he remembered this, Samejima was seized by an acute sense of chagrin.

If he'd told him that the police hadn't, in fact, turned their back on him—then, at least, the hatred Sunagami felt toward the police surely wouldn't have turned into an intention to commit murder.

But Samejima had been in a hurry. Not wanting to be late for his date with Sho, he'd been content to watch Sunagami walk away without letting him know he was a cop.

Samejima couldn't staunch the bitterness welling up inside him.

He had to tell Sunagami—that he was a cop. And also that, if there was any cop who needed to take responsibility, it was none other than himself.

"On the tenth of last month," began Fujimaru, "Koichi Sunagami went to Kabukicho to attend the concert of a singer he was a fan of and, while there, was attacked by a number of individuals thought to be members of a gang. Nobody intervened to stop them, and moreover, while on the day in question a large number of police officers had been deployed within Shinjuku in order to guard the Shinjuku Imperial Garden party, none of those officers who happened to be there offered their protection. It is thought that this caused Sunagami to harbor a grudge, which then turned into murderous intent. It is also possible that at some prior stage, Sunagami had been the recipient of unjust questioning, as a result of which he felt distrust toward the police, so that the experience he had at the hands of the gangsters transformed his distrust into a desire to kill. Unfortunately, there is no record at this police station of any such violent incident occurring on the day in question, and this proves the fact that the police did not provide protection to Sunagami."

Samejima resisted the urge to cry out, *That's not right. I might have been late getting there, but I was there at the scene of the crime.*

"Whether or not we term Sunagami's crime a case of unjust resentment, his murderous intent has probably escalated with each crime. As yet there is no hard evidence to suggest that 'Ed,' with whom Superintendent Koda has had telephone contact, is actually Sunagami. But either way, there is no guarantee that the person he chooses as his next victim will be a police officer. Accordingly, if Sunagami intends to repeat his crime this evening in the jurisdiction, anyone in Shinjuku could be his target."

Koda entered the room. He had requested an interview with Kazuo.

"How did it go?"

Koda shook his head in response to Fujimaru's question.

"Kazuo hasn't heard the name 'Ed' used by Sunagami, nor has he heard it used by anyone acquainted with him."

"I see."

But Koda didn't seem too dispirited. "May I?" he said, and began his briefing. "We questioned Kazuo Miyauchi in order to find out why Sunagami came to Shinjuku on the tenth of last month. According to Kazuo, Sunagami intended to go to a concert. We inquired with Patrol Section about concerts given that day in Shinjuku Ward."

The investigators gave Koda their undivided attention. Samejima also watched him closely. Koda was an upleasant man, but he was no fool.

"Within the jurisdiction of this station, and in fact including Yotsuya Station, there are sixteen theaters and halls, not including movie theaters, that can accommodate more than a hundred people. Among these, ten are licensed to hold concerts. Furthermore, only four out of this number were being used on the tenth of last month by singers and bands. These four were the Welfare Pension Hall, Koma Theater, Theater Apple, and

Lumine Hall. At the Welfare Pension Hall, there was a concert by the American rock group 'Bug Eaters,' then on tour in Japan. At the Koma Theater, there was a musical starring pop idol Yuri Matsugi. At the Theater Apple, the rock singer Yoshiki Ando was giving a concert, and at the Lumine Hall, *chanson* singer Mitsuko Sakai was on stage."

Koda reeled off the details in one breath and then looked at the assembled investigators.

"The musical featuring Yuri Matsugi was repeated for a further three days as an encore performance at the Koma Theater. We consider there to be a strong likelihood that Sunagami went to this concert."

Koda looked at Fujimaru.

Fujimaru had a strained look on his face. "You're saying that Sunagami might open fire inside Koma Theater?"

"For Sunagami, coming to Shinjuku to see Yuri Matsugi was the start of everything. Assuming Sunagami is a big fan of Yuri Matsugi, it is quite conceivable that he would attempt a crime there."

Fujimaru's expression grew visibly pale. "What time does the performance begin?"

"The doors open at 6:30 p.m. The curtain rises at seven."

"Contact the promoter immediately."

"With a request to cancel?"

"Naturally!"

"But if the performance is cancelled, Sunagami will be hugely disappointed and may become desparate," Koda objected.

Fujimaru showed signs for the first time of being in a dilemma. But after an instant, he made up his mind.

"Order an emergency deployment in the vicinity of the Koma Theater. Station all available plainclothes detectives in and around the building. All personnel are to wear bulletproof vests. We'll intercept and arrest Sunagami before the theater opens its doors. The commanders on the ground will be Superintendents Koda and Tonezaki!"

The investigators stood up all together.

"Superintendent Koda," said Samejima, quickly approaching Koda. Koda, who had begun to walk toward the exit, stopped in his tracks. The other investigators also stopped and looked at the two men.

"What is it?"

"What about the live concert halls? You know, the live houses?"

"The live houses?"

"There are a relatively large number of live houses in Shinjuku that rent out stages to bands, including amateur groups."

"What about them?"

"I think it's a possibility that Koichi Sunagami went to a live house."

"And exactly how many live houses do you think there are in Kabukicho alone? They don't notify the police of their existence and many of them don't produce proper schedules either. If you want to look into them, do it yourself."

Koda turned his back on Samejima.

"Did you find records or posters of Yuri Matsugi in Koichi Sunagami's apartment?"

"I've no idea. I didn't check myself," said Koda, still with his back turned.

The HQ telephone rang. The duty detective lifted the receiver and called out, "Superintendent Koda."

"What now?" Koda shouted, unable to conceal his irritation. Clearly he was in no mood to delay even for a moment heading over to Koma Theater.

"It's 'Ed.'"

Tension filled the room.

Fujimaru said in a low voice, "Whether or not he is Sunagami, whatever you do, don't let on that we've traced Sunagami's name."

Koda nodded, shot Samejima a scathing glance, and walked over to the phone. The NTT business center at Yodobashi was contacted immediately.

"Koda speaking."

"It's Ed. It's been a long time."

His voice was played through a speaker. There was a certain resonance in his voice that suggested he was enjoying himself. Koda breathed deeply so as to keep his anger in check.

"It has been a long time, yes."

"I thought for a moment you weren't there."

"No, no. That's not the case. I'm always waiting to hear from you."

"Really? Are you sure you're not just trying to make me feel good? I've come to Shinjuku on my way home from work today."

"You have? What are you doing in Shinjuku?"

"You know, I'm thinking about what to do right now. Well, have you found out anything about me?"

"No. You've got us beat."

"You surprise me. I thought the Japanese police were the best? If you really want to find me, I'll let you in on a little secret."

"What is it?"

"I've never been arrested by the police. So there's no point in checking your records. People who've been arrested by the police are afraid of them. But I'm not afraid. And something else—people like me are the same type as you all."

"The same type?"

"That's right. You and I face each other from different sides of the law. A mirror image, so to speak. No, in fact, it would be more accurate to say I'm right by your side."

"I'm not following you."

"Why do you think I'm such a good marksman? Why do I never miss my target?"

"Were you involved with the police or the Self-Defense Forces, or some such outfit?"

"Ed" sniggered.

"Think it over. Well then, I'll call again later."

"Wait. There's no hurry. I'm sure you've got time to talk a little longer."

"I'm afraid I'd rather you didn't trace my call. There's someplace I have to go now."

"Is it somewhere where…there are lots of people?"

"I wonder. I'll call again."

The line went dead.

"Maybe it's not him," Fujimaru said.

Calling all units in the vicinity of Shinjuku Station, the telephone is a public call box by the side of a kiosk in the east exit of the Shinjuku Station underground passage. Telephone number, Yotsuya-6579. I repeat, a public call box by the side of a kiosk. Telephone number, Yotsuya-6579. Move in and apprehend any suspicious persons.

The wireless operator started to issue instructions into the transmitter that had been brought into the headquarters to coordinate outside activities. The call had been successfully traced.

"Shinjuku 203, Shinjuku…" a report came in a few minutes later.

"This is Shinjuku, please go ahead."

"We have searched the area in front of the call box in question but there is no sign of any suspicious persons. The traffic is heavy. It appears it would be difficult to identify the suspect."

The wireless operator looked at Fujimaru.

"All right."

"Shinjuku 203. Understood. Thank you for your efforts."

"I'm going to the Koma Theater," said Koda, standing to attention in front of Fujimaru.

"All right. I'll ask you to explain the situation to the promoter. Please carry out your task, but remember, the priority is to safeguard lives."

"Understood."

Koda left the room.

Samejima looked at his watch. It was a few minutes past six. The Koma Theater event and Sho's live concert began at the same time. He couldn't ignore Koda's reasoning. He wasn't sure if he should tell Fujimaru about his previous encounter with Sunagami.

However, there was something he had to check out first. Samejima left the HQ and headed by car to Nakano.

The part of Nakano he headed to was a typical dense residential district. The houses were built in rows so close to one another that the walls almost touched, and there was only room on the roads for a single car to pass through. Moreover, so as to avoid the gate posts and fences by the bends and corners, Samejima had to drive at an acute angle along the streets.

Both sides of the narrow street were tightly screened by all manner of buildings: small houses and apartments, dormitories, convenience stores, tobacconists, dry cleaners, cafés and restaurants. It was a maze of streets characteristic of any big city. Part way along, Samejima decided to abandon his car and proceed on foot instead. Even if he'd managed to find his way through, he probably wouldn't be able to return the same way thanks to the series of one-way streets.

Police officers were accustomed to reading maps. However, it wasn't easy trying to locate a building he'd never been to before in the narrow, winding streets of a densely built-up district.

The Yayoi Daini Co-op building he eventually found was a two-story apartment block constructed of mortar with timber frames.

The side of the building, with an iron staircase, faced the street, and a long, narrow edifice extended to the rear.

To the right were the precincts of a temple, and to the left stood the Daiichi (No. 1) Co-op building, a perfect replica of the Daini (No. 2) building.

There were no cars in the vicinity of the apartments. The streets were narrow and it was the sort of area where an unfamiliar parked car would attract attention.

Although there was no sign of it in the neighborhood, Samejima could sense the stakeout. There were four detectives lurking in the shadows of the wall that surrounded the temple precincts and overlooked the first floor of the apartment, and four others on the temple grounds.

The stakeout comprised a total of three squads, or eighteen officers. The other ten officers were evidently lying in wait in the room adjoining the apartment under surveillance.

The commander on the ground was an inspector called Yagi. He was chief of the 13th Squad, under the control of Section One.

According to the officer at the foot of the stairs, Yagi was in Room 204, next door to Sunagami's apartment.

Samejima knocked on the door of Room 204.

Sunagami, of course, did not appear to be home.

There were four rooms on each floor of the apartment block, and from the rear of the second floor were Rooms 201, 202, 203 and 204. Room 204 was closest to the stairs.

"Who is it?" the anxious voice of a young man came from the other side of the frosted glass window, set in the plywood door.

"It's Samejima, from Shinjuku. Is Inspector Yagi there?"

The door opened. The stale odor of male bodies drifted out of the room. The one who opened the door was a young man of about eighteen and wore jeans. Four men clad in bulletproof vests sat cross-legged in the wood-paneled kitchen near the door.

Yagi was sitting in the back. He had cropped gray-streaked hair and was thickset like a judo player. He wore a bulletproof vest over a white short-sleeve shirt and a gun at his left hip.

"What is it?"

As the young man moved away from the front of the door, Yagi looked up and saw Samejima. He wore a wireless receiver earphone in his left ear. In his right hand he held a digital wireless which he used to receive transmissions from HQ on their digital circuit.

Yagi knew that Samejima hadn't been sent on the instructions of HQ.

"I'd like to have a brief look at the room if you don't mind."

Samejima entered the room, closing the door behind him.

"What for?"

"I'd like to establish which concert the suspect has gone to this evening."

The time was approaching 6:50 p.m.

"It's the Koma Theater, isn't it? Leastways, that's what I heard."

"That's what I'd like to confirm."

Yagi eyed Samejima suspiciously. "Does HQ know you're here?"

"No."

Yagi exhaled. "All right, I guess. But don't take too long over it." He took out the key from his trouser pocket and handed it to Samejima.

"Thanks."

He went out of Room 204 and inserted the key in the door of Room 203. He pulled on a pair of gloves and took a flashlight out from his hip pocket.

The interior was the same layout as in Room 204, one room and a kitchen.

There was a sink on the left, just past the entrance, and in front of that was the toilet.

The wood-paneled kitchen was roughly three mats in size and at the back of the apartment was a six-mat Japanese-style room.

The interior had been closed up, but it was still cooler than the interior of Room 204. The young man who had cooperated with the stakeout from Room 204 must have been having just about all he could take.

Removing his shoes, Samejima went into the room. A single bed and a low dining table had been placed in the six-mat room. There was a bookcase containing dozens of paperbacks and comics. On one side there was a TV set, a video deck and a mini compact player.

Samejima flashed his light on the wall. There was a bedding cupboard fitted into the recess in the wall adjoining Room 204. A poster of the all-girl rock band "Show-ya" was stuck to the sliding paper door of the cupboard.

The inside of the room didn't smell as much of food as he imagined it would. It appeared as though Sunagami went out for most of his meals.

Samejima moved toward the mini compact player.

A video deck was incorporated in the TV rack, below which were ten or so videotapes and CD cases. Something gold-colored caught the light. Samejima moved his face closer.

Five cartridges stood in a row. The 30-06 caliber cartridges were more than two inches long and about the same length as Samejima's little finger. The top half-inch of each narrowed under where it had housed the bullet.

In executing the search warrant, HQ had probably arranged for the caretaker or landlord to be present. However, afraid that they wouldn't be in time for Sunagami's return, they'd decided to seize evidence only after they'd apprehended him.

The cartridges stood on their ends and had been lined up neatly in a row. Samejima opened the glass door of the rack. Being careful not to touch the cartridges, he took out the CD cases.

The CDs were divided into pop songs and rock, and all were by female singers. He turned back to face the mini compact player. The CD player had a built-in double cassette. From the top there was the tuner, the cassette deck, and the CD player, the whole unit forming a set with a speaker on each side of it. Above the tuner, twenty or so cassette tapes had been stacked neatly in a line.

Samejima shone the flashlight on the cases. Most were unmarked. There were some old-looking tapes with recognizable names like "Yumi Mattoya" and "Minako Yoshida." But none bore the name "Yuri Matsugi."

As he moved, something came into contact with his toe. He trained the light on it and saw that it was a Walkman, with a set of headphones wrapped around it.

Picking it up he pressed the eject button. There was a tape inside. He took it out and looked at the index. It looked like a brand new tape and had nothing written on it. He put it back in the Walkman and pressed "play." Wondering what Sunagami had listened to last before he left his room,

Samejima put the headphone to his left ear.

The paused music started to flow again. The volume wasn't loud, but Samejima's blood turned to ice.

There was a voice from the kitchen. Unsettled, Yagi had come to see what was going on. Samejima quickly stopped the tape and replaced the headphone. His whole body dripped with cold sweat. He could feel the blood draining from his face. Samejima headed toward the kitchen. Yagi was standing in the entrance looking into the room.

As Samejima approached, Yagi shone the light of his flashlight on his face. "What the hell were you…doing?" his words trailed off as he noticed Samejima's complexion.

"I'm sorry. I'm done now."

Samejima returned the key to Yagi.

It was but an instant, but the sound of Sho's singing had been unmistakable in Samejima's left ear.

"Are you returning to Shinjuku?" inquired Yagi, as they went out into the corridor.

Samejima nodded. He looked at his watch. It was almost seven.

He started to walk away, then stopped. He considered using Yagi's wireless to contact HQ to tell them not to send the police unit to the Koma Theater but to the TEC Hall instead.

But Koda was in command at the Koma Theater and was convinced the new shooting would take place there. It wouldn't be easy to persuade him by wireless to change his mind. Even if he persuaded him that Sunagami was going after Sho, rather than Yuri Matsugi, he had no more than an even chance of being right. It was also possible that neither was the target. If they were to transfer half the police unit to the TEC Hall, and if, as a result of that, they failed to prevent a crime at the Koma Theater, or someplace else for that matter… Not just Koda, but any commander on the ground would see it as an impossible dilemma.

His best hope was the fact that the TEC Hall was situated on the far side of Kabukicho, farther away than the Koma Theater.

Perhaps Sunagami would be apprehended by the police who'd been deployed in the vicinity of Koma Theater as he made his way toward the TEC Hall.

First, Samejima had to contact the TEC Hall and prevent Sho from going on stage.

"Commander Yagi. We've received a message from HQ."

One of the detectives called to Yagi from Room 204. Wondering if Sunagami had been caught, Samejima followed Yagi into the room.

"Hello, Squad Thirteen. Yagi speaking."

Yagi took hold of the wireless receiver and put the earphone in his ear.

"Yes, yes. Affirmative," answered Yagi, removing the earpiece.

"Have they arrested him?" asked one of the detectives who had been standing on tiptoe.

Samejima had made the same assumption. It surely had to be so.

"This time the suspect has attacked a gangster. Thirty minutes ago, a young punk riding the elevator in the Hanaigumi gang's Kabukicho headquarters was shot in the head and killed. The bullet taken from the wall of the elevator was a 30-06 rifle bullet, the same type as the ones used by the suspect's weapon."

There was no mistake about it. Sunagami intended to finish today at the live concert what he had begun with the murder of the police officers. Now he'd killed the gangster who had beaten him up; and finally, he planned to attack the live concert thanks to which it had all begun. Sunagami was retracing the events. Samejima's intuition told him that had to be right.

"Can I use your phone?"

He turned toward the young man who lived in Room 204.

"I'm afraid," said the young man, with a pitiful expression, "I didn't pay the telephone charges, so they cut me off. I'm waiting to be reconnected at the moment…"

Samejima ran out of Room 204. He remembered seeing a public call box a short distance before the Daini Yayoi Co-op building. He hurried down the iron staircase and began to run as he emerged at the front.

It was a green public telephone. A young man, wearing a jersey tracksuit, had the receiver in his hand. As he ran toward him, Samejima took out his police ID.

"Excuse me, it's urgent. Please let me use the phone."

Surprised, the young man stepped back. "Go ahead."

Luckily he had taken down the TEC Hall number in his notebook. He glanced at his watch. It was eight minutes past seven.

Using the young man's telephone card he punched in the TEC Hall number.

The line was busy.

He pressed the buttons once again, but the line was still engaged.

Having replaced the receiver, he hastily thanked the young man and began to run. He reached his car and sped along the streets.

The quickest way back to Shinjuku would be to join Hongo Street, which flowed into Yamate Street, then, avoiding Ome Highway as it was always backed up with traffic, to exit to west Shinjuku from Sakaecho Street.

He sped along Hongo then hit Yamate. To the left was Ome Highway, and if he turned right he would enter the intersection with Sakaecho, an extension of Honan Street.

But the inside lane was choked with traffic. If anything, Ome Highway to the left was less congested.

Samejima had never cursed his car so much as now. His BMW didn't have a siren, which would have allowed him to drive contra the flow of traffic.

He wrenched the steering wheel hard left and turned onto Ome Highway. But after proceeding only a few hundred yards he ran into a traffic jam. The traffic was backed up right from the Nakano Sakaue junction that intersected with Yamate Street and Ome Highway. He'd have to wait for the traffic lights to change at least twice.

Samejima thumped the steering wheel hard, then gripped it and moved the BMW into the left-hand lane. A hundred and fifty yards ahead, at the Nakano Sakaue intersection, was a station on the Marunouchi line. Next stop from Nakano Sakaue was Shinjuku.

Samejima climbed out of his BMW and began to run again. He abandoned his car with its hazard lights flashing in a no parking zone, but he was long past caring.

He ran the distance as fast as he could and then sprinted down the steps to the entrance of the Nakano Sakaue subway stop.

There was a public telephone by the ticket barrier. He was about to go over to it when he heard the clatter of a train as it pulled into the platform. It was bound for Ikebukuro. Pulling out his police ID, he went past the ticket barrier and dove through the open doors.

22

His whole body was soaked with sweat.

It was only a few minutes, Samejima told himself, only a few minutes and he would be in Shinjuku.

It was 7:20 p.m. Even if she'd begun a little later than scheduled, Sho would be singing her first number.

Samejima closed his eyes. Sho would be dancing around on stage, microphone in her hand, as the prelude opened with the drums, guitar and bass.

Would Sunagami suddenly gun down Sho?

No. There was no reason he would do that. Sunagami was a fan of Who's Honey. A fan who'd been to live concerts and bought tapes that the group had made on their own.

He opened his eyes. He placed his hand against the doors and stared at his reflection in the glass. His hair was plastered down to his forehead. His eyes gleamed with frustration, anger and fear.

His lover, fourteen years his junior. The detective and the rock singer.

Samejima was afraid. He was scared to death by the thought of losing Sho.

Sunagami was probably listening to the song. Sho's song. He couldn't not be.

Sho would be on stage now. She would be giving it her all. It would be a performance that didn't permit Sunagami to end it all without listening to every bar of her song.

Her breath bursting forth from the pit of her stomach and coming screaming out of her mouth, colliding headlong with the sounds of the drums, guitar, bass and keyboard. Her whole being exuding sweat and passion and her fiery voice cleaving the air in two and striking at the hearts of the audience. Her small body dancing across the stage and jittering and moving, right to the very end of the concert. Her eyes joining with those of the guitarist, her body falling backwards into the arms of the bass player, snuggling up to the keyboard player, throwing her chest out toward the drums. And then, with their eyes riveted, demanding that her audience scream and dance along with her. The entire live concert hall rocking and swaying like a giant wave dragged along by Sho. Hundreds of pairs of eyes drawn magnetically to those rocket tits as they threatened at any moment to pop out from under her braless costume.

Samejima clenched his teeth. Sunagami wouldn't shoot. There was no way he would shoot. Not until the end of the last encore. Not until Sho had finished thanking all her fans for coming to see her.

Samejima inhaled. His breath caught between his chest and throat, the way it did when he was trying not to cry.

Sho always said he should keep his promises.

If you don't show up I'll call the police.

He wondered if she'd really done so.

Samejima realized he'd left his wireless receiver in his BMW. If he had it with him, he could hear the report if Sunagami had been apprehended at the Koma Theater.

It suddenly became bright outside the window. The train was coming into Shinjuku station.

Samejima forced his way through the closely packed crowds and hurried up the steps. Both the passageways and the area around the ticket barrier were thronged with people. He felt he could almost walk over the sea of bobbing heads to the east exit in the direction of Kabukicho.

He ran along the passageway, pushing aside dating couples, almost sending old people careening out of the way and getting himself snarled on a child's pram.

Once through the ticket barrier he saw a public phone next to a kiosk. But someone was using it, and there was a line of people waiting to use it.

He headed for the steps leading out to the east exit. Public phones tended to be located in prominent places and it was a safe bet that they would be in constant use.

Some phones, however, were in less conspicuous places and weren't always in use. There was a phone by the steps leading to ground level, and two more behind the steps—one was free at that moment.

A small man wearing a dark blue suit stood by the phone on the left. He had his back turned toward Samejima but from time to time looked around with the receiver pressed to his right ear.

When Samejima came running over, the man appeared startled and nearly dropped the receiver. Without paying any attention, Samejima grabbed the receiver of the phone on the right. He placed it against his left ear, inserted a coin and punched in the number for the TEC Hall. A ring tone sounded at the other end of the line.

Okay, come on, hurry up and answer. Pick up the call.

"Hello, this is the TEC Hall," shouted a man's voice as he tried not to be drowned out by the flood of sound coming from Who's Honey in the background.

Good, the performance is still going on.

"My name is Samejima. I need to talk to Sho about an urgent matter."

"I'm sorry! I can't put a call out for a customer in the middle of a performance."

The man was talking loudly so he could be heard above the music.

"She's not a customer! I'm talking about Sho, the vocalist of Who's

Honey. They're on stage right now!"

"What? That's not possible. We finish at 9:00 p.m."

"I can't wait until then! I'm a police inspector!"

There was a loud clattering noise to his left. Even Samejima, unable to hear with his right ear, and with the receiver glued to his left, noticed it. He looked sideways.

The man in the suit had stepped backwards, his mouth and eyes wide open. He had slammed the phone down and hung up his call. The man was staring at Samejima with a mixed expression of surprise and fear. He was in his late thirties and prematurely balding. Perhaps he wasn't accustomed to wearing a suit but, given his age, the way he'd knotted his tie was extremely slovenly. The man's mouth opened and he said something. It sounded like "police" but Samejima couldn't be sure.

The din from the rock band and the voice of the man from the TEC Hall sounded loud in his left ear.

"The police? Stop playing jokes!"

"This isn't a joke! It's an emergency!"

"In any case, I can't do anything about it until the performance ends! Call again at nine!"

The TEC Hall man hung up. Samejima replaced the receiver. Maybe it was better this way in any case. If Sho left the stage during the performance then Sunagami would guess something was wrong.

Samejima looked up. The man in the suit had begun to run into the crowd. He had left behind what looked like a shoulder bag next to the phone he had been using. As the form of the man was swallowed up by the sea of people in the subway, two uniformed police officers came running into view.

They were headed straight for Samejima. Both officers were from the police box at the east exit of Shinjuku station.

Surprised, they stopped in their tracks when they noticed Samejima.

"Inspector Samejima! Were you using that phone just now?"

"I was using this one," said Samejima, realizing as he did so what had happened. "Was it 'Ed'?"

The police officer nodded. "Yes."

Samejima stared in the direction where the man had disappeared. The Saturday night crowds had swallowed all traces of him. "He was about thirty-seven or -eight. Dark blue suit. He wore glasses. Height about five feet. And this is what he left behind." Samejima pointed at the bag.

One of the officers straightaway used the microphone of his wireless transmitter to report the characteristics.

"You said he was about thirty-seven or -eight?" said the other officer, surprised. According to instructions they'd received, "Ed" was a young man in his twenties.

"That's right," replied Samejima as he began to walk away.

"Inspector, which way are you headed? The Koma Theater?"

Samejima stopped walking. "Did they catch him?"

"Not yet." The officer who had called after him shook his head.

"Come with me," said Samejima, as he began to walk away again.

Surprised, the officers stared after Samejima.

"Come on!"

When Samejima yelled, they came running. One of them carried the bag left by "Ed" in his gloved hand.

Samejima headed straight for the underground passageway. By going through the interconnecting passageways of the subway, they could cross Shinjuku and Yasukuni Streets underground.

There were a fair number of people in the underground shopping mall too, but because there were no traffic lights, they'd be able to make quicker progress in the direction of Kabukicho.

Samejima raced up the steps at the exit.

They came out on the sidewalk fronting Yasukuni Street in the vicinity of Kabukicho Ichome.

Samejima continued running. The one-way street that ran right up to the Shinjuku Toho Hall, which housed the Koma Theater, was buried under a mass of people.

Here and there, they saw police officers on emergency deployment. There were both uniformed and plainclothes officers. There was no sign at all of the *yakuza* or the hoodlums who usually threw their weight around.

While this had something to do with the number of uniformed officers, it was also the result of the plainclothes detectives standing by in plain view on every street corner.

It wasn't that there weren't plainclothes detectives on patrol all the time. In particular, patrols by detectives from the Crime Prevention Section were a daily occurrence. However, today was special. There were so many plainclothes detectives scattered about Kabukicho that one would be forgiven for thinking that all the detectives from not only Shinjuku Police Station, but from all Tokyo, had been deployed.

As soon as they realized as much, the *yakuza* and pimps and pickpockets and the like had vanished without a trace.

But considering the number of people that flooded into Shinjuku's Kabukicho district on a Saturday night, that was no relief. The area of Kabukicho was a mere 0.13 square miles. However, within it were more than two thousand eating establishments. In one night during a weekend like this one, upwards of 400,000 people visited the area.

Even assuming a thousand detectives and police officers had been deployed, the ratio would be 400:1. Searching for and locating an individual at a given moment, even if that person were one's own wife or child, was a tall order.

In spite of himself, Samejima stopped in front of the Toho Hall. A queue of people starting at the entrance to the Koma Theater had formed and encircled the whole of Toho Hall. The line of people slowly advanced into the Koma Theater.

By the entrance stood a group of detectives with wireless transmitters. When he saw them, Samejima knew what had happened.

The event organizer had rejected the request to postpone the performance and so Koda had ordered that all customers be checked on entry. The Koma Theater had a capacity of 2,300 people.

Having declined to postpone the event and, following some discussion, settling instead on checking all customers, the opening time had in all likelihood been delayed; only then having begun to admit people, not all the customers had entered the theater yet.

It was the worst possible outcome.

The majority of the investigators watching the vicinity of the plaza would have been too preoccupied with the throng approaching the Koma Theater to notice whether any persons were acting suspiciously or even attempting to run away as they came closer and spotted the heavy police presence.

The TEC Kaikan, which housed the TEC Hall, was only one street over from the Koma Theater. However, the TEC Kaikan was positioned at the rear of the Koma Theater and could be reached from the direction of Kuyakusho Street—where there were buildings such as the Furinkan—without passing through the Kabukicho Plaza. Ironically, the Koma Theater was back to back with the Kabukicho Police Box.

The TEC Kaikan was diagonally opposite and across the street from the police box, but the police box was closer to the Koma Theater. The steps to the entrance of the TEC Hall in the second basement of the TEC Kaikan were to the side of the building, in a blind spot. Anyone going down the steps could not be seen from inside the police box.

Samejima took a deep breath. It didn't look as though there was any trouble at the moment in the direction of the TEC Kaikan.

Taking a detour around the queue of people, Samejima cut across Kabukicho Plaza and made his way toward the TEC Kaikan.

Bewildered, the two uniformed officers followed on behind.

The steps leading down to the TEC Hall changed direction at the landing of the first floor basement. Standing there, Samejima turned to face the two officers as they caught up with him. He could already feel the Who's Honey drumbeat through the floor of the landing.

"All right, tell me your names," said Samejima as he directed his attention toward the TEC Hall entrance at the foot of the steps.

The two uniformed officers exchanged glances.

The officer carrying the shoulder bag spoke first: "Sergeant Watanabe." He was about thirty years of age.

"I'm Officer Sakae." He was two or three years younger than Watanabe.

Samejima took another deep breath in order to compose himself. "This may be your chance to get specially promoted."

The officers looked surprised.

"How do you mean?" Watanabe asked.

"There's a possibility that the killer is attending the live concert in the basement below us."

"Seriously, sir?" Sakae reached for the microphone to the wireless transmitter slung from his shoulder.

"Keep your head," said Samejima, stopping him. "It's not certain yet that he's here. And not only that, imagine what would happen if a whole army of cops descend on this place. There are more than a hundred people down there. It would cause a mass panic."

If Sunagami wasn't there and he burst on stage with a whole squad of cops without telling her first, Sho would never forgive him. An incongruous thought occurred to him: Would his punishment for ruining the concert be for her to ditch him, or would she crack him over the head with a *saké* bottle? These two officers would end up arresting Sho for assault… But even that would be far preferable to Sho being used as a rifle target. Right now, thought Samejima, he would do absolutely anything to save her.

"What should we do?" asked Watanabe.

"For now, just stay here. You've got the suspect's photo, right?"

They both nodded.

"His hair is longer than in the photo, and he's slimmer, too. He's taller than me."

Sakae cleared his throat. His face had turned pale with the tension.

"I'll go in first. These stairs are the only way in and out. There's an elevator, but you can't use it while the concert is playing. If he's in there, I'll come out and let you know. If I don't come out within five minutes then come in after me. Take care and make sure he doesn't see you. Keep your wits about you."

Watanabe removed the cover from his holster. His expression had changed too.

"Don't be trigger-happy, either. Remember, there are a lot of people in there. If they panic, it'll be impossible to get the situation under control."

"Understood."

"When I give the signal, call for back-up."

"Yes, sir."

Samejima looked at both their faces in turn. He nodded and went down the steps. He stood in front of the door and checked his watch. It was 7:40 p.m.

He could hear Sho's voice through the door. Samejima looked back at the two officers on the landing, pointed to his watch and spread his fingers: *five minutes from now.*

He pushed the door open.

Heat and noise hit him in the face like a hammer. A guitar solo had just started. Sho was dancing in a frenzy atop the roughly twenty-five feet square stage out front. She wore a sparkle-encrusted purple tanktop with matching purple short pants. The sweat on her chest glistened in the spotlights.

The seats were buried under a sea of bodies. Nobody was seated. Shoulders bumping, everyone danced to the rhythm.

The ear-splitting high pitch of the ad-lib guitar piece cut through the sweaty, charged atmosphere.

There must have been a hundred and fifty revellers.

"Do you have a ticket?" shouted the girl at reception. A chair and table had been placed in the narrow space by the entrance.

"I'm Samejima. Have you got a ticket for me from Sho?"

Samejima gestured toward the stage with his chin. The girl nodded expansively.

"Oh yeah, of course. I heard you were coming. It's pretty full in there, but please, go ahead."

The guitar solo came to an end and the bass began. A shout went up from the audience in the front row.

Sho beat time with the tip of her toe and approached the bass player. She lowered her hips and shook her breasts; licking her lips, she looked up at the bass player. Beads of sweat flew into the air, twinkling like small pearls in the spotlight.

Samejima moved into the central aisle between the audience seats. They were arranged in ten rows of six seats on either side of the aisle. The seats were unreserved and all were taken. There were more people in the hall than there were seats, and bodies were spilling out and dancing in the aisle.

Sho moved away from the bass player and turned to face the drums. The drums' beat carved out the rhythm at a furious tempo. It rapidly picked up speed and intermingled with the keyboard, and the guitar and bass kicked in at the same time.

The audience cheered.

Samejima's head swam. It was the introduction to "Stay Here."

His mouth was parched. Sweat from his forehead seeped into his eyes.

He scanned the room for a tall figure.

Everyone's attention was given over to the stage as they stomped and shook their shoulders and heads.

Samejima gradually made his way toward the front row. Sixty percent of the audience were guys. There were typical punks there, but also young fans of the sort one might expect.

Get away!

Sho screamed, and the backing chorus screamed too.

Get away!

And the audience screamed in time with the chorus.

The sound of the guitar was much heavier than he remembered it being.

Everybody says get away right now...

He could see the backs of the people in the front row.

On the left-hand fringe of the front row was a head that stood out taller than the rest.

Samejima halted.

This town is the pits, Shinjuku, nothing but crying voices every night, every night...

He had neatly cut, longish hair and wore a clean cotton jacket and jeans. A black cord was visible across his right shoulder.

Get away!

Get away!

Everybody says get away right now, this town is the pits, Shinjuku, nothing but grief, today, and tomorrow too...

The fans were wild with excitement.

With its fast beat and hint of the Blues, "Stay Here" was the most popular of the band's original numbers.

But the instant Samejima saw the man's form from the rear, the sound tuned out from his functioning ear and receded into the distance. Sho's screams, the staccato cutting sound of the guitar, the undulating rhythm of the bass, the sobbing whine of the keyboard and the beat of the drums all disappeared.

The man's head shook. Samejima continued to stare. He had to see what it was that hung from the man's right shoulder, but he couldn't move any further for fear of being seen. A group of youths were dancing madly in the ring of light cast by the spotlight in the front row of the central aisle. They were the hardcore fans.

The man seemed to be completely mesmerized by "Stay Here."

Not just his head, but his shoulders also, jerked backwards and forwards with sharp, staccato movements.

The first verse was coming to an end. Sho retreated and the guitarist came forward.

The man's right hand moved to the cord on his right shoulder.

Samejima's eyes opened wide as he stood on tiptoe and watched the man's hand.

Just as a woman in the row behind him, whose back had been obscuring Samejima's view of everything below the man's right shoulder, gyrated her body, Samejima saw what the man was carrying.

It wasn't him!

The thing was a shoulder-carried mobile phone. A receiver sat atop a thin black rectangular box.

It wasn't him. The man wasn't Sunagami.

Samejima transferred his gaze away from the man's back over to the right side of the hall.

As he did so, he suddenly recalled the steel shelving he had seen in Kizu's workshop—the steel shelving Kizu had used as a shield from behind which to fire. Various cardboard boxes had been stacked on the shelving. On the bottom shelf there had been a number of long, narrow boxes for umbrellas, while the shelf above had contained boxes of videotapes. And then there had been one much larger box with the letters "NTT" written on it.

Samejima spun around. The man, too, happened to look behind him. He had the mobile phone unslung from his shoulder and was holding it in both hands.

Between the swaying shoulders of the fans, Samejima's eyes met with the man's. It *was* Koichi Sunagami. Apparently not having registered Samejima, the dark eyes darted in the direction of the entrance. Then they opened wide.

Samejima looked back over his shoulder toward the entrance. The uniforms of Watanabe and Sakae entered the periphery of his vision.

Get away, everybody says get the hell out now, this town is a core of darkness, nothing but crying voices every night, every night…

Sunagami moved the mobile phone to his side and raised it in the air. The base of the battery box was pointing in the direction of the entrance.

Samejima's right hand drew out his revolver. Pointing it at the ceiling he pulled the trigger.

The roar of the gunshot leapt together with the flame from the muzzle of the New Nambu.

"Get down!" yelled Samejima.

Everyone screamed at once, fans falling headlong over chairs.

A flame jumped from the bottom of the mobile phone. Instinctively Samejima ducked his head. He couldn't tell which way the bullet went.

At the same time, he extended his arms fully and trained his New Nambu on Sunagami.

"Throw down your weapon! Sunagami!"

Sunagami's eyes seemed to bulge out of their sockets as he stared at Samejima. Then he suddenly turned his head and looked at Sho, who had frozen in the middle of the stage.

Using his right thumb, Samejima pulled back the gun hammer. The cylinder rotated and the gun hammer locked in position. He aligned the front and rear sights of the New Nambu, the gun Kizu had called a "piece of junk," and aimed at Sunagami's chest.

Sunagami's eyes moved feverishly back and forth from Samejima to Sho. Finally they came to rest on Sho, and he extended his arms and the mobile phone in her direction. The index finger of his right hand curled around the strange projection on its side.

Samejima pulled the trigger.

This time the flame shot out toward Sunagami.

The booming report of the gunshot echoed around the hall.

Sunagami's body turned full circle, collided with the stage, and fell down.

A shriek went up again.

"Call an ambulance!" shouted Samejima, without turning around. He strode over the trembling fans as they cowered under their seats, and drew near to Sunagami.

Sunagami had fallen on his left shoulder, with his legs twisted under him.

The mobile phone was trapped under his side. A bloodstain had spread over his right shoulder.

"Sunagami! Can you hear me?" Samejima called out to him.

Sunagami opened his eyes and nodded faintly.

The bullet appeared to have shattered his right shoulder bone before coming to a stop. There was no sign of blood coming from his mouth. The bullet didn't seem to have penetrated his lung.

The "piece of junk" had kicked up in Samejima's hand and the bullet had struck above the point of aim.

Samejima knelt at Sunagami's side.

Sunagami's eyes wavered, then fixed on Samejima. A faint bruise had appeared on his cheek.

"Do you remember me?" called Samejima. "Sunagami, do you remember me?"

Sunagami blinked, as if in pain, and gazed at Samejima. He shook his head slightly. He didn't remember.

"The ambulance will be here soon. Hang in there."

Sunagami nodded.

Samejima got to his feet and looked in the direction where Sunagami's first shot had been fired.

Watanabe walked awkwardly over toward him.

There was a hole in one of the wall-mounted speakers. The bullet had passed clean through the speaker and gouged a hole in the concrete wall beyond.

Samejima heaved a sigh of relief and looked up at the stage.

Sho stood dumbfounded, looking down at him. Her chest heaved up and down.

"My God, oh my God," she said, shaking her head in disbelief. Her breathing was rough. "I didn't think you'd really come here with the police."

23

He didn't remember how or where he ran.

When he looked around, he found he was in the underground shopping mall.

And then, he had frozen as he saw that man, accompanied by the uniformed police officers, come running toward him.

He really was a detective. The man who'd been standing right by his side with the bandaged head was a genuine police officer. The three of them were running to arrest him.

But that couldn't have been it, for they ran past his very eyes, up the steps and out the station.

Something had happened. Something big.

After he'd killed some time at Marksman, he had called the Criminal Investigation HQ again, but Superintendent Koda was unavailable.

He became angry. After all, he had given them the benefit of his deductive powers and inferred that the killer was a former police officer or member of the Self-Defense Forces.

Twenty years ago, he'd decided to sit the civil exams for the police. Too short, he'd been rejected.

He hesitated for a moment. It was clear that the three police officers were running because something had happened. The fact that Superintendent Koda was absent probably had something to do with it, too.

He made up his mind.

Following the three officers, he climbed the steps and headed into Kabukicho.

The area around the Koma Theater was crawling with cops. He stopped dead when he realized that. Holding both excitement and fear in check, he pursued the three police officers. He understood that the suit he'd worn for that day's interview at work, in connection with a proposed reduction in staff, made him look decidedly less conspicuous.

Was the killer inside the Koma Theater?

But wait—the three officers had run past the front of the theater. They weren't running anymore. The man out front, with the bandaged head, was walking quickly.

He started to walk after them, but came to a halt again as he noticed the bag one of the officers was carrying in his hand.

It was his shoulder bag. He had left it behind when he fled from the public phone. Inside it there was a map of the meeting hall at his work, a job seekers' magazine, and a pair of gloves.

There was nothing he could do about it now.

He felt like crying. The police were bound to discover his identity through his workplace.

Even so, he continued to walk.

He watched the three officers as they turned in front of the Koma Theater and approached a building diagonally opposite the Kabukicho Police Box.

His desire to know what had happened won out over his fear. It was plain that the officers weren't pursuing him. They were on the underground landing of a building called the TEC Kaikan. He furtively watched the scene from the stairs above them.

Before long, the man with the bandaged head went in through the entrance of the room on the second-floor basement.

Watching from his high vantage point, he gulped as the two officers removed the covers from their holsters.

He was transfixed.

There was no doubt about it. The real culprit was inside this building.

The fact that the two uniformed officers had readied their guns proved as much, and he was certain that the detective with the bandaged head was also armed.

The uniformed officers had no idea he was gazing down on them. They were nervously looking at the door through which the detective had gone into the building a few moments earlier.

Were there only three of them? Were the three of them really trying to apprehend a serial killer? Or would a squad of police officers suddenly burst upon the scene?

The uniformed officers moved. One of them checked his watch and placed his hand on the door.

The deafening sound of rock music came flooding out of the open doorway. This time, the door wasn't closed the way it had been after the detective had gone inside. The police officers had entered leaving the door ajar.

He heard screams, and then the peal of gunfire as two shots were fired in close succession.

A cry went up all at once and the music came to a sudden stop.

Unable to contain himself any longer, he rushed down the stairs.

The instant he came through the open door, the screams mingled with the sound of another shot.

On the center stage there was a pretty woman who had moved the band back away from danger. The fans were taking cover under their seats.

The only people standing by the rows of seats were the two uniformed officers, and then, by the stage, the man with the bandaged head—holding his gun out in front of him.

"Call an ambulance!" the man with the bandaged head shouted.

Yes, he said to himself—and again, *yes, yes, yes.* He was finally witnessing a real arrest.

280

One of the uniformed police officers that had been standing in the aisle suddenly turned around to come running in his direction. The officer ran out of the building without so much as looking at him.

The man with the bandaged head crouched down beside the man on the floor and said something to him. He couldn't make out the details, but his serious profile was imprinted deep in his mind.

That detective had caught him. That detective had gunned down the killer. That detective was a hero.

And something else, that detective had made a phone call from right beside him.

All he wanted to do now was take a quick look at the killer. To see if he was as he had guessed he would be. He wanted to see whether his imagination had proved correct. Was the killer a former cop or soldier?

He weaved his way through the fans who were now beginning to raise themselves from the floor and, as if drawn by some invisible force, approached the stage.

The remaining uniformed officer and the detective with the bandaged head were bent over the prostrate form of the man.

The detective had exchanged words with the woman on the stage. The man on the floor was tall and young, with short hair. The right shoulder of his jacket was soaked dark with blood.

He came right up to where the two officers were crouching. The detective became aware of him standing there, and looked up. Their eyes met.

After staring at him for a moment, the detective looked away. It was as if he'd already forgotten about him.

There had been tension and relief and, for some reason he didn't understand, a look almost of sadness on the detective's face.

24

"I was so shocked."

Coming out from being questioned, she found Samejima in the corridor of the Shinjuku Police Station.

Sho hadn't known Sunagami's name. But she had seen his face a number of times at her live concerts.

"I guess it really messed up your event," Samejima said.

Without replying, Sho sighed and nodded her head. Samejima gently squeezed her hand. She squeezed back hard. Her body was quivering all over. "I'm still shaking, even now. When I think he tried to kill me."

"It seems he planned on a lovers' suicide."

"That's not funny."

Samejima stood up and stared at Sho.

"What." Smiling through her tears, Sho returned his gaze.

"All I could think of was, thank God. You don't have a bullet hole between your rocket tits."

"Fuck you."

Sho pressed her face into Samejima's chest. And then she began to sob quietly.

"If you carry on like this, you'll lose your street cred as a rock queen."

"Leave me alone."

"The record company will be delighted. All this publicity just before your debut."

"I'll kill you if you don't shut up."

She put her hands around Samejima's neck.

Detectives and uniformed police officers walking by stopped and stared in astonishment.

"Cut it out, will you?" Flustered, Samejima pulled her hands away.

Koda was there too. Slammed by a combination of humiliation and wasted effort, Koda just stood there.

Samejima looked around, and Sho looked over too.

"It's unfair playing to the grandstand the way you did," Koda let out at last. He was looking down at his feet.

"It was thanks to your seeing the concert connection," Samejima pointed out.

Koda looked up, and said in a murmur, "I refuse to acknowledge what you did. I absolutely refuse to acknowledge it. Your methods are unbecoming of a detective."

"You may be right, but—"

"I've had enough. I don't want to see your face around here again. Do you understand? I'll see to it you're finished. If it's the last thing I do, I'll bring you down."

Without warning, Sho stuck her middle finger in front of Koda's face. It was too late to stop her. "Fuck you!"

Koda's face turned crimson.

He looked as though he was about to punch her. But he managed to control himself. He quickly turned around and walked away.

"What the hell do you think you're doing? Are you trying to get yourself shot?"

Sho laughed dismissively. "If that does happen, promise me you'll kill him for me."

"Let's go."

Samejima grabbed Sho by the hand.

Before they left for home, there was someone he had to call on.

Leaving Sho outside in the corridor, he went into the detectives' room of the Crime Prevention Section.

Momoi was sitting alone in the section chief's chair.

When Samejima entered the room, Momoi lifted his eyes from the paperwork on his desk and looked at him indifferently.

Samejima and Momoi stared at one another in silence.

"Good job," Momoi said in his monotone.

Samejima nodded. "Thanks a lot, chief. Am I dismissed for the day?"

"Finished over at HQ?"

"Yes, for today."

"Is that right," Momoi mumbled.

The section chief started to go back to his paperwork but then said, as if it had just occurred to him, "Kizu's tombstone's been picked. I've decided to put him next to my son. The ceremony for depositing the ashes is being held tomorrow. I don't know if you are free…"

"I will attend."

Momoi nodded.

Samejima said, "I'll be under your command again in Crime Prevention."

"Yes," said Momoi, looking out the window.

The front entrance of the Shinjuku Police Station was brightly lit by lights from the TV broadcast vans.

"So the shark is coming back to Crime Prevention? The Shinjuku Shark?"

Samejima nodded. Then he saluted and retraced his steps. He put his hand on the door of the detectives' room. Momoi remained still and continued to gaze out of the window.

Samejima quietly closed the door and began to walk along the corridor.

Sho caught up with him, and asked, "Who were you talking to?"

"A cop," said Samejima as he walked.

"Well I know that, but which cop?" Sho asked impatiently.

Samejima pulled Sho in to his shoulder. She seemed surprised, but then gave herself in.

He answered: "The best cop in Shinjuku."

About the Author

Arimasa Osawa has received the Eiji Yoshikawa New Writer Award, the Japan Mystery Writers Association Award, and the Naoki Prize for his *Shinjuku Shark* novels. Many of his other hardboiled works have also been awarded prizes and adapted to the screen.